DAMAGE CONTROL

To my wife, Lee Breen Cassidy, for her unwavering
support throughout our journey together.
And, to our lively and talented family.

The Cassidy Family
Hugh and Joseph (deceased), John, Brendon, Kieran, Olga,
Sean, Riza, SJ, Cameron, Lisa, Adeline, Cullen, Emma, Scott,
Claudia, Ryan, Timothy, Mary, Grace, Liz, Rita, Joe, Tommy,
Charlie, Peter, Richie, Aunt Eileen, Uncle Roddy and
all of my Meade and Cassidy family.

The Breen Family
Timothy (deceased), Sean, Rachel, Kevin, Aileen, Timothy,
William, Patrick, Norah, Jason, Caroline, Mary, Dieter,
Lindsey, Ryan, Melissa, Erin, Patrick, Karen, Bob, Denise
and all of my Breen and Heenan family.

PART I

THE MAN, THE MYTH AND THE TRUTH

CHAPTER 1

AT SIX A.M. THE freshly brewed coffee is ready for slowly waking John Patrick Donnellan, Lieutenant, Manhattan South Homicide. He sips his first mug of black coffee and watches Channel 7's Eyewitness News. The volume is low, barely a whisper, as he tries not to disturb his wife and children. The news is dismal as usual. The steady drumbeat of bad news seems never ending. The year 1981 is shaping up to be another record year, just like the year before, and the year before that. Not in a good way. Crime is off the charts, and murder is leading the way. Two more homicides overnight. One in the Bronx and the other in Manhattan. Walking into the kitchen of his Manhattan apartment, Donnellan checks his beeper. No missed calls from the squad. He picks up the phone and calls Manhattan South anyway.

Detective Manny Colon answers on the second ring. He knows what Donnellan wants and starts right in. "Hey Boss, last night's homicide is an open and shut case if there ever was one. Some has-been boxer named Rocky McTie, a strung out addict, decided to pay a visit to his estranged wife and shake her down for money. At first she wouldn't let him in, but he starts crying and begs her to just let him see his children. She's wise to this wife-beater, so she calls her father who lives on the fourth floor. She tells Pop that she's leaving the door wide-open and asks him to come down right away because she's letting the stiff in the house to visit his kids." Colon pauses to light another cigarette.

1

"As soon as the wife opens the door, McTie knocks her down, grabs her purse and starts ransacking the apartment. The kids are crying, the old-lady's screaming and the neighbors call the cops, but the wife's father and brother get there first. As soon as McTie sees them coming into the apartment, he picks up a bat and hits the father-in-law in the face sending his son into a knife stabbing rage. He stabs McTie with a hunting knife until the palooka is laid out in a pool of blood. When the cops get on the scene, the wife's hysterical, the father's semi-conscious with a broken nose, the brother hands over his bloody knife and claims that he stabbed his brother-in-law in self-defense, and McTie is dead."

"Holy shit," says Donnellan. "You guys had some night."

"Well," says Colon "the wife and her father are at the hospital, the children are with grandma, the brother-in-law is in custody and McTie is at the medical examiner's office." The detective starts to review the Crime Complaint with Donnellan to see whether there are any loose ends that need to be addressed. Donnellan stops him in mid-sentence, thanks him for the update and tells him he'll be at the office within an hour.

As he races to get ready for work, the television continues to whisper the cycle of bleak news. The McTie homicide is just a quick blip on screen. Nearly all the media attention is on the upcoming mayoral election. With the crime wave wreaking havoc in every corner of the city, the mayor's reelection chances are growing slimmer by the minute. The growing chaos seems without end. Beyond the grim stats, there's public perception to deal with. And in politics, perception is reality.

The Guardian Angels and other vigilante groups patrol the subways. There's a sense that the city's problems are beyond its grasp. Police layoffs during the city's long fiscal crisis, coupled with hiring and salary freezes throughout city government, reinforce this sense. Fewer cops, firemen, and sanitation workers, means more crime, arson, and garbage on the streets. Hollywood hasn't helped, painting a bleak picture in continually darker shades, starting with the *Death Wish* movies, then piling on last year with *The Warriors,* and again this year with *Escape From New York.* The worst part is that the darkness is real. *The Warriors* seems cartoonish only if you don't know about the dozens of gangs in Williamsburg with ridiculous names killing each other night after night. Donnellan reels in his wandering mind as he finishes dressing. He shakes his head, takes a last swallow of coffee, and heads out the door. Time to do his part to lift the darkness.

Donnellan passes the elevator and jogs down the stairs. He walks briskly the four blocks from his Stuyvesant Town apartment to the Police Academy on 21st Street and 2nd Avenue. He takes the stairs two and a time and moves purposefully through the squad room into his office. Manny Colon hands Donnellan the McTie file as he passes and follows him into his office. Donnellan turns the page of his calendar to September 10th, 1981, sits in his chair and opens the folder. He reviews each interview, witness statement and case document with the detective. After he is fully debriefed, he thanks detective Colon for staying late and sends him home to get some rest. Donnellan then schedules a meeting with the medical examiner.

The medical examiner investigates all cases when persons die within the city limits from criminal violence, by casualty, or by suicide, as well as all deaths that are suspicious and unusual, and all deaths in police or correctional institutions. Simply put, the medical examiner's office is a busy place.

There are five medical examiners in New York City, one for each borough. Sidney Weinstein, MD is the supervising medical examiner for Manhattan which is located at 520 First Avenue, adjacent to Bellevue Hospital. Over the years, Weinstein has been impressed that Donnellan respects the painstaking hours that medical examiners spend attending to every forensic detail to determine a homicide victim's cause of death, with the goal of helping to capture the real perpetrators and avoiding false arrests. Conversely, the medical examiner is a detective at heart. Donnellan spends many hours telling him, in methodical detail, the often simple, but occasionally complex, elements of an investigation. A fair exchange between two experts.

The McTie file is on the medical examiner's desk when Donnellan enters Weinstein's office. The bottom line: McTie had substantial amounts of alcohol and heroin in his blood and bodily fluids. He also had numerous scratches on his arms and chest consistent with a struggle with a woman. There were six incisions on his front torso: four in the stomach, two in the chest. All the wounds were consistent with and appeared to be stab wounds caused by a hunting knife. Preliminary opinion of the medical examiner: McTie bled to death as a result of being stabbed six times with a knife.

After they finish the post-mortem review, Weinstein mentions he had dinner last night with the Chief Medical Examiner who told him that Mayor Longley is seriously worried about losing the upcoming election. The mayor wants every government job fully-covered from now until Election Day to reduce the chance for embarrassing mishaps. He's also suspending all restrictions on overtime and requiring that Deputy Mayor Barry Rosen handle all media inquiries.

Donnellan can't hide the smirk on his face as he tells Weinstein, "That's why I hate politics. I will never take the captain's test because at that level every move up the ladder is who you know, not what you know. Besides as a detective commander, I get captain's pay and the politicians leave me alone."

The meeting with Weinstein was just about over when detectives Nick Padula and Benjamin Harrison knock on the door. They just finished reviewing reports on several active investigations and were planning to drive Donnellan back to Manhattan South, but instead they accept the medical examiner's invitation for an early lunch at Bellevue. The detectives know the drill at the hospital cafeteria and grab a tray, pick a meal and go to the back of the fast moving line.

As soon as they all sit down, Detective Harrison starts right in, "The hunting knife used in last night's homicide was similar to the one used in case I worked on fifteen years ago at the Seven-Seven in Brooklyn. I got a call to assist the precinct detectives as they all searched for a suspect who had killed a guy in a barroom brawl. When I arrived at the precinct, there was a swarm of people with various complaints waiting to see a detective. The whole squad had been pulled from the precinct to search for the murder suspect. I asked the people to be patient and I will take the complaints in the order they came in. Four hours and fifteen interviews later, I take a complaint from a person who had been waiting to see a detective for six hours. He tells me that he thinks he just killed a man in a barroom fight." Donnellan was just about to make a clever comment when he received an urgent message on his beeper. He gave a quick wave to Weinstein and the three detectives stood up and sprinted for the door.

A siren screams and the red lights flash as Harrison pilots the squad car north on First Avenue. They listen intently to the dispatch on the police radio. "A DOA at the Tarrant Hotel. Male. White. Mid 30's. Likely a homicide. No known suspects. No one in custody. The victim is thought to be movie star."

Suddenly Donnellan feels a powerful rush of adrenaline and angst that he'd never experienced in any other investigation. He had one friend who lived at the Tarrant. He hoped it wouldn't be...but some-how he felt certain dead actor was his childhood friend GQ.

They make a left turn on to 42nd and head west. Four blocks away from the hotel they come to a screeching halt. The traffic is at a stand-still. Even the squad car is stuck in midtown gridlock. Donnellan decides to break from the car and race on foot to the magnificent hotel at the corner of East 44th Street and Lexington Avenue. The Tarrant Hotel, located across from Grand Central Station and one block from the Chrysler Building was a posh oasis in a chaotic city. It seemed worlds away from the Theater District and seediness of Times Square on the west side. It's the place to see and be seen, but not today. The tourists, groupies and paparazzi are being cordoned off by wooden saw horses and police officers. The surge of curious spectators grows by the second. The bystanders are all wondering what had happened as they gawk at police and emergency responders.

Donnellan has an eerie feeling as he races up the sidewalk. He hopes he is wrong. A bad dream. A case of mistaken identity. He weaves through a throng of bystanders and makes his way to the entrance of the hotel. Donnellan is recognized immediately by a wait-ing detective who escorts him into the lobby. As they briskly walk toward the elevators, the detective tells Donnellan that all available police officers and detectives are actively canvassing the vicinity for potential witnesses. They are especially trying to locate the young blonde who supposedly had a rendezvous with the dead actor earlier in the morning.

Donnellan signals to the detective to go back to his post and he pushes the button for the 38th floor. The elevator seems to be moving in slow motion. Donnellan's heart beats rapidly. He stares straight at the mirror and notices the beads of sweat covering his face. He grabs a handkerchief from his back pocket and wipes his brow. He's never had this anxious feeling on any other case. In less than sixty seconds he knows he will see his best friend's lifeless body. He considers his options. If he overreacts with anger and does not behave like a first-class investigator he will be off the case. He must be composed, thorough and steady. He does not want this case handed off to another detective commander. The elevator chimes. The doors separate. Donnellan collects himself, turns left, walks past two familiar doors. He's greeted by a police officer standing guard at the open doorway. Donnellan hears a familiar voice. He looks toward the kitchen and sees Chief of Detectives Emma Dickersen talking on the phone.

CHAPTER 2

IT IS HIM. DONNELLAN walks solemnly to the body of his dead friend, the rogue actor Gregory Quinn, affectionately known as GQ. The star of *Only One Life* was lying face down on the carpet of his hotel suite covered only by his damp bathrobe, just as he had been discovered ninety minutes earlier by a chambermaid. Donnellan is traumatized and numb, but he knows he must keep his emotions in check. He doesn't want to be pulled off this case. That would be an insult to GQ, his best friend. It's not that he doesn't respect the ability of other detective commanders; it's just that this is no standard homicide investigation for Donnellan because – this time – GQ is dead.

A cardinal rule for homicide detectives is to shut off any emotional feelings during the investigation. They must rapidly analyze the scene for clues and immediately interview witnesses for information that may lead them to the perpetrator or perpetrators. There is an intense urgency to move fast; all seasoned detectives know that if a perp is not arrested or at least identified after the initial twenty-four hours, the homicide trail grows cold. After forty-eight hours the trail develops ice.

As in the early stage of any other investigation all of Donnellan's senses are heightened. Every clue is instantly absorbed and analyzed by the detective. Up until this day, all of the victims he has encountered were strangers. This situation is awkwardly different. In a city of eight million people, it was his best friend lying dead. For the first time in his career, Donnellan feels surreal. His subconscious mind keeps screaming "Get Up!" to his celebrity friend who looks peacefully asleep on the floor. But this is not a bad dream. Donnellan is puzzled; he didn't think that GQ had enemies who would want him dead. He has no doubt that if GQ was ever seriously in danger, he would have confided that threat to him.

For a brief moment Donnellan's mind drifts to childhood memories with GQ, but quickly snaps back to reality. He knows he has to be careful not to let his friendship with GQ interfere with his skills as a detective. He has to get a grip on himself and take control of the situation. His mind swirled with possible motives and potential perpetrators, but nothing made sense. A burglary gone bad? But, this hotel was like a fortress with a security team filled with seasoned veterans, with surveillance cameras mounted everywhere. Uniformed guards posted at every public exit or entry. Larceny is typically the motive when a victim's wallet and jewelry are stolen, but that crime rarely happened at this hotel. And never before was there a homicide. Quick thought, was it an inside job? If so why GQ? Was it a jealous lover? Possibly? But he thinks again, GQ at no time ever was threatened. Nothing was making sense!

Donnellan stares at GQ with a puzzled look, capturing the attention of detectives Padula and Harrison. They had arrived at the scene twenty minutes after their boss and started working the room for clues. Very few words are spoken at this early stage. Detectives don't want any distractions or opinions at this time. They focus on canvassing every detail and clue. None of the detectives were surprised that Donnellan appeared to be a little out of sync. His friendship with GQ was well known.

The detectives knew that Chief Dickersen, the first African-American female Chief of Detectives in the history of the NYPD, would make her decision whether to keep Donnellan on the case soon. The old proverb that a lawyer who represents himself has a fool for a client can be loosely applied to detective work. The Chief is not about to allow Donnellan to supervise this investigation unless he can control his emotions and intelligently unravel this case. They've been good friends for many years and they respect each other, but police work is not about being popular. Dickersen is a supervisor who supervises.

Detective Harrison senses that time is running out for Donnellan to keep this case and says. "All eyes are on you, Boss." Donnellan takes a peripheral view of the Chief. She is watching his every move as she prepares to make her decision.

Donnellan takes a deep breath, looks at Harrison, and says, "I don't see any sign of a struggle."

Harrison parts GQ's hair. He and Donnellan examine a bruise on the back of Quinn's head. It is a minor abrasion, barely visible and less than an inch in diameter. There is no blood surrounding the wound and the bruise appears to slight to cause the death of such a young and powerfully built man.

GQ enjoyed being physically fit. He was a morning person who started each day with a vigorous workout, either swimming, weights or running. Although he was socially extravagant, he was disciplined with consumption of food or drink. Instead, his intemperance was for fame and attention. Knowing GQ so well, it simply did not make sense to Donnellan that a minor thump on the back of the head would kill a healthy man in the prime of his life. However, Donnellan had stopped questioning the mystery of death many years before this homicide.

"This is the only area of assault," said Harrison. "It looks like he was lightly popped with a pipe or a black jack. Maybe even, the barrel of a gun. It's too early to tell. All we know is that he was found on the floor. Naked, except for a bathrobe. Wet hair, probably from a shower. No sign of a struggle. No weapon. And, at this point – no leads."

The Chief signals to Donnellan, who walks over to state his case. "There isn't anyone in this department who knows more about GQ than me. I want to stay on this case until the perp is behind bars. I'm telling you right now that I won't let my personal feelings get in the way of doing my job."

The Chief had already made her decision to keep Donnellan on the case, but wanted to share some disturbing news from headquarters. She looked at Donnellan and then GQ. Then she spoke in a in a soft voice that only Donnellan could hear. "The mayor's office is already working overtime on damage control with the election only weeks away. The Commissioner and Deputy Mayor Barry Rosen had me on the speaker phone from headquarters for an urgent update. They know we don't have any suspects identified yet and the only lead is the mystery woman. Rosen tells me that when you get a lemon, make lemonade. Can you believe him? Then he tells me his plan is to "hint" to the media that GQ was a prolific lover and the perpetrator is probably a jealous husband or boyfriend of one of his romantic interests. This theory also gives cover to the Tarrant."

Dickersen took a deep breath, and then continued. "But, Rosen made one critical mistake which should keep him off our backs. He tells me. "No disrespect Chief, but it looks like *GQ went out with a bang*!" I tell him that I am offended and disrespected by his aloofness. And, here I am in the presence of a young homicide victim and he has the nerve to make jokes! I got a superficial apology, but I leveraged his crudeness to get assurances that he won't interfere in the investigation, yet!"

Donnellan is shocked. "Unbelievable," he says.

"There is one caveat to his cooperation," Dickersen continues. "There can be no media contact by anyone except him until after the election. Rosen specifically said to tell Donnellan to keep his big mouth shut and keep his sarcastic Irish wit to himself or he...you... will be patrolling the garbage dump in Staten Island."

Donnellan recalls the fateful day that reporters branded Rosen with the moniker *Lefty* when they overheard Donnellan referring to Rosen as Mayor Longley's left ball. Whoops!

"The rules are simple, John." she says. "If you want to stay on this case we have to keep a tight gag order on information. Absolutely no leaks. That being said, you will have a green light to use all the personnel you need to conduct a thorough investigation and follow *all* leads. Just keep me informed at every step, stay away from headquarters, and let me handle the commissioner and Rosen. If you have a problem with this set of circumstances, tell me now before we proceed any further. Just know that I am truly sorry about the death of your friend, but you are in a position to bring him justice."

Donnellan answers, "Thanks Chief. I want this case."

Donnellan walks back to GQ for one last look at his friend before he heads to the hotel lobby for updates from detectives and witnesses. The quiet stillness of the room is occasionally interrupted by the snap of a forensic detective's camera and the murmuring conversations between detectives and police officers. Anna Ramos, the supervising detective of the forensic unit, continues to gather fingerprints, fiber, hair and other samples which she places in vials and marks them for evidence. Her partner, Abdul Kahlid, has video recorded and photographed the crime scene and is busy examining the door jams with a powerful magnifying glass to determine if there is any evidence of a forced entry into the suite.

Donnellan thinks to himself, "Rest in peace my friend," and begins to walk toward the elevator. He stops in his tracks, turns around and pensively scans his surroundings. He senses something is out of place. He notices that the telescope by the living room window is pointing uptown. He asks detective Ramos if anyone had touched the telescope. She says not since she got there. He asks her to dust it for fingerprints. Then he heads for the elevator.

CHAPTER 3

Unlike the torment and anxiety he felt on his trip up to the 38th floor, Donnellan was livid, laser-sharp and focused as he traveled to the main floor. The only thing on his mind was capturing GQ's killer or killers. When the elevator doors open, he navigates quickly through the jam-packed lobby swarming with employees, residents, potential eye-witnesses, police and reporters. As he moves toward the temporary command center, he sees the obscure silhouette of Deputy Mayor Barry Rosen in a small room behind the reception desk whispering to reporters. Donnellan picks up his pace and avoids making eye contact with Lefty.

Just before he reaches the nerve center, he hears a reporter on the hotel's television reporting that confidential sources within the police department have confirmed that GQ was sexually active hours, or possibly minutes, before his death. The police department is asking for the public's help to identify and find the mysterious blonde who had an early morning rendezvous with GQ. She is described as a tall attractive young woman with long blonde hair who was last seen dashing from the Tarrant. This mystery woman is not considered a suspect in the murder of GQ, but rather a possible witness. NYPD Detectives are pursing the possibility that GQ was killed by a jealous husband or boyfriend of one of his many lovers.

Donnellan is steadfast and attentive when he meets with Sergeant Herb Wagner for a progress report. The Sergeant has been supervising a team of eight detectives who have been interviewing witnesses on the 38th floor and in the lobby of the hotel. All employees, residents and visitors in those two locations are being identified and have, or will be interviewed. He reads from his notes. "As far as we can tell, GQ gets a visit from a blonde at about seven hundred hours and she is seen leaving at about eleven hundred hours.

"They apparently have a sexual encounter in his bed, both take showers and then the broad is out the door, wet hair and all. The mystery woman is noticed in a big way by the hotel staff as she leaves the hotel. She doesn't hail a cab or ask for directions. She was last seen walking uptown. No witnesses have been able to identify her by name, but most sense they have seen her somewhere; maybe the movies, television or in some type of skin magazine. She is described as drop dead gorgeous by numerous sources.

"It appears that the assault occurred shortly after GQ takes his shower, based on the moisture of his hair and the fact that he is found by the chambermaid lying naked on the floor wearing a moist bathrobe. So we figure either the lady popped him, set him up, or an unrelated perp saw her leave and entered the room. We haven't ruled out the mystery woman as a suspect, but I don't think she assaulted him just based on the force of the blow to the head. Anyway, she was decked out in fashion with expensive jewelry, so there's no apparent motive for robbery. We found no weapon at the scene. We've got a task force looking for the blonde. And we are combing the hotel for anyone who had access to the 38th floor."

Donnellan and Detectives Padula and Harrison listen to every one of Wagner's words. Each was developing all sorts of imaginary possibilities of how and why GQ was murdered. Donnellan momentarily reflects on the vision of GQ's lifeless body on the 38th floor and asks if Wagner has a gut feeling.

"I don't have a good feeling yet, but maybe the lady didn't close the door all the way when she left. The perp just sneaks in and thinks nobody home. GQ doesn't hear a thing and he surprises the perp when he comes out of the bathroom. The perp bangs him on the back of the head. GQ doesn't know what hit him. He drops to the floor. The perp gets scared and – so it's not a total loss – looks at the dresser, and grabs the wallet, loose change, rings, and watch, and then sneaks quietly out the door. It looks like a rushed job. The perp misses all the real valuables that GQ kept in a box in the third drawer of his dresser. That's why I don't think it's the female. If she wanted his dough, she would have known where the treasure was hidden. That's how it looks to me. We've got to find the blonde. She's either the perp or a potential witness."

The Chief of Detectives enters the provisional command center and she is brought up-to-speed on the progress of the case. She tells Donnellan that the clock is ticking and the case is going nowhere fast. Chief Dickersen is a cop first and she does not like the way this case is developing. She knows that not every case is solved in the first twenty-four hours and not every case is solved period. But as the first female Chief of Detectives in the NYPD, she is held to higher standard by police officers, politicians, the community, the media, and . . . most significantly, herself.

Dickersen calls Police Commissioner Joseph P. Ryan to give him a briefing on the GQ murder case. She tells Commissioner Ryan all the relevant details in a clear concise summary. Then she listens as the Commissioner tells her to emphasize to her detectives that she must make absolutely certain that they do not share *any* information with anyone other than detectives assigned to this case. Above all, she is ordered to only share information with him or Barry Rosen. The Chief calls her detectives to the conference room for a brief meeting and passes on the Commissioner's orders. Then she directs her squad to continue their investigation and asks to speak privately with Donnellan.

"This is going to be a tough investigation for the Department, and especially for you Donnellan. Reporters are already digging into the sex angle. They're touting this homicide as a Sex God with lovers all over the world. Already former detectives on radio and television are reporting that GQ was caught in a love triangle and was killed in his New York playpen by a jilted lover. They even identify the perpetrator as the boyfriend or husband of the mystery woman.

"The desk manager of the Tarrant has already been on the tube talking about the mystery woman. Needless to say, all this will make it much less likely that she will come forward voluntarily, unless she's a glutton for attention. Sex sells and there is plenty of it here. You know Rosen will be handling the public relations, but don't get distracted. Just go solve this case."

Chief Dickersen then leaves the Tarrant for a press conference with Mayor Longley and the Commissioner at Police Headquarters.

CHAPTER 4

Claudia Witte, the supervising forensic pathologist and her assistants from the medical examiner's office, have finished their examination of GQ. They are preparing to take his body to Dr. Weinstein and his team at the morgue. Donnellan sees them leaving the Tarrant and asks them to stop. He pulls up the sheet and takes one more look at his dead friend before they leave. He internalizes his rage and thinks to himself. "GQ's killer is going to pay for this . . . big time."

Donnellan goes back to the command center and starts scribbling notes about the progress of the case searching for any clues. Zero. Nothing yet. He takes his notebook and sticks it back in his coat pocket. He knows that ultimately police work comes down to face to face interviews. But not the good cop/bad cop crime solving routines that abound in movies. Donnellan knows that detectives need to gain the trust of potential witnesses so they won't hesitate to share information, even when they believe their answer is worthless. No bad cops, just good detectives.

Donnellan takes a brief moment to reflect about his friend. He's jolted back to reality by the sound of two detectives entering the conference room with a witness. Sal Tonio, the morning desk manager at the Tarrant, became an instant celebrity when he started talking to any reporters who would listen to his *instinctive* observations about the beautiful mystery woman who spent the early morning with GQ. He delighted in expressing the most spicy and sensuous description of the blonde that his imagination would permit, until he was contacted by homicide detectives and ushered to the command center.

Donnellan tells the manager to sit down across from him. He nods to the detectives to close the door and wait outside. Donnellan likes the one-on-one interview, with no distractions. Tonio is uncomfortable. He is sweating and squirming in his chair. He hopes the Commander is not angry at him. He doesn't know if the Lieutenant is going to scream at him, hit him, or arrest him. Donnellan loosens his tie and unbuttons his shirt at the neck. Tonio is sweating. Donnellan carefully reviews his scribbled notes without saying a word. Occasionally he glances in a curious manner at Tonio. Without uttering a word, the detective commander is speaking volumes.

The manager starts to apologize for blabbering his theories about GQ's death. Donnellan interrupts, "Look, what's done is done, but you do realize you may have complicated this investigation. I'm a homicide detective, Tonio, I want to solve this case and find the person or persons who killed a resident of this hotel. That means I need witnesses like you to talk with me, and no one else, unless I ask you to. So, when you start giving a description of a gorgeous woman who spent the morning with GQ, you're out of line. That's not your job. Your job is to tell me everything you saw or think happened in the last twenty-four hours. Then if the NYPD thinks we need help finding witnesses, we will ask for the public's help."

Tonio, close to tears, shaking uncontrollably, mutters under his breath, "I'm sorry, I'm sorry." Donnellan gives him a little time to get his composure. Then, he starts his interview looking at Tonio – eye to eye – just talking. No note taking yet. He starts with a few ground ball type questions. Donnellan learns that Sal Tonio has worked as a desk manager for The Tarrant for the past two-and-a- half years. He works the 6:00 a.m. to 2:00 p.m. shift, Monday through Friday. He arrived on time today and relieved Margaret McMahon who worked the midnight shift. Donnellan is listening attentively and occasionally scribbling a note. The witness is starting to calm down and promptly answers each question. Donnellan tells him, "Okay you're doing good buddy, so just tell me about GQ."

"GQ already owned one of the penthouse suites at the Tarrant when I stared working here. I saw him all the time, usually with lady friends. He never met a broad he didn't like. He was doing everyone from movie stars to cleaning ladies. Anyone with a skirt. He never has had any fights, arguments or problems. They loved him.

"This morning, about seven he walks past the front desk. He's a great guy. Always smiling and laughing. He gives us the usual hellos and tells us he is expecting a lady friend. About fifteen minutes later a gorgeous broad walked by the front desk and says she is visiting a friend on the 38th floor. She was early twenties, with that nice Marilyn Monroe shape, a big pair, blonde, tan, a real looker. We all just figure GQ is having a matinee: like who cares? What's for lunch? GQ's gett'n laid. Not'n unusual.

"The broad leaves about eleven o'clock. An hour later, a chambermaid notices that his door was partially open and she calls inside. When no one answered she peeks in and sees him laid out on the floor. He was almost naked just wearing a damp bathrobe, face down and dead. She screams for help. GQ's neighbor calls the desk. I race there, call security and they called the cops."

"The broad, - you ever see her before?" asks Donnellan.

"She looked familiar, but I can't remember if she was here or in a magazine, GQ had so many gorgeous broads. It's hard to remember."

"Anyone hear any unusual noises - a fight, a crash, anything?"

"No," says Tonio.

Donnellan calls his detectives back to the room and they escort the desk manager back to his post and bring in Kenya Holmes for an interview.

Donnellan is reviewing his notes as the detectives walk Ms. Holmes into the room. As he stands to introduce himself, he instinctively senses that Kenya may have been an intimate acquaintance of GQ. She's a breathtaking beauty, almost six feet tall with flawless light brown skin. Donnellan figures right away that she was probably an aspiring model or actress working at the Tarrant to make contacts and pay the rent. He was right. Kenya begins to sob as she sits in the chair. Donnellan offers her a box of Kleenex before starting to ask questions.

Donnellan learns that Kenya Holmes, a twenty-six year old model had been working at the Tarrant for the last three years. She is considered a temp worker who is only available between modeling gigs. Usually her assignment is as a cocktail waitress, receptionist, or some other visible position. This morning she arrived at the Tarrant at 7:30 and reported to Carlos Diaz. Her assignment was to organize the room service breakfast orders. She was checking that the orders on the 38th floor were properly delivered when she noticed GQ's door was partially open. At this point of the interrogation, Holmes cries as she describes how she found GQ. Donnellan had already read the reports of her prior interviews. He did not want to go over each and every detail again, but there was something missing. He lets her talk until she finished.

'Kenya," Donnellan asks, "when you first noticed the door was open, was it wide open or just slightly opened, or almost shut all the way?"

She thinks for a few moments before she answers. "I'd say it was barely open. As I walked by, I noticed that it appeared closed, but on closer look I could see that it was not."

"Then what did you do?"

"I knocked on the door lightly. There was no answer or response. I gently opened the door a little more and called a little louder. Still there was no response. Then I opened the door and saw GQ unconscious lying on the floor. I screamed and cried for help. The next thing I know there are people all over the room and I find out that GQ is dead." Kenya continues to cry.

Donnellan waits until she calms down before he resumes his line of questioning, in a very consoling tone. "Kenya, there is something that you are not telling me. Something I need to know. Did you know GQ well?"

"Yes. He was so nice. He gave me my first real break. He had his agent make some calls for me. That's how I got my first modeling job. He wasn't looking for anything in return. He didn't demand sex in return for his help. He did not even hint at it. He was just a real friend."

"Did you have a relationship with him Kenya?"

"Yes. It was beautiful relationship. But that was six months after he got me my first gig. Besides, we both knew that he was a ladies' man and he wasn't looking for a long-term relationship. He was up front, no pressure. That was the beauty of his charm. No lies, no sneaking around, just occasional sex with a great lover. That was GQ. When I went by his room and saw his door open, I thought maybe we could get together for a quickie. It wouldn't have been the first time."

Donnellan ends his interview and allows Kenya to compose herself before she leaves for home. She is too distraught to go back to work. Then he scribbles more notes on his pad, thinks briefly of GQ and heads out to see if his team has developed any promising leads.

CHAPTER 5

POLICE OFFICERS, DETECTIVES, EMPLOYEES and the hotel's corporate security team are actively reviewing surveillance tapes at the command center. There are thousands of people caught on tape. Perhaps one of them is the murderer, but there is no conceivable or clear-cut suspect. Most of the investigators and detectives have a gut feeling that GQ was assaulted by a thief, so their attention is focused on spotting any offbeat characters that do not appear to be typical residents, guests or visitors at the hotel.

Donnellan knows one thing for certain, if he acted on detectives gut feelings, he would have dozens of perps for every homicide. His questions remain who and why? Sure, GQ was a world class womanizer, but he never pushed himself on anyone. He didn't have to.

Detectives are determined to interview every resident, guest and visitor at or near the hotel as a potential witness or suspect. All employees, contractors and subcontractors are on the interview lists. No stone will be left unturned until the killer is in handcuffs. At the same time, the media frenzy is in full swing with heated competition to find former lovers of *Gregory the Great*.

Sergeant Wagner is studying a sketch of the hotel layout with the Tarrant Security Director, Frankie Carraballo. Three corporate executives from the Tarrant International home office are also in the conference room. This disturbs Donnellan. He nods to Carraballo that he wants to speak privately.

They enter an empty office and close the door. Caraballo and Donnellan have known each other for more than ten years. They worked together on several cases when Frankie was a detective in the One-Six. They like and respect each other as honest hard working cops. When Donnellan asks the Security Chief about the executives, he knows that this case just got more difficult.

"They are the first wave of the corporate damage control team from the home office," Carraballo says. "Their first stop was a strategy meeting with Barry Rosen for help to reverse the plunging value of the Tarrant. Five minutes after reporters announced that GQ was murdered in the flagship hotel of Tarrant International; the stock price dropped ten percent on the big board. The money managers on Wall Street react with speed to any bad news and they sell first; then wait. When the news was leaked that GQ was victim of a love triangle, the stock recovered and is now up more than two points from this morning's open. Their goal now is product placement. They will use every media inquiry about GQ to flaunt the luxury hotel suites and the breathtaking views of the city."

Donnellan shakes his head as Carraballo continues.

"My job is to help you find the killer. I will try not to let anyone get in your way, but Donnellan, let me tell you *I* will handle them, not you. These attorneys and MBAs will not be intimidated and they will stop you in your tracks if you push them too far. They were assured by Rosen that he will coordinate all media correspondence with them. Trust me, keep your cool and we can work together. If you start screaming and cursing at them or any of the employees of the Tarrant, they will slow you down by having an attorney at every interview. I've seen them in action."

There's no mixed message. The primary goal for the damage

control team is to protect their investment and minimize any down-side risk. For Donnellan the hunt for GQ's killer is more than a homicide investigation. It's a quest.

The damage control team gives Carraballo and Donnellan a cautious, but respectful greeting when they return. They assure the detective commander that the staff at the Tarrant will offer all possible assistance to the NYPD. Donnellan thanks them for their cooperation and starts reviewing a cross section of the surveillance tapes that are being studied by his detectives. The black and white tapes show several different views of the crowded hotel lobby. There are three major conferences at the hotel. Attendees with name cards on their lapels are visible in every corner of the lobby, along with employees, tourists, shoppers and customers having breakfast. There are many young, attractive and stylish women visible on each tape, but no one has been able to identify the mystery woman in any of the scenes.

Donnellan was hoping to get at least a blurred image that could help detectives identify and find her, but no such luck. After several futile hours of reviewing tapes and updating the progress of potential eyewitness interviews, there is still no meaningful development. Donnellan is exasperated as he overhears the corporate executives murmuring about the rising stock value of Tarrant International. The corporate number crunchers are getting under his skin, so he decides to make a bold move and secretly visit a friend with underworld connections.

The headquarters for Metropolitan Auto Parts, Wholesale Tire and Repair, Inc. is located on First Avenue near the entrance to the Queens Midtown Tunnel. Brady Finnegan is the boss and owner of all fifteen automotive shops throughout the city. His wholesale operation provides discount prices for taxis, buses,

trucks and cops. He also pays "rent" to the five families for pro-
tection. Finnegan, a childhood friend of Donnellan's father, is
Donnellan's intermediary with the five crime families that control
New York City.

Finnegan is not your typical millionaire. Even at age 73, he still
gets his hands dirty changing tires and repairing cars. When he sees
Donnellan enter his shop he can tell from the glum look on his face
that it's not a social call. He cleans the grease from his hands and
greets the detective. Many clichés swirl around in Brady's head like,
"You look like you lost your best friend" or, "You look like you have
the weight of the world on your shoulders." Sadly, Finnegan knows
that these thoughts are not platitudes today. They walk back to his
office and close the door.

Brady Finnegan is more like an uncle than a friend. He looks
at Donnellan with trepidation, unsure of what to say. On the one
hand as he clearly sees the mental anguish consuming Donnellan.
He's tempted to advise him to take some time off to grieve the
loss of his best friend. But he knows Donnellan would never take
that that recommendation. So he simply asks if there's a reason
for the visit. Donnellan asks him to reach out to the five families.
Finnegan asks Donnellan to wait out in the shop while he makes
a few calls.

Finnegan calls his friend and contact, Joey Carrullo – known as
"Handsome Joey" – a constitutional lawyer and consigliere for the
five families. Handsome Joey picks up the phone on the first ring.
Finnegan gives a polite greeting and lets the consigliere know that
he needs a favor for a detective friend. Carrullo asks which one.
Finnegan tells him it's Donnellan.

"Whoa, whoa," thinks Handsome Joey. "Getting a "marker"
from a rising star like Donnellan is better than money in the

bank." The consigliere then tells Finnegan to consider the families' cooperation a done deal. Before he hangs up the phone, he asks Finnegan,

"Do you remember when a cop was shot a few years ago when he walking into a candy store in Brooklyn to buy a pack of gum?"

Finnegan says. "Sure I remember and I contributed two grand for the widow's fund."

"Well," says Carullo, "That was the first time I heard about detective Donnellan. He locked up Vic "The Animal" Putrino before the mob got their hands on him. It turns out that the "Animal" was a low level street goon trying to make a name for himself with the syndicate. But he was out-of-control and reckless. When the families found out he killed a cop, they put a contract out on his head as a sign of good faith. The families planned to ice Putrino for killing a cop, but Donnellan got him first when he rolled over Putrino's cousin Tommy, who was hiding the "Animal" in the back of an ice cream warehouse on Staten Island. Hey Brady, relay this message to Donnellan. Tell him that the "Animal's" *supposed* suicide by hanging at Rikers cost the families 20 large."

A few minutes later, Finnegan calls Donnellan back to his office and he assures the detective that the "bosses" will put the word out to New York and the national syndicate for associates to be on the lookout for anyone with information about the murder of GQ or trying to fence GQ's engraved Rolex. Donnellan understands that the families will expect mutual consideration in the future, what they refer to as a "marker," but he'll cross that bridge when he gets there. As he's leaving, Donnellan warns Finnegan to stay clear of the Irish mobster in Boston in this situation, word is he can't be trusted.

Donnellan goes back to the hotel and checks with the detectives working at the control center. There are no breakthroughs yet, so he decides to return to Manhattan South. His attention goes back to GQ's diary. Who was the blonde with GQ? Strange, she is not entered in the diary. Was it an impromptu visit? Did GQ write his diary at night, or was this another mystery?

Donnellan is driven to Manhattan South by an old time detective, Brendon Dugan, who is six months away from mandatory retirement. Dugan transferred to Homicide almost forty years ago when it was the graveyard of the Detective Bureau. In the old days, most homicides were solved by the Precinct Detective Squad within forty eight hours and the perpetrators were usually identified at the scene. But times changed and murders became more difficult to solve, so police departments had to shift the most talented detectives, like Dugan, to the Homicide Bureau.

As they crawl through the traffic to get downtown, the detectives exchange ideas about the case. "Hey Boss," says Dugan as he drives the squad car down Second Avenue. "Remember, don't make mysteries. Your friend had a roll in the crib. When the party's over, the broad leaves in a hurry. Maybe she had to go back to work or home to the hubby. She may not have closed the door all the way. Some low life in the joint sees her leave. He listens for noise. Nothing. Maybe he slightly raps on the door. No response. He thinks nobody's home. He quietly sneaks into the room and sees the wallet and jewelry. He thinks he hit the lottery. GQ catches him by surprise when he comes out of the bathroom. The perp bangs him on the head with a hammer or pipe and then takes the wallet and any anything else he can grab in a hurry. And he slips out of the hotel like nothing happened."

For Dugan, life is simple. A victim is robbed and assaulted in a hotel. First step, rule out robbery as the primary motive. Next step, check out the possibility of some mysterious love affair. Donnellan has known for a long time, GQ was not a simple man. This is not a simple case.

CHAPTER 6

THE NIGHT SHIFT DETECTIVES are busy tracking down leads when Donnellan finally makes it back to Manhattan South. Mercifully it has been a quiet night in the Big Apple. At least, there were no additional homicides in Manhattan. The investigative spotlight is concentrated on one high profile homicide pursuing— in rapid-fire fashion—every possible lead.

A dozen Manhattan South detectives are working around the clock along with uniform cops and extra detectives from precincts throughout the City. Every cop and detective has reliable and not-so-reliable sources who will give them the buzz on the street. An all-points-bulletin has been issued spreading the news for street teams to be on the lookout for anyone fencing expensive watches or jewelry. The police have notified the credit card investigative teams. They are on the alert looking for any activity on GQ's "plastic." Somehow, it is hoped that this dragnet will pull in some person or persons. But . . . nothing to date.

The Precinct Commander of the One-Six, Captain Juan Rivera, will be the first one notified if his precinct breaks the case. He will contact the Chief of Detectives and Donnellan forthwith when, and if, this occurs. His reports are not promising. Not even a rumor on the street. Usually, when a crime is committed, the perpetrator talks or makes some mistake. For now, however, the street is silent. The squad room at Manhattan South Homicide resembles a military operation on ready alert. There is a clearly defined chain of command and every member understands his or her responsibility. Chief of Detectives Dickersen made it clear to everyone associated with this case that there will be no leaks. The media is in urgent need of information, but Chief Dickersen knew from day-one that this case has the potential to get out of hand in a flash. For some in the media the death of GQ is entertainment. For Chief Dickersen, GQ's death is a police matter, a homicide investigation.

Detective Harrison made copies of all the pages in the GQ's diary and address book. GQ's answering machine had recorded eighteen messages from people who had been in touch with him in the forty-eight hour period before his death. All individuals who interacted with GQ have or will be contacted as soon as possible: memories have short attention spans. Homicide detectives are assigned to interview the individuals identified in the diary and answering machine starting with the most recent communication and working back. Precinct detectives are assigned to interview the people identified in the address book.

Normally, experienced detectives are not coached by supervisors on how to interview a potential witness, but this case is different. Lieutenant Peter Goldstein, the night supervisor at Manhattan South Homicide, wrote a brief summary of the case along with some sample questions for the detectives. Face the facts; even for seasoned detectives it is awkward to make cold calls asking people, especially women, if they had a sexual relationship with a dead actor. Some of the questions were as follows:

- Do you know the actor GQ?

- Were you aware that he had died?

- How did you learn of his death?

- When was the last time you saw or spoke to him?

- Did GQ every express any concern for his own well-being?

- How would you describe your relationship with GQ?

- A blonde lady was with him the morning of his death. Did GQ ever mention anyone who fit this description?

- When you heard about GQ's death, what was you first reaction?

- When did you hear, what time was it?

- Were you planning to see him? When? Where?

- May I ask if the relationship was of an intimate nature?

- How long were you involved with him?

- How did you meet GQ? When?

- Can you think of anyone who would want to harm GQ?

- Do you suspect anyone?

The NYPD does not want to be trumped by some private eye breaking the case. Those private gumshoes are working hard to solve this one. All the high profile media snoops have their staffs combing the streets looking to buy information. Money talks. They have the dough. The organized crime networks are working overtime to break this case. They hope that their cooperation will be rewarded. The mobsters look for markers now, or later. To them a marker is money in the bank. Time should be running out for whoever killed GQ.

Donnellan sits at his desk to review all the potential witnesses and leads. There are very few familiar names. Donnellan stopped talking with GQ about his romantic acquaintances many years ago and most of what he knew about GQ's love life was what he read in the papers. According to the media, sex was an obsession to GQ as if he was stuck in one gear: permanent puberty.

Lieutenant Goldstein drops in to give an update on developments. It turns out that GQ is the leading story on every major news network. Most of the media are convinced that GQ is the victim of a love triangle and he was murdered by a jealous lover. For now at least, they report that the NYPD is in hot pursuit of the perpetrator. The second guessing has started and is in full bloom. Television, radio and newspaper reporters are saturating the public with supposed intimate erotic details of GQ's love life. There's an epidemic of purported lovers providing salacious and passionate details of their romantic encounters with GQ. If nothing else, GQ must have been an equal opportunity lover, because they have women of all ages, races, and ethnic backgrounds claiming his love interest.

Donnellan turns on the TV in the squad room and watches Linda Denniston, a sixty-four- year-old star of stage and screen, sobbing on TV about the death of her true love. She first met GQ when he was an usher at Radio City and brought him to her home in Los Angeles. Her image as the mom next door was shattered as she sobbed in graphic detail about her intimacy with GQ. When asked if she knew him well, she burst out sobbing. "I knew every inch of him, from his nose to his toes and every bit in-between!"

Donnellan switches the channel and GQ's actress wife from the daytime drama is talking about her wonderful relationship with her leading man. She reveals that when they acted together in love scenes all the moaning and groaning was not theatrical. As she put it, "Sometimes little GQ got out of the cage and into the nest!"

The former lovers are outnumbered only by the brilliant corps of former detectives from coast to coast who offer their *valuable* advice on how to solve this case. As Donnellan turns off the TV, Goldstein sarcastically mentions that their old buddy from homicide, Dutch O'Callahan, has been on three different networks boasting about his knowledge of "crimes of passion" as he shamelessly promotes himself, his detective agency and his book, *Make My Day*. As Goldstein is about to go back to his office, he turns back to Donnellan. "Oh, by the way," he says. "The model you interviewed this afternoon is scheduled to be interviewed on TODAY, tomorrow."

Donnellan scans the pile of messages on his desk. He reads Chief Dickersen's message first and is thankful that she is covering his back. It reads,

Have reviewed all reports to date with interest. Mayor Longley, Barry Rosen and the Commissioner have scheduled a press conference for 3:00 PM tomorrow. I will handle this, but I want you to meet me for an early morning meeting in my office.

Donnellan is relieved that he won't have to attend the press conference. He appreciates that the Chief is a cop first and understands the demands of an investigation. He calls and leaves the Chief the following message;

Will be available in AM at your convenience. Have scheduled an appointment with Dr. Weinstein to review autopsy at 8:30 AM. Suggest I meet you there for a briefing.

Donnellan gets an affirmative reply from the Chief at headquarters. He looks at the McTie file on his desk and decides to review the

Crime Complaint, [UF 61: 9Pct-11678] to see if there are any additional leads that need to be addressed in last night's homicide.

Date-Time of Occurrence: Wednesday, September 9, 1981 at 22:30 Hours;

Location: 13-13 Houston Street, 3rd floor hallway [9th Precinct];

Crime: Homicide: Manslaughter;

Deceased-Pedigree: Rocky McTie: male, white, Age 26: DOB: 5-21-1956;

Arrest: Luis Hernandez: brother-in-law;

Incident-Summary:

At time and place of occurrence, the deceased, Rocky McTie, a strung-out heroin addict, was screaming incoherently and fighting his wife Rosa as he ransacked the apartment, stealing her money. When McTie saw his father-in-law and brother-in-law approaching, McTie grabbed a baseball bat and lunged towards them, smashing his father-in law's face and breaking his nose. The brother-in-law, who was armed with hunting type knife, then stabbed McTie multiple times in the torso resulting in the immediate death of McTie who collapsed to the floor in a pool of blood. A physician from the medical examiner's office was called to the scene and officially declared that McTie was dead.

Assistant District Attorney Carmen Levine was present at the station house with her stenographer, Josh Goldblatt. Witness statements were taken. Luis Hernandez confessed and claimed it was self-defense; confession was taken by order of DA Levine, who did the Q&A. The hunting knife was dusted for fingerprints and invoiced as evidence. [Prop. Clk. Invoice# 9-1607]

Date: September 10, 1981

Arrest #: 2446: Luis Hernandez:

Arresting Officers: Detective James Greenwood, 9th Detective Squad and Detective Richard Barnes, Manhattan South Homicide Squad.

After three reads of the McTie file, Donnellan is confident that for all practical purposes this case is resolved. His eyelids are getting heavy as he closes the file. He looks at the clock on the wall, it's midnight. He skims through the rest of his messages. Many are from law enforcement colleagues, his network of reliable reporters and former investigators offering their help. He even has a message from Dutch O'Callahan. Donnellan takes that message, crumbles it and tosses it in the circular file. He thinks to himself. "That phony couldn't find a bleeding elephant in the snow." Donnellan stacks the rest of the messages on his desk. He knows it's time to go home and get some rest. This case is a long way from the finish line.

CHAPTER 7

LIEUTENANT GOLDSTEIN OFFERS TO give him a ride home. Donnellan thanks him for the offer but decides to walk. He hopes the fresh air will blow the cobwebs from his brain. As he walks toward First Avenue, he thinks that the possible love connection in GQ's death is a long shot at best. As he crosses First Avenue, he wonders . . . Or is it?

Donnellan slips quietly into his apartment and walks into the kitchen. The automatic coffee machine is set for 5:50 a.m. He walks into his room and puts his gun in a locked strong box on the floor of his closet. Twenty minutes later, he softly slips into bed. His wife Marian whispers that she loves him. Donnellan says the same to his wife. He closes his eyes but he does not sleep. Instead he tries to reconstruct his last contact with GQ just one-day ago.

The elevator at the Tarrant stopped on the 38th floor. The door was open and Donnellan walked into the suite. GQ called from the bedroom and said that he had to make one quick call before they leave.

Donnellan walked toward the window and peered through GQ's telescope. He observed breathtaking views of the East River, the Pepsi Cola sign on the Queen's side and the United Nations on the Manhattan side and further downtown his home in Stuyvesant Town. When GQ came into the room, he jokingly asks Donnellan if he's a peeping John and wanted to know what he's looking at.

Donnellan told him that he was looking at GQ's old apartment house in Stuy Town on 20th Street, where he roamed before he was famous. GQ smiled and they rushed to the elevator because their waitress friend, Miriam, was holding a booth for them at the Irish Pavilion.

A cab dropped them off on 57th. Miriam slyly ushered them to a reserved booth in the back of the pub. GQ ordered a vodka tonic and Donnellan a Jameson on the rocks. When their drinks arrived, GQ lifted his glass and toasted "Up the Republic," their traditional Irish toast to their grandfathers. Donnellan replied, "May you die in Ireland."

GQ said it felt good to be back in the City. He was amused that most of the people he meets in LA think he's some kind of preppy from a privileged east coast family. His entertainment friends are incredulous when he tells them he went to high school in the Bronx. They don't know any better. People think the Bronx is a war zone. Their only image of the borough are photos of Jimmy Carter touring a section of the South Bronx completely leveled by arson a few years ago, or Paul Newman's new movie *Fort Apache: The Bronx*, depicting a criminal wasteland. What GQ remembers is different, rushing every morning for the crosstown subway on 14th Street, switching at Union Square for an express train to 149th Street in the Bronx and sprinting a few blocks carrying his jam-packed school bag to Cardinal Hayes High School. Donnellan knew this scenario quite well because they traveled together most mornings and afternoons.

Donnellan took a sip of his drink and mentioned that he saw GQ's high school sweetheart yesterday in Stuy Town. Out of the blue GQ confided that Bernadette's name came up last week during a therapy session with his psychiatrist. Donnellan was surprised by this revelation and wondered out loud if his friend has gone off the deep end in the land of fruits and nuts. GQ laughed and in a low voice confided that he started seeing a therapist last year because he had a constant feeling of emptiness, and even sex wasn't bringing him pleasure. At that point Donnellan held up his hands and started flailing his arms, repeating, "Stop! Stop! Stop!" He signaled to Miriam to come to the booth. Donnellan then ordered a double Jameson and told Miriam not to drift too far from their table.

GQ laughed at Donnellan's antics, but continued to share his innermost feelings. At first his psychiatrist thought he might have an anxiety disorder. But after months of intensive therapy, his psychiatrist uncovered that GQ suffered from persistent depression which he was able to keep in check until two life-changing events pushed him over the edge. Donnellan was immediately skeptical about GQ's psychiatric diagnosis but he also questioned himself about being unkind when his friend is obviously troubled. He decided to listen attentively with no more smartass remarks or gestures.

The first life-changer was when GQ's high school girlfriend, Bernadette Kelly, abandoned him without warning and left for Ireland to help her grandmother recover from a stroke. Donnellan knew about this breakup when it happened. He remembered that GQ seemed to take the breakup in stride. He cheerfully told his buddies that there are too many fish in the sea and he's casting a net, not a line. GQ was cool and never gave the slightest hint that he was heartbroken.

Then GQ shared a family secret about his father. Mr. Clancy was a fearless combat veteran and a courageous firefighter who had even earned the admiration of Donnellan's father; a rare accomplishment. But there was another side to Mr. Clancy that the detective didn't know or suspect until GQ confessed.

"My Dad had more than a little chip on his shoulder because of the trauma in his life." GQ said. "He grew up fatherless and poor during the Depression. Then he enlisted in the marines the day he turned seventeen and went off to war. You couldn't tell from the outside, but the three years he spent in the Philippine Islands drained his compassion tank. My psychiatrist suspects that Pop felt guilty that he survived the war while many of his fellow marines were maimed, captured or killed. He also internalized his anger that the war stole his youth and he took it out on me."

He continued, "I hated the way he mocked my accomplishments, but for some strange reason it made me work harder. He reminded me again and again that when he was seventeen he was getting shot at in the Philippines and my success as the valedictorian at Epiphany School and as a swimmer was a joke."

Donnellan was taken aback by GQ's unprompted confession and tried to digest his friend's revelations. He realized there is much he does not know about his friend. Donnellan recalled that he needed a moment to think. He momentarily stared at his glass, stirred the ice cubes, and slowly took a sip of his drink. Miriam approached the booth and asked GQ if she could get a picture taken with him. GQ stood up, told Miriam that she's a beautiful Irish lassie and he put his arm around her waist. She handed Donnellan the camera and he took a few pictures of the happy couple. They sat back in the booth and Donnellan asked GQ if there was more to his story.

GQ looked at Donnellan, hesitated slightly and told him; "Do you remember when I quit the swimming team in my junior year? I told everyone that I wanted to work at Radio City and make some money instead of doing stupid laps in a swimming pool. Well, actually it was a not a choice. My father told me he found a job for me after school and weekends as an usher at Radio City Music Hall. I yelled at him and told him, "Bullshit, I'm not going." He told me, "You damn well, are going to take that job." We kept yelling at each other, getting louder and madder. Finally he got in my face and I went to punch him. He blocked my arm and then he hit me hard in the chest. I lost my breath and gasped for air. I felt like I was going to die. Then he told me to "Shut up. Be a man and do what you are told." So I quit the team, went to work and dreamed every day of packing my bags and leaving town."

Donnellan remembers thinking to himself that he's been on the job for twelve years, ten as a detective, and I'm truly shocked. We were best buds from kindergarten through high school. He was the lion. I was the tiger. Donnellan recalls asking GQ "Why didn't you tell me? Why are you telling me now?"

Speaking with genuine emotion GQ replied. "Both of my parents died last year and I could never say anything bad about either one of them while they were alive. I guess it was my Catholic upbring-ing – Honor Thy Father and Thy Mother. Besides, the reason I have this acting gig is because of my work at Radio City. I was only sev-enteen with money in my pockets. I started partying with the stage crew, actors, dancers and actresses every night after work. Next thing I knew, I got an invitation to live rent-free with an actress friend in California and I left for Hollywood."

Donnellan remembers asking him if he changed his name to get even with his father. GQ tells him that he'd never thought about changing his name until, *Gentleman's Quarterly* changed the name of their upscale publication to GQ. He then decided to hop on the *Gentleman's Quarterly* bandwagon and changed from a Clancy to a Quinn in the blink of an eye.

"Hey," he said. "It worked for me, my obsession with sex and my acting career. Every month when a new magazine hits the newsstand, everyone thinks of GQ the actor first, and then the magazine."

Donnellan quickly changed the subject and asked if GQ's psychia-trist gave him any advice about dealing with his relationship with his father. GQ said that his therapist has helped him accept the fact that his father's envy and anger was due to the lingering effects of battle fatigue. And, now his psychiatrist is addressing GQ's obsession with having sex with vast numbers of partners. Donnellan recalled thinking to himself. "I hope Dr. Freud keeps both hands on the desk during GQ's therapy sessions," but decided to keep his wisecracks to himself.

GQ mentioned that lately he felt like he's lived his life like an actor in someone else's movie; playing the role of the carefree playboy, but not being true to himself. All of a sudden Miriam raced over to the booth. There was a crowd of fans lining up at the Irish Pavilion to get a quick look or picture with GQ. They decided to make a quick exit out the service door and go their separate ways. But before he got in his cab, GQ cheerfully told Donnellan that he may have some exciting news to share when he makes his long overdue return to Stuyvesant Town in a few days.

Donnellan rehashed every moment of his visit with GQ and he could not detect the slightest indication that GQ was in danger. If anything, GQ was as happy as he'd ever been. After two hours of restlessly reviewing again and again every detail of their conversation at the Irish Pavilion, Donnellan starts to think of GQ as a teenager. That memory helped him to fade into a deep sleep.

CHAPTER 8

DONNELLAN IS JOLTED FROM a deep sleep by a powerful body tremor. He sits upright in his bed sweating profusely, breathing heavily and feeling his heart beat rapidly. All he can remember is the last part of his dream as he kneels down next to his lifeless friend, repeating "GQ! Get up!" He can't shake the memory of GQ lying dead in his suite at the Tarrant. He looks at the clock. The time reads 4:45 a.m. No point in trying to go back to sleep. His convulsive reaction woke Marian, who studies her husband with uneasiness. She notices that his shirt and pillow are soaked with sweat. She places her hand on her husband's hand and they both grip tightly and affectionately. It takes him a few minutes of silence to compose himself and get a grip on reality before he whispers to Marian that he is going back to work. She's worried that he might have a heart attack. She's afraid for him, her and their children, but she knows if he quits the case, he couldn't live with himself. She keeps her fearsome thoughts to herself and prays silently for her husband.

After a quick shave, shower, cup of coffee and bowl of cereal, Donnellan starts his brisk walk up 20th Street toward the squad room. The fresh air helps to clear his mind as he races toward the Academy. As he enters his office, he is provided with a hollow progress report by the detective sergeant; no arrests, no suspects, no leads. The case is getting cold and he keeps thinking, what else can I do? Have I missed anything? Who? Why? Again and again this same theme resonates through his conscious and subconscious. He is fighting self-doubt. He has worked cases like this before; he knows that sometimes it takes days, weeks or even years to break a case. But sometimes, there is just no logic to it. This time he's impatient. This time the victim is GQ.

His second cup of coffee is almost empty as Donnellan stares at the front page headlines in the early editions of the New York papers. He is debating whether to subject himself to reading about the case. On the one hand he doesn't want to be distracted by reports and headlines that sensationalize the homicide, but he also wants to see if there are any reports that could help the investigation – an unlikely possibility. Against his better judgement he spends a little time reading a few articles. Chief Dickersen was right. Sex sells. GQ's love life, real and fictional, is the dominant news of the day. Donnellan is starting to become distracted and he knows it. He shifts back to the status report and starts a rapid review of every report as he eats a cold slice of pizza.

At 5:45 a.m., he gets a call from his wife. This is unusual, but for the first time in more than twelve years of marriage, she is uneasy about her husband's physical, emotional and professional well-being. He's so consumed with finding the perpetrator who killed GQ that she fears he's putting his own life at risk.

Donnellan reassures his wife, "Don't worry about me sweetheart. I'm fine. I just need a few days to solve this case. I can't stop. I owe it to GQ."

Up to this point he was basically patronizing his wife as his attention was laser focused on the status reports. But now he is also tense that in a time of crisis he has failed to attend to the needs of his family. He starts to have second thoughts about taking the case.

As he hangs up the phone he glances at the newspaper headlines.

GQ MURDERED
IN
LOVE TRIANGLE

MYSTERY BLONDE
LINKED TO
GQ DEATH

GREGORY QUINN DIES
OF APPARENT HEAD WOUND IN NYC HOTEL

Manhattan South is still a quiet place at 6:30. Donnellan pains-takingly reviews the status reports on his desk. There are no sur-prises. He compares the roster with the schedule on his calendar. No changes. He calls headquarters, speaks with a detective and leaves a message for Chief Dickersen:

Status reports have been reviewed: Negative results. Will meet with M.E. as planned.

Donnellan calls the medical examiner's office expecting to leave a message with the switchboard operator confirming his appointment. Dr. Weinstein answers. He tells Donnellan that he just completed his report on the autopsy of GQ and that he has just authorized the release of the body to McLaughlin & Sons Funeral Home in Bay Ridge. While Donnellan is talking with Dr. Weinstein he is interrupted by a detec-tive who tells the commander that the Chief in on line two. Donnellan puts Weinstein on hold and picks up Chief Dickersen who is anxious for a progress report. Donnellan then puts Weinstein on with her for a conference call. They all agree to meet at 7:00 a.m.

Brendon Dugan is sitting at his desk in the squad room sipping his morning coffee and reading the sports section of the *Daily News*. The night shift detectives are wrapping up the overnight status reports for the next shift.

Donnellan initiates an impromptu meeting with all available detectives. They summarize the overnight activity. Donnellan tells his squad that he expects to be in the field most of the day, but emphasizes that he wants to be contacted immediately regarding any developments, no matter how slight. Dugan and the other detectives nod in agreement. Dugan grabs the keys for the squad car and he drives Donnellan to Bellevue.

The Chief of Detectives and Donnellan enter Weinstein's office together for an early morning review of the GQ autopsy report. The meeting is somber and businesslike. Dr. Weinstein reviews the autopsy file for the GQ homicide before he speaks to the detectives. He doesn't offer any condolences. That would be inappropriate. He does offer his preliminary diagnosis of how GQ died, with an empathetic presentation.

"The death of GQ is one of those extremely rare tragedies where it is possible that due to his exceptional physical condition, he died in a circumstance that would not have killed, or even caused a significant injury, for a typical person of his age. Initially, I was at a loss as to what caused his death. The other pathologists on staff were also puzzled. There was no logical reason why such an apparently light blow to the head could cause the death of such a physically fit man. We checked immediately for the possibility of a drug overdose. But initial results found no evidence of drug usage. We have sent samples to the lab for more detailed testing, but we have no expectation that any drugs were involved.

I contacted GQ's physician, Doctor Bernard Fusco. GQ had been his patient for the last ten years. He said that GQ was primarily concerned with sexually transmitted diseases such as syphilis and gonorrhea. As you know, GQ was sexually active and had many sex partners. GQ's primary concern was being infected by, or infecting a partner. He was tested at least every six months and most of his tests were negative. The results of his latest tests were negative, as well, and were received three weeks ago.

Dr. Fusco said that GQ was beyond what we normally expect from a physically fit person. He was more like an Olympic athlete. His last blood pressure reading was 90/52. A blood pressure reading that low is consistent with competitive cardio-vascular athletes like swimmers and runners. GQ also had a history of arrhythmia or irregular heartbeats. The shock of being struck unexpectedly, combined with a random arrhythmia while his heart was at rest, appears to be what caused his death. Incidentally, although I don't believe it was related to his death, GQ had evidence of sexual activity within hours of his death."

Dickersen and Donnellan listen carefully to every word spoken by the medical examiner. They are both then given a copy of the medical examiner's report, which they review in silence. After she completes her review, Dickersen requests the doctor to attend the press conference at 3:00 p.m., which he respectfully agrees to attend.

Donnellan and the Chief thank Weinstein for his time and exit to the Bellevue Hospital cafeteria.

CHAPTER 9

IT WAS WAY TOO early for the Chief or Donnellan to confidently establish a motive for GQ's death. Suicide or accidental death was ruled out and two plausible theories were being given consideration. On the surface, it appeared that GQ was an assault victim by a thief who broke into what appeared to be a vacant suite. Or, the more remote possibility of a premeditated attack by an enraged individual with some type of personal connection. The Chief asks Donnellan for his opinion.

"This is looking less and less like a premeditated love quarrel," he says. "If a jealous lover was looking for revenge on GQ, he or she would have to be either a genius or an idiot. This case has the characteristics of a flat out robbery. If we find the thief we solve the homicide. Then we can put this mystery lover theory to bed."

Dickersen was expecting this response and gives the Lieutenant a stern look. "Listen Donnellan, we can't stop the mystery lover angle yet. I respect your theory, but until we have a suspect in custody we will also be checking the love connection. Look, the public has already decided that GQ was killed by a jealous love rival. They are told this day and night by "expert" former prosecutors, federal agents and detectives from all over the country. We can't ignore the media and public. We need to do some damage control while we search for the perpetrators. The perpetrator is at large, the world is watching and we have to shine. This is my watch, and I will not let the City, the

Department, or myself down. Besides, if the perp thinks we are on a wild goose chase, he or she might get lazy and make a mistake. Plus, so far this case is going nowhere."

There is no mixed message from the Chief of Detectives. Either you go along with the program or you are replaced by another supervisor. Donnellan considers his options and decides to stay on the case.

"Chief, I understand your predicament, I've been there before. You can count on me to keep a low profile. I'll stick to the investigation and you handle the public relations."

Detective Dugan is waiting in the squad car when Donnellan leaves Bellevue. Dugan drives to the FDR Drive and heads south toward the Brooklyn Bridge. They talk intermittently about the case, but Donnellan appears to have his mind in another place. Dugan senses something is wrong, but keeps his thoughts to himself. When they are near the bridge, Donnellan appears to become more intense. As they drive past Little Italy and Chinatown towards Police Plaza, Donnellan starts talking.

"Do you ever think about the difference between people who are on the frontline and the Monday morning quarterbacks who tell you everything you did wrong the day after game?" he asks. "Here we are conducting an investigation of a man who was violated in life and now in his death. First, we have to watch as all sorts of strangers examine him as he lies dead in his living room. Then, we see him cut and drained by the medical examiner. Meanwhile, his personal life is examined in detail in every form of the media. It's as if he were a cartoon character, not a human being. But we don't have the worst of it, Dugan. Think of all the frontline workers who get their hands dirty like doctors, nurses, health aides, teachers, carpenters, street cleaners, and most of us who work for a living. But by far the worst case is the hangman.

"You know Dugan, the unlucky guy who has to turn the switch. You ever think about that poor guy. He goes to work in the morning. What does he say to his wife and children? How about when he comes home from work? Does he coach the little league team? Does he read books to his children? Does anybody care? Do you care? You know what, Dugan, do I care? Last week I read that two convicts on death row somewhere down south were exonerated by a judge and released from jail. How does that make the hangman feel? What if he executed an innocent man? What does his boss say? Whoops?"

Dugan makes a stop on Chambers Street, near headquarters. Dugan gets out of the car and walks over to the Lieutenant's side. Donnellan gets out of the car.

"Donnellan, you're losing it. I've been on this job for more than forty-years and I've never seen anything like this before. Maybe you're juggling too many balls. You've got to get a hold of yourself Lieutenant. You can't bring GQ back to life. The next best thing you can do is solve this case. I've seen you in action before. You're the best. It's time to turn on your Irish charm and take command. Or else, you're off the case."

"You're right Dugan. I'm getting it together. I've never felt this way before. I always have such certainty in everything I do. But this case has me in a bind. I feel like at some point I should shed a tear for my friend, yet I never cry. I haven't even had time to think about what life will be like without GQ. Man, it was nice to have him in my life. He was never boring, but the thing I'll miss the most is his laugh. He's been laughing all his life. When I saw him smile on the big screen, I knew inside he was laughing for me, you, the world, all of life and especially . . . he laughed for himself."

"Lieutenant, don't you see; he's laughing at death, too."

"You're right Dugan. He is laughing every time someone talks about his sex life. That's right. Now it's time for me to be his best friend; the detective. I'm ready, Dugan. Thanks for your help. We need more guys like you in the department. This mandatory retirement is bullshit."

Donnellan looks through the skyscrapers at a cloudless pale blue sky and pauses for a moment. Then he gets back in the car.

CHAPTER 10

Dugan drives while Donnellan reviews his notes as they cross the Brooklyn Bridge. Next stop a visit with GQ's sister, Mary Murtagh, in the Bay Ridge section of Brooklyn. Dugan drives to their destination on 58th Street. It's a one-way street with cars parked in every available parking spot and cars double-parked in front of almost every other house. Most of the row-houses that border many Brooklyn Streets were built long before America fell in love with the automobile. They do not have driveways and garages, which makes the parking problems more difficult. Those who are unfortunate enough to own cars in Brooklyn are forced to know their neighbors, since every time a car is double parked, it either blocks or is blocked by a neighbor or visitor. The sound of horns beeping throughout the day is the Morse code used by neighbors to move their cars.

The only parking rule that is usually obeyed and always enforced by the police, is parking in front of a fire hydrant. Several cars are double parked in front of the house when the detectives reach the Murtaghs' home. Two of the cars are obviously from out of town because they are sparkling clean with no scratches or dents. Sure enough, they have license plates from Pennsylvania and New Jersey. Detective Dugan parks the squad car two doors away from the Murtaghs, and then he grabs his *Daily News*. Donnellan exits the car.

He's only fifty feet from the house. Donnellan is weighed down by a lifetime of memories. He has been on streets like this a thousand times before, but today is different. He looks at the houses, each with a uniform light brown brick face bordered from the sidewalk by a cast iron gate protecting a small cement patio. Each house has a stairway to the basement and stairway to the first floor, which New Yorkers call their stoop.

He examines the woodwork and glass etchings on the front door of the Murtagh home before he rings the bell. He is impressed with the craftsmanship. He wonders when the door was made; it had to be at least sixty years old. Why had he never noticed it before? Then he realizes that he is stalling. He takes a brief moment to collect himself, inhales deeply a few times and rings the bell.

Mary Murtagh, GQ's sister and his closest living relative, answers the door and looks at him. They give each other a hug. They walk about ten feet inside the hallway and make a left turn into the living room. Her husband Jim is sitting on the couch. They thank Donnellan for his visit.

In a low sincere voice Donnellan tells them, "Sorry for your troubles."

They sigh in unison and acknowledge his condolence. They had given similar sympathies at many wakes and funerals, but never expected to hear it for the death of GQ.

The Murtaghs appear to be handling stress as well as can be expected. They are an attractive couple who moved from Manhattan to their version of the suburbs, Brooklyn. Mary a mother of three daughters appears exceptionally fit and bears a striking resemblance to her brother. She shares her sadness with Donnellan.

"Fifteen years ago when Gregory went to California, I thought I would never see him again. My parents, especially my father were devastated and he blamed himself for ruining our family. My mother and I just prayed that he would come back home and give up his dream of being an actor. Then we see him in living color acting in *Only One Life*. When he got his first break he called me and we just laughed and laughed, he was beyond happy. I miss him so much; I can't believe he's gone. Every time the phone rings, I think it's him."

Mary sobs uncontrollably. Donnellan puts his arm around her shoulder. He's speechless. In a few minutes, they gather their composure.

Donnellan asks, "Did GQ ever mentioned that he was being threatened by anyone or had enemies?"

Mary answers, "No. None that I've heard of."

As Donnellan gets ready to leave, Mary stops him to share a family secret. Donnellan thinks to himself that he already knows about GQ's fight with his father, but Mary reveals another secret.

"Do you remember when Bernadette Kelly went back to Ireland as a teenager?" she said.

"Sure" he says curiously, "I see her all the time."

"Did you ever notice that her brother Connor has a striking resemblance to GQ."

"What!"

"Yes, that's right, about a month after she breaks up with GQ; Bernadette decides to make an extended trip to Ireland to supposedly help her father's mother recover from a stroke. Funny isn't it, that six months after Bernadette leaves Stuy Town, Mr. and Mrs. Kelly decided to adopt an Irish baby who looks surprisingly like my brother!"

Donnellan is confused.

"I wonder if you could do me a big favor John." she asks. "I don't really get along that well with Frank Kelly or his better half, if you could call her that. But, we need to contact them about GQ's will."

"Of course. I'll do anything."

Murtagh continues. "About my brother's thirteen-year-old son . . . The Kellys wanted nothing to do with GQ and wouldn't let him see, phone or contact Connor in any manner. Frank had a powerful connection in Ireland. His oldest brother, Father Sean, was a Monsignor at the Archdiocese of Dublin. Not that he tried, but Greg had no way to get his hands on Connor's birth records and even if he did, his name is nowhere to be found. Yet, Bernadette and I were always close. One early morning, when we were alone watching Connor on the baby swing at Playground 2, she broke down and told me the truth. She pleaded with me to promise that GQ wouldn't try to get involved with Connor. She said that the best chance that Connor had for a good life was to be raised in a stable family with her parents, brother, sisters and especially herself."

Donnellan listens closely.

"The original plan when she went to Ireland was to have her baby placed in an orphanage," she says. "But when she first held Connor she decided she would never leave him. Her parents loved Connor at first sight. They all knew they could never let him go. One thing for sure, the Kellys are good parents and Connor is great kid, he might even become the valedictorian at Epiphany next June. Well, GQ has left half of his estate to me and the other half to Connor. I know that you are still friends with the Kelly family. I was hoping you could break the news to them. It would be a great relief for me."

Although Donnellan doesn't look forward to being the messenger, he is relieved to learn the details of GQ's estate without having to ask for this information. It is always important for homicide detectives to be aware of the beneficiaries of a will, especially when a victim leaves a sizeable estate.

As he gets ready to leave, Donnellan can see that Mary is clearly upset about her brother's death.

Mary pleads, "Find his killer, John. You have to find GQ's killer."

She is sitting on the couch with her husband and Donnellan looks directly at them and he decides not to hold back. He feels he owes them that.

"Look, Mary. I wish that I could tell you that I have solved this case, but I can't. I have to warn you that this could take time, because right now, at this moment, we haven't identified a suspect. This is my case, and I won't leave a stone unturned. The only person I report to is the Chief of Detectives. We have a task force working day and night looking at every possible angle. When we catch the perp, I will call you right away.

"I know that a lot of the media is promoting the theory GQ's death is related to his love life. I don't buy that at all. But until we have a suspect in hand, we can't completely discount all the rumors. Besides, there's another reason that the Department is not discounting the love theory. It might give the perpetrators a false sense of security.

"As far as GQ's death goes, the medical examiner suspects that it was painless and unusual. GQ always kept himself in exceptional condition. He also had history of arrhythmia or irregular heartbeats. The medical examiner believes that GQ may have had an arrhythmia at the moment he was being assaulted by the perpetrator. It could be one of those mysteries where unusual random events cause terrible things to happen."

Mary's husband Jim comments, "I have to say that I have mixed feelings about a woman being the Chief of Detectives. I don't have a whole lot of confidence in her."

"Look, Jimmy. I assure you that Chief Dickersen is one of the best bosses I have ever worked with. She has come up through the ranks. She was a good cop who became a good boss. As far as this case goes, she has given me the green light on every possible lead."

Donnellan looks at his watch and takes the notepad out of his pocket pretending to be reviewing notes. He's actually thinking about how to approach Mary's request. He will do it, but he is debating whether to call first or just go there. Most cops don't like to announce their visits with a phone call. He decides that he is better off not calling the Kellys. He tells Mary that he will visit the Kellys. Then she hands him a copy of GQ's last will and testament.

Detective Dugan is sitting in the squad car doing some retirement planning when Donnellan reaches the car. He is reading a police retirement newsletter and has his notepad open with three columns listing expenses, assets and sources of income. His primary concern is the amount of savings he will need in addition to his pension and Social Security to live comfortably in his retirement. He is studying the figures in each column when Donnellan enters the car. Donnellan looks at Dugan, peers through the windshield and looks skyward. He pauses for a moment, and then looks back at his driver.

"Dugan," he says. "Next stop . . . Stuy Town."

CHAPTER 11

Dᴜɢᴀɴ ᴅʀɪᴠᴇs ᴛᴡᴏ ʙʟᴏᴄᴋs, makes a left turn and parks at a bus stop. Donnellan gets out, drops a dime in a pay phone and calls the office. He's hoping a witness has materialized at the Tarrant.

The corporate and hotel security divisions at the Tarrant have been working with the NYPD non-stop since the crime was committed. They are reviewing the surveillance video with small groups of employees and guests who were at the hotel around the time of the murder. This is a slow and tedious process. The detectives show each group of twenty potential witnesses the video, and make a log of all the people that the witnesses can identify. Some of these people are known by name, others are identified as guests, contractors, subcontractors, frequent visitors, seminar speakers, or participants.

The detectives are particularly interested in several unidentified males, who either appear out of place at the Tarrant or are acting in a suspicious manner. There are no conclusions being drawn by investigators, but they do not want to overlook the obvious. Don't make mysteries.

The Tarrant is like a city, within a city, and there are still several hundred people waiting to see the video. Fortunately, the hotel and the NYPD have sufficient personnel to provide rotating shifts of detectives. The Tarrant is also providing lodging and meals to all guests who are being inconvenienced as witnesses in this case.

Unfortunately, despite all the manpower and cooperation, there have been no developments.

Donnellan lets Dugan know about his phone call. On their way to Stuy Town, Donnellan summarizes his visit with Mary Murtagh. Dugan just nods his head. He's really not too surprised by the turn of events. There has been nothing typical in this case yet. Dugan thinks to himself, "Why start now?"

Donnellan and Dugan both feel it would be better if Donnellan handles the interview with the Kellys alone. The situation is awkward and has the potential to become uncomfortable for all involved. They make a plan. Donnellan will talk to Frank Kelly first as they have a long history in the community and at Epiphany Church. They agree this is not a time for secrets. It is better to put all the cards on the table. Donnellan wants to make certain that Connor is not in the house. He knows, from experience, that kids always seem to hear the things they shouldn't. He will look for an opportunity to get Frank out of the house if Connor is at home. Dugan decides to wait outside. He plans to grab a sandwich and stay in touch with the squad.

The Kelly apartment is a carbon copy of Donnellan's. Yet, inside, the personalities are a different story. Frank Kelly is gregarious and easy going, but a strict parent schooled in Catholic traditions. His wife, Joan, is friendly and polite, but private, rarely showing any emotion. As parents of five children, one of which is adopted, they are accustomed to visitors. It's not a good place for a secret visit.

Donnellan rings the doorbell. Frank answers. He looks good for a man of fifty-five. His curly grey hair is almost white and at six-feet two and two-hundred and seventy pounds. He still looks like he could play defensive line on the JETS. He gives Donnellan a hearty handshake. They walk into the living room. Joan enters the room from the kitchen. She gives the detective a kiss on the cheek.

After Donnellan exchanges pleasantries and talks with Frank briefly about sports, he asks if anyone else is at home. Kelly shakes his head. Joan decides to break the ice.

"I gather that this isn't strictly a social call," she says. "Does this have something to do with GQ?"

They all knew it did and Donnellan acknowledges such.

Donnellan paused for a moment. He is careful not to refer to GQ as Connor's father. That would be an insult to the Kellys' who have done a fine job of raising his deceased best friend's son.

"I have just spent a few minutes with Mary Murtagh and she asked me to be a messenger. GQ has left half of his estate to Connor. I don't know the amount of his wealth, but I expect that it will be a substantial sum. I am sorry to be the bearer of this news, but I wanted you to be prepared if you receive a call from GQ's attorney."

Mrs. Kelly gets up and leaves the room. She is visibly upset and really wants no part of anything to do with GQ. Frank starts to follow her into the kitchen. Donnellan asks him to wait.

He understands that there is no magic formula when it comes to addressing difficult family issues. He doesn't want to add any additional stress, but feels he owes it to Kelly and GQ to try to settle this situation.

With great care and concern, Donnellan begins by saying, "First of all, know that your confidentiality is protected in the will. GQ's attorney, Steve Cohen, placed Connor's portion of the estate in a trust valued at close to a million dollars with Frank and Joan Kelly appointed as co-executors. Nowhere in the will is there any indication of GQ's biological relationship. Plus, as a trust, it avoids probate court."

Kelly mumbles under his breath, "This is a lot of money. . . I do know that Connor plans to be a doctor." Kelly then mentions that

Connor has been accepted at Regis High School, the prestigious, tuition-free, Jesuit preparatory school for Catholic boys.

Donnellan is well aware that Regis graduates are expected to enroll in the most selective colleges and universities in the United States, and he compliments Connor by asking Kelly, "Have you ever heard of Regis Philbin? The announcer for the Joey Bishop Show? Well, even Philbin couldn't get into Regis, so he went to Cardinal Hayes instead."

Donnellan understands that Kelly won't need any tuition money for Connor for high school, so he says. "It's going to be helpful to have money to pay for Connor's college and medical school. Right?"

Kelly agrees. "It will be good to let the money sit in the trust for the time being as long as it can be kept quiet."

As the detective is getting ready to leave, he asks, "Mind if I ask a personal question?"

Kelly nods affirmatively.

"Does Connor know he's adopted?"

Kelly quickly answers, "No." After a brief pause, he continues.

"Look Donnellan, Joan and I took Connor as our son within hours of his birth. We fed him, clothed him, changed his diapers, read him stories . . . We take him to school, check his homework, take him to little league and church, but – more than anything else – we love him like no one else possibly could. Everyone in our family has taken a vow of silence about Connor's biology, so as far as he knows, he is totally ours. He is more important to me and Joan than GQ's money. So, let's just leave it alone for now and let the future take care of itself."

As he's finishing the conversation Joan reenters the room. Donnellan congratulates the Kellys on raising such an extraordinary son. He assures them that he will not share anything about Connor with any of his family and friends. He sees that Joan is particularly relieved by this promise. Donnellan further reassures her when he tells her that he is taking "the Kelly family vow of silence." That brings smiles to the Kellys as the detective leaves the apartment and gets back to the task of finding the individual or individuals who murdered GQ.

CHAPTER 12

Donnellan takes out his notepad as soon as he enters the squad car. The detectives keep their thoughts to themselves for ten minutes as the car idles. This is not typical for Donnellan, but he needs a few moments to analyze and evaluate the complex issues associated with this investigation. Unfortunately, none of strange facts he's unearthed about GQ's life or death sheds light on who his murderer might be. More than twenty-four hours have passed since GQ's death, and still no significant leads. This is not good. They take the quick ride to Manhattan South where there is a frenzy of activity.

Detectives, technical experts and police officers are continuing their frantic pace tracking witnesses from GQ's diary and address book. Still. . . there are no developments. They give the Lieutenant a nod and a wave. He acknowledges them even as he perceives the frustration in the room. There is an overwhelming feeling that this is a waste of time.

Detective Dugan sits at his desk and studies GQ's diary. He's talking out loud and wondering why he, Brendon Aloysius Dugan, has had such a lousy love life. As he turns each page, he mutters, "Why did I get so little, and this hump got so much?"

Detective Padula laughs. "Look in the mirror Dugan. You'll find the answer to that question written all over your face."

"Hey, listen," says Dugan to all the detectives contacting GQ's female friends. "When you talk to these broads, tell them that you know a very eligible bachelor who is available to provide them comfort in their time of need. Tell them I'm an expert in horizontal therapy."

Padula laughs. "The last time you had any horizontal therapy, the color television wasn't invented."

"Let's put it this way, Padula. I'm like a fine wine. I get better with age. At this point I'm just coming into my prime."

Mandy Morris checks her watch. It's 2:58. She wheels over to the television in the squad room and turns on Channel Five. They announce that a news conference is about to begin. Everyone looks at the television. Mayor Longley, Police Commissioner Ryan, Chief Dickersen, Cardinal Terrence Cooke, Regis Philbin, Susan Lucci, and many other entertainers and politicians are crowded behind a podium.

Donnellan notices Barry Rosen, off in the corner, whispering something to a reporter. He thinks to himself. "Lefty never stops working the crowd."

The Mayor speaks emotionally about the sorrow New York City residents feel at the loss of their hometown star, GQ. Chief Dickersen gives an update on the homicide investigation and a brief synopsis of the autopsy report. She compliments Dr. Weinstein and his staff. She then introduces him and he gives a more detailed explanation of GQ's mysterious death.

All the questions from the press concern the mystery blonde and GQ's sex life. As previously scripted, the press conference ends at 3:30.

Donnellan goes back to his desk and continues to review the status reports. His phone rings. It's Captain Rivera from the One-Six. Donnellan has a brief burst of optimism that maybe they solved the case. No such luck.

Captain Rivera tells the commander. "First off, I will tell you that we haven't got anything yet on the GQ case. Unfortunately we're also looking at another gruesome mystery involving the disappearance of Dolly Goldberg, the eighty-nine year-old wealthy widow. She's the owner of several apartment buildings downtown and lives on East 29th Street. She also happens to be Barry Rosen's aunt. We put a surveillance team on a mother and son pair that we suspect in the disappearance. They've been very busy. Now, we think they might have killed the old lady and are looking to make a run for it. The Chief tried to keep you off this case, but Rosen demanded that you be involved. Sorry about your friend Lieutenant, but we need you to meet us ASAP at the precinct to review this case."

Donnellan is somewhat familiar with Dolly Goldberg. She was a well-known philanthropist supporting many museums, parks, and scholarship programs for underprivileged students. He knows the One-Six took this case seriously right away and, like everyone else, he knows that people don't just disappear. He immediately thinks that she probably either had an accident, which is highly unlikely. Or, more likely, she was the victim of a crime. Donnellan tells Captain Rivera that he will be up to the precinct within an hour. Then he picks up the phone and calls Barry Rosen who answers on the first ring.

Rosen apologizes to Donnellan for temporarily taking him away from the GQ investigation. He pleads with Donnellan to understand that there is still the possibility that his aunt is alive. He's desperate. Donnellan is sympathetic to his predicament and assures the deputy mayor that he will do his best to find his aunt. Rosen tells him to use *any* means to find her and he has his back. Donnellan updates Rosen on the status of GQ's autopsy and mentions that the body should be released to McLaughlin & Sons Funeral Home in Bay Ridge in the next day or two for a one-day private wake for the family. After which, GQ's remains will be transferred to Manhattan for a public viewing and a funeral service at Saint Patrick's Cathedral. Donnellan asks Rosen to keep the media away from the family's viewing in Bay Ridge. Rosen assures him that he will. He asks if the family would appreciate a personal visit at McLaughlin & Sons to allow himself and Mayor Longley to offer their heartfelt condolences to the family? Donnellan says that would be meaningful, but no pictures or press releases. Donnellan gives Rosen the phone number for GQ's sister so he can ask her about the mayor's visit and coordinate the appropriate time for the visit.

Donnellan pauses at his desk for a moment before he leaves. He thinks about GQ. Is there anything else he can do? Is he missing any possible lead? He can't think of a thing that isn't being pursued. Donnellan thinks to himself, "Sorry, buddy."

Lieutenant Donnellan walks out to the squad room and glances in the direction of Detective Dugan. He is still reviewing GQ's diary and making humorous comments about each page. Donnellan wonders what will happen to Dugan in seven months, as he will have been retired for four weeks. Here it's Dugan's scheduled day off and, instead of watching a ball game or playing catch with a grandchild, he goes to work. Donnellan grabs the keys to the squad car and lets his staff know that he is on his way up to the One-Six. He lets them know that his visit is related to a new case and to keep pursuing all possible leads on the GQ homicide.

CHAPTER 13

Julia and Lawrence Smitter are hard-edged swindlers who prey on the elderly. These mother/son imposters never stay in one place long. They move swiftly across state lines and change names frequently to complicate detection by law enforcement. These crooks scout the high wealth zip codes for elderly widows and widowers who are friendly, lonely and rich. They hope to become fast-friends with their elderly victims, do a quick net worth, and develop a devious plan to steal everything. These bandits aren't satisfied with tokens. They want it all.

Dolly Goldberg met the most important criteria for the Smitters. She was wealthy. The income she received from renting her apartments was more than a million a year. A real estate agency handled all of her rental properties except the one apartment she rented on the third floor of the elegant brownstone townhouse that was her personal residence. By a tragic twist of fate, when the third floor apartment in Dolly's townhouse unexpectedly became available, the Smitters arrived in Manhattan. They introduced themselves to Goldberg as visiting antique appraisers who needed a short term rental in Manhattan to complete an estate assessment for a wealthy Eastern European client. Although Mrs. Goldberg was uneasy about the Smitters excessive appreciation of her Tiffany lamps, 19th Century antiques and the handcrafted molding throughout her ground and second floor apartment, she figured she would let them rent her upstairs on a short-term basis. Regrettably, once the six-month lease was signed and the two month security deposit was paid, Dolly Goldberg's fate was signed, sealed and delivered.

Julia was an experienced elder scammer whose knowhow involved expertise at gaining the trust of lonely oldsters by acting as a compassionate friend who truly cared about them. But Dolly was not lonely, had many friends and was wary about making friends with Julia.

The Smitters had a problem. Dolly didn't take their bait. She told her neighbors she didn't trust or like those people. But Dolly made one critical mistake. Early one morning, when Julia knocked on her door, she was caught her off guard. Julia said she was frightened and on edge because she and her son had possession of a luxurious diamond bracelet they were appraising for a client. She begged Dolly to put the bracelet in her safe for just one day. Dolly took the bracelet, walked down to her basement and put it in her safe. As she walked back up the stairs she wondered how they knew she had a safe, which they didn't. Now . . . they did.

The next morning when Julia came back for the bracelet, Dolly opened the door and told Julia to wait outside. Dolly got the bracelet from the safe, barely opened the door, looked at Julia with suspicion, stuck her arm through the barely opened door, gave Julia the bracelet and shut the door. Julia instantly knew that her original elder fraud plan had unraveled. She rushed upstairs and told Lawrence that they had to move fast and crack the safe that night.

When evening came, the Smitters listened attentively for any sounds in the second floor apartment. At ten o'clock, the television was turned off. They figured that Dolly was ready to go to sleep. At ten-thirty, Lawrence used the skills he learned in prison to pick Dolly's door lock. He silently snuck up on his sleeping landlady, suffocated her until she was unconscious then tied a rope around her mouth to gag her. At the same time Julia was sneaking around on the first floor where she found the safe and also discovered a hidden fallout shelter. It didn't take Lawrence long to crack the safe and steal a treasure load of cash, bearer bonds, and jewelry. He carefully placed the treasures in a customized shipping container. Before leaving the apartment, the mother and son placed the barely conscious landlady in the concealed fallout shelter, and then covered it with a rug and a hope chest.

Dolly had many friends in her community who called or socialized with her frequently. Dolly's neighborhood was what gerontologists call a Naturally Occurring Retirement Community, in other words there were a lot of older neighbors aging at the same time. One of Dolly's longtime neighbors, Freda Lang, spoke with Dolly several times a day for social reasons, as well as to make sure that each of them was safe and alive. Freda's first call was at nine in the morning. Then she followed up every fifteen minutes for almost two hours. Then she called her neighbor Jim Mulroy, a retired New York City detective, and asked him to go with her to Dolly's house because she might be in danger. Though Freda had a key, she knocked on the door first. No answer. She opened the door and called for Dolly. No answer. They searched the house. No Dolly. They both immediately suspected the Smittters.

Mulroy picked up Dolly's phone and called the 16th Precinct. He connected with his longtime friend, Captain Rivera. Mulroy had a plan to lift some fingerprints and find out who these third floor tenants really were, yet he wanted to avoid the NYPD bureaucracy. Without saying why, Mulroy was granted a courtesy request by the Captain. When police arrived at 29th Street they were met by Mulroy. One of the officers slipped him some lifting tape.

The two police officers were then guided by Mulroy to Dolly's apartment. They searched Dolly's apartment and found no sign of her or evidence of struggle. They searched the roof and the basement with no luck. Then they went upstairs, without touching the handrail, and knocked on the Smitters door. Julia answered and feigned concern about the safety of her neighbor. She consented to let the police search her apartment. Mulroy stayed outside on the third floor landing during the police search. Once Mulroy was confident that the search was active and the Smitters were distracted, he started lifting fingerprints off the doorknob and then the handrail. He was quiet, thorough and fast. The minute he lifted his final print, he raced downstairs to an awaiting patrol car and was driven to the forensic unit at police headquarters.

The fingerprints were rushed through lab and faxed to the state police. It was a longshot at best, but worth a try. Bingo! There was a match for Lawrence Sexton, also known as Lawrence Jenkins, and William Stagwell. He had a lengthy rap sheet for financial crimes in New York and six other states. Plus, there was a felony arrest warrant for his capture from California.

The afternoon sun is still bright, peeking through the skyscrapers. Donnellan puts on his sunglasses before he opens the squad car door. He finds it hard to believe that summer is almost over. This is usually his favorite time of year, but right now he can't think of anything but work. As he drives uptown, he thinks about Mrs. Dolly Goldberg.

There are a lot of Mrs. Goldbergs these days – frail elderly men and women, usually women, who outlive their spouses and most of their friends. Many have families spread out around the country, many live alone. For a growing breed of criminals, the isolated elders are prime picking. Donnellan rehashes in his mind the CBS News radio alert he listened to about the wealthy widow's disappearance. Dolly was described as a friendly person who outlived her husband, relatives and many friends.

As he headed north on Third Avenue in his unmarked car, the commander makes a left turn onto 29th Street. He drives past the brownstone. He doesn't stop or slow down; he just wants to get a feel for the neighborhood. He knows that there is an active surveillance, but he observes no obvious sign of the police. These detectives are good.

Donnellan arrives at the One-Six and rushes through the hurried crowds of people briskly walking on 46th Street. Once inside the precinct he joins Captain Rivera, Chief Dickersen and the three precinct detectives who are conducting an intense strategy meeting. Their objective is to find Mrs. Goldberg . . . and soon. Everyone hopes that she is still alive, but it may be too late. Either way, they must gather evidence against those who have kidnapped, harmed or murdered her.

Donnellan is brought up to speed as soon as he enters the captain's office. He looks over the rap sheet on Lawrence and the file on the Smitters. They leave a disturbing trail of elderly victims. For these grifters, it is not enough to rob their elderly victims. Their older "friends" all die under suspicious circumstance, like a fire, accident, or in this case, a disappearance. The only thing missing in each case is the money and fortune of the victims, which always finds its way into the hands of these swindlers.

Chief Dickersen waits for Donnellan to finish his review before she presents her plan.

"We're dealing with some bad people here. Julia and Lawrence Smitter are professional swindlers of the worst type. They have left a trail of elderly victims from the West Coast to the Mississippi River. Although we have search and arrest warrants for both of them, I believe that best chance of finding Mrs. Goldberg is to keep both of them under a tight surveillance for forty-eight hours at the most. That brings us to Monday. I realize that there is a risk that the undercover team will be identified by these crooks. We have to take that chance. We can't let them out of our sight.

"If the supervisors have any suspicion that the Smitters are on to the surveillance, or are trying to give us the slip, they are to be arrested immediately and the search warrants are to be executed for their apartment and car. I would rather that we err on the side of arresting them too soon, rather than giving them the chance to give us the slip or harm Mrs. Goldberg.

"We have to be prepared for the possibility that it may be too late for Mrs. Goldberg. In that case, we must attempt to find her body. Otherwise we will have to build a homicide case on circumstantial evidence. Let's hope it doesn't come to that."

Detective teams have been conducting around-the-clock surveillance of the Smitters for the twenty-four hours. The fact that various news outlets have been covering the disappearance of Mrs. Goldberg makes their job more difficult. The perps must have some suspicion that they are being watched or are under investigation. The police must be aware that even when criminals are being cautious, they still make mistakes.

The disappearance of an elderly woman in connection with experienced swindlers, presents many challenges to investigators. The Chief is aware that the Department must use every available investigative tool to solve this case. She recognizes the possibility that Donnellan could be distracted with the GQ case. Yet, she needs his investigative and supervisory skill for this case now, if there is any chance that Goldberg will be found alive. Donnellan understands that everything possible is being done on the GQ case. He agrees to take command of this investigation.

The Chief summarizes the case one more time before she heads back to headquarters. "We have a solid Grand Larceny case against the Smitters. Just the forged documents alone, are enough to send them both up the river for a long time. Building a homicide case is doable, but uncertain. The Smitters are experienced criminals who are probably lawyered up already and will insist on having counsel present for any interview, so an admission or confession is unlikely at best. Also, the fact that we have a mother and son involved, we can't count on one of them giving up the other."

As the Chief is leaving the precinct, she shares her opinion that Mrs. Goldberg is either dead or in great jeopardy. The grifters got an early jump on the NYPD which gives them an advantage. They had a day to hide and destroy incriminating evidence. All the detectives agree with the Chief that they must keep them under a tight surveillance. The Smitters have no roots in New York and they may suspect that the heat is on. They have to make certain that the grifters are not given the opportunity to blow town.

The Captain and detectives continue their methodical analysis of the case and exchange ideas for another half hour. Captain Rivera and Donnellan agree that this case needs to be tightly supervised and investigated by experienced detectives who are capable of gathering evidence in a circumstantial case. Donnellan is tempted to take himself off this case, but that's not his style.

Captain Rivera has assigned the supervision of the surveillance to Detective Sergeant Driscoll, a sixteen year veteran with more than ten years in the detective bureau. A veteran of the Marine Corps, Driscoll also graduated from John Jay College with a Bachelor's and Master's Degree in Criminal Justice. He speaks cop talk to mask his intelligence because he is a private guy. He doesn't like to sound like he is trying to impress his co-workers with his academic achievements. But when he gets on the stand he can articulate a case with the best of them.

Donnellan takes a copy of the case file and leaves for the Tarrant to check on the progress of the GQ case. When he gets there he lets his squad know that he will be doing double duty on another high priority investigation involving the Deputy Mayor's aunt. He also emphasizes no leaks will be permitted and to keep him informed of any developments. No one asks questions, these detectives know the drill.

Donnellan leaves the command center at the Tarrant, walks into the conference room and closes the door. He takes Barry Rosen's business card out of his pocket and makes a call. Barry answers on the second ring. Donnellan assures Rosen that he is taking command of the Dolly Goldberg investigation, but warns him not to be overly optimistic. Donnellan expresses his concern that Dolly's upstairs tenants are evil swindlers with a trail of elderly victims from coast to coast. Rosen is filled with a heightened sense of anxiety and asks if there is anything he can do to help the investigation. Donnellan tells Rosen that he is supervising a tight surveillance of Dolly's residence. He needs to keep the media away from that vicinity. Rosen guarantees the detective that he will contact his media sources and the street will be quiet. Before Rosen hangs up the phone he expresses once again his condolences to Donnellan for the death of his friend GQ.

Donnellan leaves the Tarrant and returns to the squad room at the One-Six for a strategy meeting with Sergeant Kevin Driscoll. His six-foot five-inch frame topped by flaming red hair is easy to find in a crowd. Driscoll is usually an easygoing guy, except when people call him "Red." For some reason, he could never get used to being called a color. Call him Sarge, Sergeant, Detective, Kevin, Driscoll or almost any other name, just not "Red."

Driscoll gives the commander the progress of the case. The One-Six has been working on the disappearance of the wealthy widow from East 29th Street. It looks like she's in imminent danger and a possible homicide victim by that mother and son team of swindlers. No one has seen her for twenty-four hours. The perps have at least a day on us and they might have already started hiding Mrs. Goldberg's body parts in a garbage dump in Jersey. If they can't find her body, they will have to build a case on circumstantial evidence.

Donnellan tells the Sergeant that he wants to meet with the precinct's day shift detectives in the early morning. He's also assigning three Manhattan South homicide detectives, Cindy Gomes, Tony Sigura and Jamal Maxon to work with the precinct team.

CHAPTER 14

Patrick is waiting at the elevator when his father gets off at the seventh floor. He gives his dad a hug and tells him that he was waving to him from the window. Donnellan says he's sorry he didn't look. They go into the apartment and his whole family gives him a warm greeting.

Marian looks at the kitchen clock and notices it almost ten o'clock. She figures that she will let the kids stay up for about a half hour more to talk with their dad. They all want to know if he caught GQ's killer.

"Not yet, but it's just a matter of time," Donnellan says. Suddenly, he loses his voice and grabs a glass of ice water. He feels famished, almost dizzy. He realizes that he hasn't had anything to eat since noon. Marian asks him if he is hungry and he nods yes. She tells the children to go to their rooms and get ready for bed. Marian brings out a plate of cheese and crackers, then makes a dinner. He eats a few crackers feels better. He says goodnight to his children and he reminds them to say their prayers.

Marian fills two glasses with Cabernet. They move into the living room and have a toast, they clink their glasses and he says, "To my long lost friend GQ, I miss you buddy."

Marian gets up to check on the dinner. While she's in the kitchen, he turns on the TV.

Donnellan adjusts the antennae until the picture is clear, and then turns the dial past the ten o'clock news on channels 5, 9 and 11, looking for some levity to close out the day. He turns from channel to channel in such a hurry that he almost misses a familiar face. He backtracks a few channels.

"Marian, I can't believe it! Geraldo has "Wild" Joe Donovan on his show. I can't believe it. I thought he was dead. He must be at least eighty. Oh my, God! He's talking about GQ."

Joe Donovan retired from the NYPD Homicide Squad more than twenty-five years ago as a first grade detective. He started his own investigative agency and was famous around the world for solving and talking about homicides. He used to be a frequent expert guest on the talk shows. He was known for his New York accent and direct approach. Donnellan knew he had a serious battle with lung cancer about three years ago and he is glad to see Joe is still around. He met Joe at a few retirement dinners and he is still a legend in the bureau.

"Wild" Joe looks good and is as feisty as ever. Marian comes into the living room with his dinner and she sits down to watch TV. Geraldo asks Joe about crimes of passion.

"Geraldo, let me tell ye about a case I worked back in dhe early 60's. Dhis very calm female calls dhe precinct to report dhat she just killed a man in his car. I drive down to dhe scene of the crime which happens to be a remote parking lot near Bensonhurst. I look in dhe car and dhere I see himself, layed out in dhe back seat with his pants off.

I ask dhe broad . . . uh excuse me . . . dhe woman what happened. She tells me dhat her boyfriend was a married man. Dhat he was, uh excuse me Geraldo, uh she used the "F" word. Uh, I know it is after ten o'clock, but I still don't think your guests use the "F" word. Am I right on that score, Geraldo?"

Geraldo nods. "Yes."

"Well, let's just say, she told me her married boyfriend was doing her. He keeps telling her dhat he is going to divorce his wife and marry her. Basically he is using dhe old stall tactic. Plus, he starts getting cheap with her. They started out in a nice hotel and gradually he's getting his jollies in dhe back seat of dhe car. Finally, she had it. She slips a pistol in her purse and waits until dhe cowboy is in dhe saddle. Dhen, she asks him if he is a Catholic. He says yes. She asks him if he is committing a mortal sin dhat will send him right to hell. He says yes, again. She asks him to close his eyes and she blows him away."

Geraldo is mesmerized by the story and asks "Wild Joe" if he thinks GQ's murder is connected to his love life.

"I won't tell anyone who I dhink killed GQ or anyone else. What if dhe perp is watching? I don't wanna give him any of my inside thoughts. Dhe only thing I would tell him is to give up now, because sometimes bad things happens when dhe cops are huntin for a murderer."

Donnellan smiles at Marian and tells her that "Wild" Joe will never change. At the commercial break, he gets up to change channels again and stops suddenly when he sees Kenya Holmes. He tells Marian that she was the one who found GQ. Marian remarks that Kenya is beautiful. Donnellan thinks to himself that Kenya has certainly composed herself. If she doesn't get noticed now, she should give up show business. She is a stunning beauty.

The host, Gina Rotinni, has been asking her about her relationship with GQ. Apparently, Kenya has decided to be open about her intimate relationship with GQ. This surprises, but doesn't shock Donnellan. The show must go on.

Gina is searching for some startling revelation and asks Kenya if there is any truth to the rumor that GQ was gay.

Kenya was stunned and reacted instantly. "No way GQ was gay. As a matter of fact there were times that he didn't even wait for me to get my panties off before he . . .

Donnellan shakes his head again. Marian is trying to contain her laughter. She tells her husband, GQ must be laughing hysterically in heaven. Donnellan had to admit, that if GQ had to leave the stage early, he picked the right script.

Marian picks up his dinner plate and walks into the kitchen to clean up. When she returns a few minutes later he is asleep on the couch. She shuts off the TV, wakes him up and they both go into their bedroom. As he gets into bed Donnellan tells his wife that he's setting the alarm for four-thirty because he is supervising an early morning surveillance. Then, he falls into a deep sleep.

CHAPTER 15

An ABANDONED BLUE PANEL van is parked three houses down, across the street from Dolly Goldberg's apartment. The dented van hasn't been moved for twenty-four hours. There are two parking tickets attached to its windshield wipers. On the tinted rear windows someone has written "Clean Me," as well as few choice obscenities. It is only a matter of time before a city tow truck will impound this piece of junk and haul it to the police garage.

Actually, this van is the epicenter of the surveillance operation of the Smitters. The antenna is a video periscope which records every movement in front of Dolly Goldberg's house. Every time Lawrence or Julia leaves their apartment, detectives are ready to follow their every move.

A pedestrian walking at a reasonable pace is not that difficult to follow, especially for experienced cops. They can give their subjects a little latitude and hang back a half block. When their subject stops or enters a store, they do a little window shopping to keep from getting too close. The objective is always to follow as close as possible without being noticed or made. Trailing Lawrence and Julia is not too difficult. On the rare times that they leave their apartment they walk at a leisurely pace and stay within a few blocks of 29th street.

Julia wears clothes that fit the conservative image of her act. Her son projects a clean cut image and wears a sports jacket and usually a tie. They act pleasant and friendly whenever they are in public.

The surveillance of the mom/son grifters was fairly routine until Lawrence rented a car and started making trips to New Jersey.

A long distance truck driver from Louisiana once told Donnellan that the worst place to drive in the United States is New York City. He was probably right. Monday through Friday, from morning till night, the traffic in Manhattan crawls from street to street. Frustrated drivers sit in their cars watching as mothers pushing baby carriages pass them. These drivers are not known for their patience.

A rare sight is a friendly driver giving a signal to another motorist to just cut in front of him or her. A more familiar scene has cars bumper to bumper, almost attached, defending their territory from any potential invader. The horn blasts, obscenities and hand gestures are the battle cry of these road warriors. The surveillance of a car often involves running red lights and speeding, especially if the target is a reckless driver.

Fortunately, Lawrence doesn't want to deal with the rush hour traffic. He makes his trips early in the morning before six a.m.

The Smitters are planning to leave town. They know the heat is on. Their plan is to destroy and remove all evidence that they ever lived in New York City. They hope to cover their tracks and make it more difficult to be discovered when they move to Miami. They have already secured a new identity, changing their names to Carol and William Rettin.

At the crack of dawn, Lawrence starts walking to a garage two blocks from his apartment to pick up his rental car which now has a slight chip in each taillight which will shine like a beacon in a lighthouse every time Smitter touches the brakes. At the same time the undercover team goes on high alert. The detectives who are monitoring the surveillance equipment in the van immediately notify detectives in the three surveillance cars of his movement.

The homeless man that Lawrence passes when he reaches the corner is Detective Jack Kowalski. He slowly walks and watches his subject while his plain clothes partner drives past the garage, watches and waits.

A parking attendant grabs a set of keys and brings Lawrence his car. He gives the attendant an extravagant ten dollar tip. Kowalski watches this transaction as he searches through a garbage can in front of the garage. He thinks this guy is a big tipper with Mrs. Goldberg's money.

Smitter then double parks outside his apartment for a few minutes. He makes three trips inside his building, two times returning to the car with a carefully sealed cardboard boxes containing crucial items they want to ship to their Florida storage facility. During the third trip, he nervously carries a stamped metal shipping box. After he places the metal box which contains the contents of Dolly's safe in the front seat of his car, he anxiously starts looking frantically up and down the street, before he enters the car. Detectives record each of these trips, thinking that, the jury will love this.

Sergeant Driscoll sits in the back of a white panel van on Ninth Avenue with detectives Manny Colon and Greg Morrow. They are waiting for the radio call to start heading toward the Lincoln Tunnel.

As he waits, Driscoll reviews the file again. The Smitters live in Dolly Goldberg's apartment building on 29th Street. They don't have much of a social life. They seem to do everything together. Driscoll thinks to himself, "These people are weird." He remembers taking an elective course in mythology. He thought it was entertaining, but basically a filler course. Suddenly, he's thinking, "Is this like Oedipus Rex? Is Lawrence in love with his mother? It's like a thirty-four year old man is dating his mother. They go out to dinner every night. He has no other friends; male or female. At least Oedipus didn't know his mother was his mother. These people are strange."

Suddenly, the radio announces that, "It's time for the flowers to be delivered."

The police are aware that it is possible that their transmissions can be picked up by scanners or other servers transmitting and receiving radio signals. They use code words and phrases to protect their undercover operations.

The car is full and Smitter drives uptown on Tenth Avenue to the entrance of the Lincoln Tunnel.

Driscoll's van gets a slight lead on the rental car. As expected, at 38th Street Smitter passes him and enters the tunnel. The undercover van and Buick follow him, but keep a loose tail keeping a watchful eye on the damaged taillights every time Smitter touches the brakes.

Hoboken is the first exit on the Jersey side of the tunnel. Lawrence believes it is the perfect spot to bury evidence. It is across the state line, which he hopes will confuse the New York authorities. Also, there are many construction sites in Hoboken, which provides ample opportunities to discard the evidence.

Lawrence drives directly to the north end of town where an old factory is being converted into apartments. There are four separate construction dumpsters at this site. Two are already filled with pipes, sheet rock, nails, and lumber. He pulls right next to a half-filled dumpster. He does not see anyone when he gets out of his car. It's only six-thirty in the morning. In a matter of five minutes, he unloads the bags from the backseat and trunk. He looks around, again. He sees no one and he drives over to the UPS Store. He is the only customer when the store opens at seven o'clock. Mr. Rettin tells the the UPS manager that he wants this tightly sealed box delivered next day air to Miami. The box is weighed and labeled. Smitter pays in cash, returns to his car, and heads back New York City.

A third undercover team in a maroon Mercury Cougar watched

and recorded his every move. Detectives Penny Lucia and Betty Williamson retrieve the garbage bags from the dumpsters which mostly contain letters, magazines, towels, and winter clothes that might contain incriminating fingerprints or fiber evidence. The detectives seal the bags and mark them for evidence. They sit fifty-feet away from the UPS store parked between a ford and a VW Beetle. They are not noticed by Lawrence. When Smitter is out of sight and driving back to New York, Detectives Williamson and Lucia enters the UPS Store, identify themselves to the clerk as NYPD detectives and ask for some confidential help regarding his first customer of the day.

The clerk calls the manager, who retrieves the box and places it on the counter so that the detective can clearly read the label. They tell the manager that they are investigating a horrendous case of elder abuse and they need his help. The box on the counter, which contains Mrs. Goldberg's jewelry, bearer bonds and cash is being sent from William Rettin to be held at a storage facility in Miami for Carol Rettin. The detectives place several evidence stamps on the box, confiscate it for evidence and give the manager a signed NYPD Evidence Receipt. As they leave the UPS store, the manager that he's sorry he couldn't help. (wink, wink).

Meanwhile, Smitter left Hoboken and returned to the garage and his apartment under the watchful eyes of the detectives. Donnellan then meets Sergeant Driscoll and two of the surveillance detectives in the white van at a prearranged parking spot at 30th Street and Ninth Avenue. The detectives think through the next step. They all agree that the Smitters are making moving plans and there is still no sign of Dolly Goldberg. Sergeant Driscoll mentions that the neighborhood was unusually quiet overnight and this morning. There are no reporters or photographers looking for Goldberg. Plus, her disappearance was not even mentioned in the morning news. Donnellan tells the detectives that he asked Barry Rosen to put an embargo on any media coverage of the Goldberg disappearance for forty-eight hours. The Lieutenant emphasized that nobody crosses "Lefty." The detectives are impressed and agree that "Lefty" has clout, but are curious as to how Donnellan got a direct pipeline to the deputy mayor.

"Do you remember the night when the Brazilian soccer star got stabbed in Chinatown?" All of the detectives say they remember him, as well as the memories of his grieving family, friends and fans. Then Donnellan explains that, the morning after the Brazilian was murdered he met with Doc Weinstein at the medical examiner's office to evaluate the results of his initial examination of the soccer star's body. Weinstein tells Donnellan that his preliminary impression is that the attacker was a strong athletic type who was right handed, based on the forceful thrust needed to fracture the ribs and the angle of the incision on the back. He also believed that the knife used had a small blade of two to three inches which further corroborates that the perpetrator is most likely a powerfully built man to do so much damage to the body with such a small knife. While Donnellan is discussing the case with Weinstein, he gets a call from the squad. Dutch O'Callahan has arrested the assailant who confessed to the murder. Of course, Dutch contacts his reporter friends and the mayor's office to boast that he broke the case. Unfortunately, he locked up the wrong guy!"

Donnellan then says, "I raced down to the Seventh Precinct and what does the perp look like in the holding pen? A skinny middle-aged guy identified as Arthur Tillman. He's crying hysterically and blaming himself for killing the soccer player and also for the fluoridation in the city's water supply. I tell the perp to calm down, that I just want to talk with him. He composes himself. Dugan lets the perp out of the pen. As Tillman starts walking toward me, I pick up a small stapler from the desk and throw it to him. He catches it with both hands and he throws it back to me with his left hand. I think to myself, forget the interview this guy is a psycho. So, I just ask him when was he discharged from the hospital?

"Tillman tells me that two weeks ago he was released from Creedmoor Psychiatric Center to the community as part of the dein-stitutionalization movement and he has been homeless and wander-ing around the City. I calmly tell Tillman that he shouldn't lie about killing someone because then the real killer doesn't get caught. He starts crying and screaming that he's sorry and he didn't kill the soccer player. Then he begs to see his doctor.

"Dugan starts making the arrangements to get Tillman an ambu-lance and send him to Bellevue. Meanwhile, the deputy mayor busy is arranging for a mayoral press conference at the precinct to announce that the Brazilian's homicide has been solved. So, I ask Harrison if he could diplomatically request to Rosen to meet me in the squad room.

"Barry Rosen comes barging into the room yelling at me that this better be important, Lieutenant, that he's a very busy man. I stand up and shout back at him. "Listen, you empty suit, I'm going to save your sorry ass from making a fool out of the mayor and yourself." That got his attention. Then I point to the holding pen and give him the update on the so called perpetrator. "Holy shit," he says. Then he asks me what am I going to do? I tell him I know what I'm going to do. I'm going to find the killer of the Brazilian. "No. What can I do for damage control, the mayor and media from around the world will be here within an hour?" he says.

"I was just about to tell him to go back to Madison Avenue and play pocket pool when the phone rings. I pick it up and Mickey Long from the Merrill Lynch Credit Card bureau tells me that a customer at an electronics store at Union Square is using the Brazilian's credit card. I get a quick description of the suspect and within ten minutes two cops on patrol arrest the suspect for fraud and possession of stolen goods. He was later charged and pled to the homicide.

"Rosen changes the press release to read that the NYPD has made an arrest in connection with the unfortunate death of the Brazilian soccer star and the police investigation remains active. After the press conference, Rosen comes back to the squad room to thank me for saving his ass and he gives me his beeper and hotline number. Since then, Rosen and I have a respectful understanding. As Dr. Ruthie would say. "Ve have vhat dey call a co-dependent relationship."

All of the detectives in the van try to contain their laughter as the story ends. Before he leaves the van, Donnellan thanks the team for their tireless efforts and he tells his team that they will give the surveillance just twelve more hours before they make an arrest.

Donnellan returns to the precinct to review the investigation with Captain Rivera at the One-Six. "I think we should plan on locking them up early tomorrow morning, Captain. If anyone, the weak link is the son. It's an outside chance, but maybe if we bust him in the street and toss him right into the van, he might break down on the way to the precinct and tell us where they hid the old lady. We have very few options left, sure it's a long shot but that's the only chance I see."

"I agree, Donnellan. That's our only chance. I think Kowalski should be in the van for the interrogation. Just the sight of him might be enough to break Smitter."

"Good plan, Captain, I'll be there with him."

Donnellan writes a report of the morning surveillance and an internal memo regarding the arrest tactic that he and Captain Rivera have planned. He faxes both reports to Chief Dickersen. He looks at his watch. 2:11 p.m. It's time to check in at the Tarrant.

CHAPTER 16

Frankie Carraballo is sitting in his office, with the door open, studying all of the reports issued by his security staff. He's as anxious as anyone to find the killer of GQ. Donnellan sees him and knocks on the door to get his attention.

"Lieutenant, I'm glad you came by, I was going to call you."

"Do you have a suspect or gut-reaction for this case?" Donnellan values the initial instincts of topnotch detectives, especially someone like Carraballo who thinks out of the box.

"Sorry, it has nothing to do with solving this case. I think the best we can do is identify everyone on those tapes and hope the mystery blonde comes forward. She's our best hope as a witness or suspect. So far we haven't made the case, but be patient, it's still early."

"Then what did you want to call me about?"

"Well, you made quite an impression on the executives from the home office. The Tarrant is about to complete a merger with another international hotel chain based in the Netherlands. This is a major acquisition for us which will double our capacity and triple our revenues. Remember the vice president you met yesterday, Betty Meade. Her specialty is acquisitions.

"Well, to make a long story very short, she recommended that we hire you for the security and damage control team. The home office called me this morning to find out your current salary. They will double it, give you a stock option, and a complete benefit package including retirement and health. This is a once in a lifetime opportunity. The timing is perfect. Oh, by the way, one of the fringe benefits of the management package is a scholarship program for your kids. What do you have a daughter and two sons? Do you know what it cost to send a kid to college these days? I have one daughter left in school. She's a senior at NYU, a great but expensive university. The Tarrant is picking up just about all the freight. I basically just pay for her books and transportation."

Donnellan is stunned by this proposal. He never thought about being anything but a cop, a New York City Police Officer. But, how many chances does a kid from Cardinal Hayes get to join Corporate America? He loves New York and doesn't want to travel the world. He has his dream job and he knows deep inside, he is a cop forever. But still, this is going to be a tough call. He decides that he won't make any decision until he talks to his wife.

"Thanks for the offer Frankie. I know that they wouldn't be interested in me unless you gave me a recommendation. First of all, I have to solve this case. I owe it to my friend GQ. Then I will talk to my wife about the offer. Can you stall them for a week or so?"

Frank Carraballo assures him that the offer will stand for at least a few weeks. The corporation policy is to give potential recruits for management at least a month before they pull the offer and go elsewhere.

Donnellan checks the time. It's almost four o'clock. He quickly gathers all of the available detectives from the hotel and the department for a brief meeting. He thanks them for their efforts and encourages them to keep it up. He then leaves for Manhattan South.

The squad room is fairly quiet. Donnellan reviews all of the status reports on his desk. He is impressed with the efforts of all involved. Almost all of the potential witnesses from GQ's diary and address book have been contacted with preliminary interviews. Now it is a matter of choosing which individuals require a follow-up interview by Donnellan.

Donnellan looks at his watch. It's almost six o'clock now. He knows that it is time to go home. He realizes that there is nothing else that he personally can do this evening to solve his active cases. He has another early morning appointment. He thinks, Marian is a very understanding partner. He walks home, greets his family and sets his alarm for four-thirty a.m.

CHAPTER 17

SERGEANT DRISCOLL CAN'T RELAX when he gets home. The adrenalin surge he felt during the surveillance is still pumping through his veins. He was on high alert from the time Lawrence left his building until he returned to 29th Street. Driscoll had to be ready if Smitter made an unexpected move. Then the sirens and red lights would have gone on, and who knows what would happen. Maybe Smitter would draw a gun. Resist arrest. Or try to make a run for it. The Sergeant was prepared for anything, or as was the case this morning, nothing.

Driscoll puts the Yankee game on the television while he reads the New York Times. He hopes to get lost in one or the other. He doesn't. "Holy cow!" Even Phil Rizzuto couldn't keep his attention. He checks the time, six-thirty. He just can't sit still.

Kevin Driscoll is a recovering alcoholic who goes to AA meetings at least four times a week. He checks his master list and finds a meeting at Saint Martin's Church at seven o'clock. He hasn't been there before, but today is as good a day as any.

Some might call this an almost perfect Indian summer day in New York. The temperature is in the seventies. The sun is shining, and there is just a slight southern breeze. Kevin takes a quick shower and gets ready to leave for his meeting. He checks with his team by phone. There are no further orders in the case. He slides his holster into his belt, and then attaches his beeper. He wears a lightweight pullover wind breaker to cover his gun, and he is ready to go.

Driscoll walks two blocks to the Union Square Subway Station on 14th Street and Lexington Avenue. He takes the express train uptown to 86th Street. This time the train ride is quiet and uneventful. Driscoll walks up the stairs and exits onto 87th Street.

The meeting has already started in the auditorium of Saint Martin's. Kevin walks quietly to the back row and sits without making a sound. The members in the front rows are standing and introducing themselves by first name only. Mike M. stands, introduces himself and waves a greeting to all in the room.

John B. gives the next introduction, and then sits.

A tall woman stands and introduces herself. "Hello everyone, my name is Rosa H. and I am an alcoholic." She looks around the room. She and Driscoll make brief eye contact. She sits. All of the remaining attendees introduce themselves, including Kevin D.

The meeting is called to order. The main speaker is Mike M., who has been sober for more than forty years. He explains how he had to hit rock bottom before he was able to realize that he is powerless against alcohol. He fights for his sobriety every day. Some might think that a person who has not had a drink for more than forty years would no longer have to worry about staying sober. For Mike, and countless others, that is not the case. He has managed to stay sober by attending meetings every week and helping others to keep their sobriety.

He has been a sponsor for hundreds of alcoholics in his lifetime. Many of those he sponsored have been able to remain sober. There are at least twenty of them in attendance tonight. Today is a celebration of a courageous friend of Bill W.

He is given a standing ovation when he finishes his speech. Mike is hugged by his wife and five of his adult children. Then others, many with tears in their eyes, hug and embrace him, including Rosa H.

Kevin D. puts his hand out to Mike, they shake hands and he says, "Thank you for sharing. I feel inspired by your experiences. I have met many people in the program who you have helped. It's a privilege to meet you in person."

Driscoll looks at his watch: 8:22 p.m. He stops at the back of the auditorium for a cup of coffee before he leaves for home. He sits alone in the back row, watching Mike greet friend after friend.

"Excuse me. Do you mind a little company?"

Kevin looks up at Rosa H, he smiles and moves over two seats. She sits next to him drinking her coffee. They know each other from the job. The two detectives start talking about their battle with sobriety. They share aspects of their personal history that are off limits when they are at work. Rosa tells Kevin that when she first came on the job, she was determined to prove that she was more macho then any man. She did a tremendous amount of boozing, sex and obscenities. She felt a need to drink hard, have an active sex life, and curse like a sailor. Somehow, she felt as a woman, especially a Latina, entering a white male dominated field that she had to prove she was as good and bad as they were.

It's strange that all around her were responsible men and women who did their job and went home to their families, night schools or other worthy endeavors. Then there were the reckless cops, who spent all their free time drinking, cheating and acting as outrageous as possible. Those were the cops she was initially drawn too. The "in" crowd, with the outrageous and exaggerated stories, made them the center of attention for all the wrong reasons. They tarnish the badges of the good cops and abuse the power that they are entrusted with. Ultimately, they destroy themselves and everyone around them.

"After I had three years on the job, I thought I was immune from any disciplinary action. Then I was caught in an after-hours sweep of a bar in the Hamptons. I could have just gone back to the house I was renting, and gone to bed. But . . . no. I had to give those East Hampton cops a piece of my boozed up mind. They took exception to being cursed at and ridiculed by a drunk. I spent a night in jail for disorderly conduct. The Department was notified; I was reprimanded and put on probation. Within a week, I was transferred to the One-O-Eight in Queens. Hugh J. B. O'Casey was the Precinct Commander. My first day on that assignment, my gun was taken away and I was assigned desk duty. I had a meeting with O'Casey. He made it clear that he won't tolerate any abusive behavior. He was a supervisor who supervised.

"I was in the bow and arrow squad for a month. When I finally got my gun back, I was assigned to a radio car with Henry Jenkins. He was an older black cop near his retirement. He mentored me like I was his daughter. Henry was a stable family man and a Korean War veteran who shared his wisdom without being in your face. It took me about a week of working with Henry before I had the courage to give AA a serious attempt. That was six years ago. I've been sober ever since."

Rosa looks around the auditorium and notices that she and Kevin are the only ones in the building except for a man and woman cleaning up the coffee and cakes. They both stand up and get ready to leave.

Kevin is not tired. He hesitates before asking Rosa if she would like to grab a quick bite to eat. She eyes her watch; it's 9:18. She stares at her wrist for a few seconds. She wonders what she is getting herself into. She realizes that she has been in social hibernation for more than four years. She can't remember the last time she was on a date. Rosa smiles at Driscoll and agrees to go to dinner.

CHAPTER 18

Rosa recommends the Bistro, an Italian restaurant on 83rd and Lexington. The manager greets them as soon as they enter. He asks if they have a reservation, even though it's late on a Monday night. They say no, and he tells them that a table will be ready in about twenty minutes and they can wait in the bar. Although the place looks empty, neither one complains.

The bartender is an Irishman with a brogue, named Emmet. He sets down two coasters. Rosa orders a seltzer with a twist. Kevin asks for a combination of fruit juices. The bartender recognizes this request as typical of the AA crowd. He asks Kevin if he is a friend of Bill W. Kevin nods and says, "Yes."

The manager is quick to notice that Rosa and Kevin are not boozers and won't be running up a bar bill. He suddenly finds an available table and he escorts them into the dining room. They walk by three empty tables before they are seated at a window table with a view of Lexington Avenue.

They each study the menu. Frank Sinatra is heard singing "Fly Me to the Moon" in the background. Kevin looks at Rosa. He doesn't want this night to end. The waiter, an Italian man of forty, tells them the specials of the day. They are ready to order.

Senora orders first. A garden salad with house dressing, and for her entre she will have the special, Saltimbocca, which is described as chicken baked with strips of prosciutto ham and raclette cheese.

Driscoll orders the garden salad with house dressing and the veal parmigiana.

Rosa butters a piece of bread. Before she takes a bite, she asks Driscoll what motivated him to join Alcoholics Anonymous.

He says he hit rock bottom about eight years ago. His wife divorced him and moved back to Minnesota with his two daughters. She told him she was tired of living with a boozer and she hated New York. At first he blamed her, then the City, then the job. A classic case of denial and avoidance. The more he blamed, the more he drank.

One morning, after a night of hard drinking, he went to the gym. The place was basically empty and he did a fierce workout as punishment for drinking like a fool. He went to the locker room dripping with sweat and sat down by his locker. He didn't know what happened, but he started crying.

He emphasizes to Rosa that he never cries. Yet there he was, sitting in a gym by himself sobbing. He thought he was the only one in the locker room until an old guy named Roy Mc Donaugh taps him on the shoulder and asks him if he's all right. He quickly collected himself, was embarrassed and told him he was fine. "Then I told him that I was out on a bender last night and I was missing my wife and daughters. He listened and I kept talking.

"When I was done, he started talking about how booze can take over your life. It's like he was reading my mail. Then he told me he is a recovering alcoholic. He hadn't had a drink for twenty-five years. He said he still goes to AA meetings a few times a week and he invited me to come to a meeting. He handed me his business card and tells me I can call him when I'm ready.

"My first reaction was, I'm not an alcoholic. So, I tried a little experiment. I decided that I would give up booze on my own. I lasted two days. I drank almost everything in my liquor cabinet. The next morning I got up with the worst hangover. I knew I needed help. I called Roy. He invited me to my first meeting. I've been sober ever since."

They continued talking about everything except work throughout dinner. They skipped dessert and ordered decaf. Driscoll realized that he had to be up early. He debated to himself how to handle the rest of the night. He had never felt so at home with any other woman, but this is so awkward.

He wondered if he should ask her for a date. How should he approach her? Rosa is a detective. They are both recovering alcoholics. How would that affect them? Is this a good idea? "Oh yeah," he thinks to himself. "Another thing . . . She's Puerto Rican and I'm Irish." But on the other hand, they're both Catholic. Besides, she is smart, beautiful, sober and fun to be with.

Rosa is watching Driscoll study the bill. She can tell that he is pondering his next move. She wonders what she will say if he asks her out on a date. He's a sergeant. The thought even occurs to her that maybe he's thinking that if he asks a detective for a date, the department might consider it sexual harassment? In this society you never know. But they don't work in the same unit.

She thinks that it helps that they don't drink and she is a very practical person, but tonight Rosa has the best time she has had in years. The total bill, tax included, is thirty-two dollars. They split the bill at twenty dollars each and leave an eight dollar tip. The waiter takes their money and thanks them for their generosity. Driscoll insists on walking Rosa to her apartment at 89th Street and Third Avenue. He was hoping the fresh air would help him to make a decision. As they approach her apartment building, he asks Rosa if they could talk for a minute. She says, "Sure."

Kevin reaches for Rosa's hand. She likes his approach.

"I just want you to know Rosa that tonight is very special to me. I don't know how to put this, but I would like to spend more time with you."

"Kevin, I was hoping you would say that. I enjoyed every minute too. Look we're adults. We can make our own decisions: I'm looking forward to seeing you again. You make the call."

Kevin walks to her building. She takes out the key and unlocks the front door. He opens the door for her. She starts to walk inside. She stops. She looks him in the eyes. She likes what she sees. She gives him a kiss goodnight.

He waits until Rosa is in her elevator before he takes the long day's journey into the subway.

CHAPTER 19

Monday morning at five-thirty Sergeant Driscoll sits in the back seat of the white undercover panel van on Ninth Avenue. Detectives Manny Colon and Greg Morrow are sitting in the front seats dressed like two construction workers. Across the street Detective Toby Green is seated in the back seat of a marked police car with uniformed Police Officers Ken Harvey and Mike Pennington.

As he waits in the back seat, Driscoll goes over the arrest strategy. The anticipated scenario is broken down into two parts.

Part A: Lawrence Smitter will load his car and drive up Tenth Avenue toward the Lincoln Tunnel. The marked police car will pull him over at 37th Street. The car will flash its red lights and blast its siren. The undercover teams will be in close pursuit with flashing lights and blasting sirens. Smitter's car will be surrounded.

The uniformed officers will then take the suspect out of the car and place him under arrest. Lawrence will "assume the position," hands on the roof, then he will be frisked.

Kowalski will cuff the suspect, hands behind the back. The only words to be spoken at that point are to inform the defendant that he is under arrest. Lawrence will then be placed in the back of the van with Kowalski and Driscoll. They will interrogate him as to the whereabouts of Dolly Goldberg.

Part B: As soon as Lawrence drives from his apartment, Lieutenant Donnellan, Detectives Penny Lucia and Betty Williamson, accompanied by two uniformed officers, Ted Moses and Ken Fisher, will arrest Julia Smitter and search her apartment. The Detectives will interrogate Julia as to the whereabouts of Dolly Goldberg. Upon completion of the interrogation, the Detectives will continue to search the apartment and the defendant will be transferred to the One-Six by the uniformed officers. The plan is in place.

At 5:42 a.m., Lawrence leaves his building and walks towards his parking garage. The undercover team goes on high alert.

Detective Kowalski stays in the Buick Le Sabre with his partner Jamal Moore. They watch Smitter's every move from a spot across from the parking garage. Lawrence picks up his car, drives around the corner and, double parks in front of his apartment. He rushes into the building and comes out with two plastic garbage bags. He throws the bags into the trunk. He starts to go back into his building. He hesitates, turns, and stares across the street.

Suddenly, he seems to notice the blue abandoned van. He looks back at his apartment and pauses. He removes his rubber gloves and runs into his car. The tech team picks up his actions. The arrest team is alerted that he is acting strange. Driscoll gives the signal for an immediate arrest. Detective Moore starts to drive down 29th toward the suspect with his police lights flashing. Lawrence accelerates up the street with the squad car in full pursuit.

At the corner of Eighth Avenue, Lawrence makes a left turn against the traffic on a one way street and races recklessly downtown. Moore is following as close as possible without causing a car accident or injuring a pedestrian. The other police cars are racing in pursuit down Seventh and Ninth Avenues.

At 12th Street, Lawrence makes another left hand turn and heads cross town against the one-way traffic. As he crosses Fourth Avenue, cars are stopped in front of him. He crashes into a street light and continues driving crosstown on the sidewalk, seriously injuring four pedestrians along the way. He turns left on Third Avenue and then right on 15th Street. He presses to pedal to the metal and accelerates at full speed towards Second Avenue. The sound of police cars in full pursuit seems to be coming from all directions. The closest car is the van driven by Manny Colon. He is driving downtown on Second Avenue when he picks up Lawrence shooting across 12th Street. Colon speeds up and rams the van into Lawrence Smitter's car, but it doesn't stop him. He keeps driving until he reaches First Avenue.

Lawrence panics. In front of him are the brick buildings of Stuyvesant Town and he has to turn either right or left. He looks to his right toward 14th Street. He sees a few early commuters racing into a subway station. He drives his car right into the entrance to the station, injuring three more people. He runs from his car down into the station. He jumps the turnstile and runs down another set of stairs. A train is just leaving as he reaches the platform. He looks around the station. There are no other passengers. He sees a uniformed police officer at the opposite end of the platform. He turns and looks at the stairs. He sees Sergeant Driscoll racing toward him.

Lawrence jumps off the platform and onto the tracks. He looks ahead. The tunnel is dark with dim lights that barely illuminate the tracks. He knows enough to stay clear of the third rail which could electrocute him if he touches it the wrong way. The lights of the Third Avenue platform are his immediate goal. He runs down the middle of the tracks. His only desperate thoughts are to escape by any means possible. He's afraid of prison.

Driscoll sees Lawrence running down the tracks. His only thought is a killer is on the loose. He jumps on the tracks and follows him. The big redhead is not a fast runner, but he keeps in great shape. He is losing the race but Driscoll keeps running.

When Driscoll is almost halfway down to Third Avenue, he hears the deadly roar of a speeding subway coming into First Avenue. He stays focused on his target and keeps running forward. Lawrence is getting tired and now Driscoll is gaining on him.

The train at First Avenue doesn't move. Driscoll is confident that his partners stopped the train. He hears other cops running at a distance behind him. Lawrence has only about fifty feet on Driscoll when he reaches Third Avenue. Lawrence looks up and sees two uniformed cops running toward him on the platform. He jumps over the third rail and crosses to the other side of the station.

Driscoll stays in close pursuit. Lawrence jumps up onto the platform. Driscoll is less than twenty feet behind him. Two uniformed cops are in pursuit. Smitter grabs a high school kid who is standing against the wall trying to get out of the way. He takes a knife out his pocket and holds it against the kid's throat.

Everyone on the platform is frozen. The police officers and Driscoll have their guns pointed at Lawrence Smitter. He has a hostage. The police back off and try to negotiate. They know they are dealing with a madman. The high school kid is sweating and is being choked by Lawrence.

"I will kill the kid if you come any closer," he tells the cops. To show he means business he cuts the kid on his arm. Blood starts dripping through the student's shirt.

"Leave the kid alone," yells Driscoll. "I'll trade places with him." Driscoll takes his gun and gives it to one of the officers. 'I'll walk to you with my back turned. Then you let the kid go and take me hostage."

Lawrence yells, "Forget it! Don't anyone move or the kid is history."

The platform is quiet for a few moments as Lawrence Smitter thinks about his next move. Suddenly, they all hear the distant roar of the subway barreling toward Third Avenue. Smitter is momentarily distracted. The student breaks loose. Driscoll turns and lunges to grab Smitter. He sees the big redhead is little more than a body length away from apprehending him. Smitter turns toward the tracks and jumps in front of the oncoming train.

CHAPTER 20

Julia Smitter hears the sounds of police sirens and rushes to her window. She watches Lawrence screech down 29th Street being pursued by an unmarked police car. She feels stunned and abandoned as she stretches out the window and sees her son make a left turn into the traffic on Ninth Avenue. Detectives Donnellan, Lucia and, Williamson reach the third floor landing and notice that Julia's door is partially open.

Penny Lucia glances into the apartment and sees Julia looking out the window. The Detective has her gun drawn and enters the apartment telling Julia Smitter to, "Freeze! Police! Don't move!"

Julia does not move until she is directed to move away from the window and put her hands up. Detective Lucia tells Julia Smitter she's under arrest. The Detective frisks Julia and then places handcuffs on the defendant. Detective Lucia asks Julia to tell her whereabouts of Dolly Goldberg. Julia murmurs that she doesn't know and then starts crying. She keeps asking what will happen to her son. Donnellan quietly observes the female detectives, hoping that a woman to woman interrogation might work to their advantage.

Detective Lucia senses that there may be an opportunity to get some information from the mother. Her partner, Betty Williamson yells at Julia and tells her you won't see your son until you tell us where Dolly Goldberg is.

The two uniformed police officers are standing in the kitchen waiting to transfer Julia Smitter to the precinct. She just keeps talking about her son. Lucia tells her to sit on a chair in the kitchen, where she is placed in the custody of the police officers.

Donnellan signals to the detectives to keep talking, as there might be a chance that Smitter will break down and talk. They don't want to transfer her yet.

So far, Julia has not asked for an attorney. All she seems to be concerned with is her son. The Detectives act quickly and both reenter the apartment. Detective Lucia keeps talking with Julia sympathetically, expressing the imminent danger of the police chase, while Detective Williamson searches the apartment.

Donnellan asks one of the officers for his hand-held police radio, and then sits across the table from Julia Smitter. Donnellan turns the radio on and they all listen to the police chase. Julia hears that her son is being pursued by at least five police and emergency vehicles. She is intently listening to every report on the radio. She keeps whispering, "My son . . . my son."

They hear the dispatcher shout that the target has entered the subway station at 14th and First being pursued by Sergeant Driscoll. The dispatcher directs the police to the 14th Street and Third Avenue subway station to intercept Lawrence Smitter. The dispatcher describes Lawrence as a dangerous fleeing felon. He tells the police that the NYPD Tactical Team with sharpshooters is on route to the 14th Street station.

Julia is hysterical listening to the radio. She starts crying and repeating, "My son . . . they're going to kill my son. My son, they're going to kill my son."

Donnellan turns the radio off. Julia becomes overwhelmed, screaming for detective Lucia to turn it back on. She begs and pleads to have the radio put back on. Detective Lucia is all business. There is no compassion or concern in her demeanor. She stares right into Julia's eyes and asks, "Where is Dolly Goldberg?"

Julia Smitter screams back, "I don't know, I don't know. Please turn on the radio."

Detective Lucia glances at Donnellan then stares at the overwrought mother, takes the radio and sticks it in her brief case. She calls to the uniformed police officers and tells them to take her to the precinct. Betty Williamson says she will accompany the prisoner.

Julia starts screaming, "Please turn on the radio, I have to know if my son is alive."

Detective Lucia takes the radio out of her briefcase and holds it in her hand with her finger on the power button. She stares at Julia, "Where is Dolly Goldberg?"

"She's in the bomb shelter under the basement floor," screams Julia.

"How do you find it?"

"Go to the basement and walk to the back. You'll see an old desk on a green throw rug. Move the desk and rug and you'll see the trap door. Open the door and you'll find her. Now turn on the radio. Please."

Donnellan and Betty Williamson race to the basement. They remove the desk and the rug and find Dolly Goldberg lying on the floor unconscious, but still breathing. They run out to the street where an emergency services unit is on call. Two police EMTs race down to the basement with a stretcher. Williamson stays with Goldberg and Donnellan reports back to Detective Lucia that they found Goldberg alive, but unconscious.

Julia screams. "Please turn on the radio."

Detective Lucia presses the power button and a police officer is heard announcing that the subject has died after being struck by a train.

CHAPTER 21

As soon as Chief of Detectives Dickersen hears that Lawrence fled to 14th Street, she races from headquarters to the First Avenue station. As she turns up 14th, she sees several police cars with their red lights flashing and a crowd watching passengers exit the station. The Chief pushes her way through the onlookers, past Lawrence Smitter's smashed rental car, and down to the subway platform.

The train was stopped and passengers were slowly being evacuated out of the station. Two police officers are maintaining a guard at the front of the train, while two others are beginning to walk cautiously on the tracks heading west toward Third Avenue. The Chief jumps onto the tracks and walks west with the officers. As they approach Third Avenue, they hear, and then see, a train on the other side of the tracks rumble into the station. As soon as the train stops, the police officers shine their flashlights in front of the train and see a body lying on the tracks.

They carefully cross over the tracks and examine the maimed body of Lawrence Smitter. It is very apparent that he is dead. Chief Dickersen races up to the platform to assess the situation. She finds Sergeant Driscoll sitting against the wall next to an injured high school student. The kid, who is in obvious pain, is shivering under Driscoll's jacket. The Sergeant is talking to the boy in an attempt to calm him down.

Two police EMTs hurry toward the front of the train. Dickersen slows them down with a wave of her hand, and directs them to the kid. She tells them there is nothing they can do for the other guy.

"Chief Dickersen, come over here and meet a real hero," yells Driscoll. "This young man, Pedro Maldonado, is one brave kid." Driscoll then explains how Pedro was able to get out of Smitter's stranglehold.

The EMTs rip Pedro's shirt and attend to his wounds. Driscoll continues talking non-stop. The Chief takes his radio but the reception is weak and she can't communicate. She walks up the subway to street level and gets and gives an update. Detective Colon is on the radio and standing by his squad car. He waves over to the Chief of Detectives and tells her they found Dolly Goldberg alive and that she is listed in stable condition at Bellevue and Julia Smitter is in custody.

Detective Colon goes down to the subway platform as the EMTs continue to stabilize the student. He hands the radio to the sergeant and tells him that Lieutenant Donnellan wants to talk with him. "Hey Driscoll," says Donnellan. "You must have made quite an impression on a Detective Rosa Hernandez in the Major Crimes Unit. She heard about your chase on the radio and she keeps calling the squad every five minutes requesting an update on your condition. What should I tell her? You're still a little rough around the edges? Do you have any dents or injured parts? Seriously, Driscoll. Are you okay?"

"Do me a favor Lieutenant. Just tell her I'm fine. I appreciate her concern. I told Pedro, here, that I would go to the hospital with him. This guy's been through a lot today and I promised him I would stay with him until his mom and pop get to see him."

As soon as Donnellan gets off the radio, he thanks the surveillance team for their exceptional effort, and then rushes to the 14th Street and Third Avenue subway station. Several teams of detectives are busy interviewing police and civilian witnesses at various parts of the station. Donnellan checks in with each team for a progress report. He interviews the subway engineer, Ernie Jackson. The engineer is visibly shaken, but he offers to finish his route when the tracks are clear. Donnellan thanks him for his dedication, but tells him that a relief engineer will finish the run.

Donnellan goes back down to the tracks for an update from the forensic unit. The chief pathologist has just completed her examination and is directing her staff to transfer Lawrence Smitter to the morgue.

When the forensic unit completes their investigation and all potential witnesses have been identified and interviewed, Donnellan checks with headquarters and receives authorization to open the station. He looks at his watch and finds it hard to believe that it is only two o'clock in the afternoon. He exits the train station and walks a few blocks to the emergency room entrance at Mother Cabrini Hospital. The supervising nurse recognizes him and points to Sergeant Driscoll's room. The door is open and the first thing Donnellan sees is a linen curtain surrounding a patient and two huge feet hanging off the end of a gurney.

Donnellan walks into the room quietly and he hears the whisper of a woman's voice telling the patient that he is doing fine. Donnellan lifts the curtain and sees Driscoll lying unconscious. Detective Hernandez is holding the Sergeant's hand and continues to whisper.

She tells Donnellan that once the kid went into the operating room, Driscoll felt weak and asked to lie down. As soon as he lied down, he went into a deep, almost unconscious, sleep. The doctors checked his vital signs right away and they were fine. They said that Driscoll is totally exhausted and in mild shock.

She insists that she is staying with Driscoll until he recovers. She assures him that he will be notified as soon as Driscoll wakes up, but before she can finish her sentence Sergeant Driscoll opens his eyes in a state of confusion. He looks right into the eyes of Rosa Hernandez and smiles. He says just one word before he slides back to sleep. "Thanks." Donnellan stays with the detective for about a half hour more before he leaves for a brief update at Manhattan South, and then on to Third Avenue in Brooklyn and McLaughlin & Sons Funeral Home.

Donnellan remembers this section of Brooklyn from many visits to aunts, uncles, cousins and grandparents in his childhood. It was predominantly an Irish immigrant community and the Basilica of Our Lady of Perpetual Help was the center of their universe. The Basilica remains at the epicenter of this neighborhood, but Hispanic and Asian immigrants are replacing the Irish parishioners.

There's a long line of friends and family waiting to enter the funeral home when Donnellan gets to McLaughlin & Sons. He recognizes many of them from Stuy Town and Brooklyn. The funeral director waves Donnellan to the front of the line and tells him, in a loud voice so that those on line can hear him, that the detective's wife is waiting inside for him. The mourners respectfully let Donnellan cut the line. He thanks them for their patience.

Donnellan signs the guest book and takes three of GQ's prayer cards which include his name, a picture and the Serenity Prayer. He walks past numerous floral arrangements including the one his wife sent, a shamrock design surrounded by green carnations. He warmly greets GQ's aunts, uncles and cousins as he works his way toward the casket. He notices that sitting in the front row is GQ's grandfather, Hughie Clancy, an Irishman from County Mayo and soldier in the Irish Republican Army during the Easter Rising in 1916. Donnellan always enjoyed when his own grandfather and Hughie would talk about their experiences in the Irish revolution. Somehow, no matter how sad the war story, they always found a way to insert their own brand of humor. But today is different.

Donnellan reaches the open casket, kneels, prays and takes a respectful view of his best friend. Then he sits next to Mr. Clancy and he tells him he's sorry for the loss of his grandson. As he stares solemnly at the casket, Donnellan thinks back to September of 1965 when Hurricane Betsy, a powerful Category 4 hurricane was raging deep into the North Atlantic Ocean. Although Betsy stayed far out in the ocean, the intense storm generated massive waves along the shores of east coast beaches. GQ and Donnellan watched as reporters warned that beaches were closed due to the dangerous conditions caused by gigantic waves.

They couldn't sit still. They wanted to get a piece of this historic action. They took the Long Island Railroad to Long Beach, borrowed a couple of surfboards from their classmate Brendon O'Reilly and walked down Delaware Avenue to the beach. They stood there in awe for a full twenty minutes; staring at the waves, listening to the thundering roar and feeling the wet salt air. They watched the futile struggle of surfers in the water, none of whom could get past the breakers. When a surfer got close, a wave would crush down and an explosion of whitewater would push them back to the shore.

GQ looked at Donnellan, nodded his head and said "Let the games begin." The two high school swimmers were faster than the other surfers. They paddled furiously into the heart of the ocean. When a wave crashed and rumbled toward them they swiftly flipped the board over while holding down the nose and gripping the board with their legs to slow down the momentum, doing what the surfers called a turtle roll. It took forty five minutes, but they made it past the breakers. They were about three hundred yards offshore and they could see O'Reilly frantically waving his arms, calling them in. GQ laughed as he told Donnellan that Brendon is afraid that his boards will break if we ride these waves.

Surfers believe that waves have patterns and in the Atlantic Ocean the seventh wave in a series is the biggest. GQ and Donnellan wait for the seventh wave of a giant set. They sit on their boards in silence as enormous swells of incoming waves lift them thirty feet up and down. As GQ rises to the top of a colossal swell he sees a monster wave racing toward them. He gives a nod, and they start paddling. It takes just three strokes – Donnellan feels the wave's powerful surge take control of the board, he stands as the board drops down the face of the wave, and looks twenty feet to his right. GQ is there. Standing tall. They ride all the way to the shore and are met by an angry policeman who tells them the beach is closed and to stay out of the water.

As Donnellan thinks back to that day in the treacherous surf, he briefly wonders why he wasn't the slightest bit scared, and then he realizes the answer to his question is in the casket. He was with GQ.

Donnellan then walks over to greet Mary Murtagh and her husband Jimmy. She appears composed as he hugs and kisses her on the cheek. Without warning Mary starts shaking uncontrollably, attempting to muffle an eerie keening cry. Donnellan wonders if his presence has disturbed her. Her husband takes her hand and starts walking her toward the back of the viewing area. Donnellan turns around and does a double take. In a reflex moment, he thought he saw GQ walking toward the casket, but it was Connor Kelly paying his respects along with his parents. Donnellan briefly wondered how many people knew about Connor's biology, and then he sat back down next to Hughie Clancy.

Frank, Joan, and Connor all offer their condolences to Hughie Clancy, and then greet Donnellan, who thanks them for making the trip from Stuy Town. Frank mentions that he remembers GQ well from his days at Epiphany and he hopes he finds comfort in heaven. The Kellys leave the funeral home and Donnellan is invited to join some of his childhood friends for a drink at the Irish Haven. Donnellan respectfully declines the offer and drives back home. As he approaches the Brooklyn Bridge he is unexpectedly overcome with emotions. He parks under the bridge in front of an Italian restaurant and for the first time in many years, he cries uncontrollably. It takes him about an hour to gain his composure.

Donnellan says a silent prayer for GQ and he heads back to an affectionate greeting by his wife at his Manhattan home. He slips into a deep undisturbed sleep until he's jolted awake at almost nine o'clock in the morning.

Barry Rosen on the other hand, didn't sleep late; he was in his office working his rolodex before six o'clock. Just before seven, Rosen received an unexpected call from his friend Kieran McNamara, a long-time editor at the *Daily News*. As requested, McNamara instructed his reporters to respect the privacy of GQ's family wake, but the message didn't reach a cub reporter in the obituaries department who's from Bay Ridge. The reporter, Bernard Toomey, took it upon himself to attend GQ's private viewing as a neighborhood friend of GQ's sister. But he tells his editor that he thinks he might have uncovered a bombshell.

It seems that everything about the wake was fairly predictable, but Toomey was waiting to see the famous Detective Donnellan in person. He watched Donnellan greet GQ's friends and family and was about to leave when he heard GQ's sister burst into an eerie wailing cry like he never heard before. At the same time, a family from Stuy Town entered the funeral home. Toomey couldn't figure out what caused the emotional breakdown, but he decided to prolong his visit. He noticed that some of the Stuy Town crew were heading to the Irish

Haven and decided to follow along and have a few drinks. He overheard some of GQ's classmates whispering that Connor Kelly had an incredible resemblance to the teenaged GQ. They reminisced about GQ's girlfriend, Bernadette Kelly, and her sudden sendoff to Ireland. Basically, Toomey says he thinks he saw GQ's out-of-wedlock son. McNamara told Toomey not to tell a soul about his hunch and that GQ's family is off limits. Toomey assured McNamara he would honor the request.

Rosen thanks McNamara for the call and asks him to keep a close eye on Toomey and keep a lid on the story. Rosen suggests that maybe the *Daily News* could reward Toomey for his loyalty by giving him a field assignment like assessing the lasting impact of Robert Moses who died two months ago at the age of ninety-two. McNamara agrees to keep Toomey out of the city and send him out to Long Island to interview Robert Moses's neighbors, followed by field reports on the impact of the Jones Beach and the Bethpage Parks.

After Rosen hangs up the phone he thinks to himself that these straight-laced Irish people and their secrets have made the Guinness Brewers rich. He thinks to himself that Donnellan hasn't had a moment to grieve the loss of his best friend, GQ. So he decides not to tell Donnellan about the cub reporter's bombshell yet. It would only add flame to the fire.

CHAPTER 22

THE MORNING WALK TO Manhattan South gives Donnellan a brief chance to sort out some of the events of the last three days. He never thought that Dolly Goldberg would be found alive. He felt certain that he would have locked up a suspect in the GQ case in forty-eight hours. He thinks how important it is for an investigator to resist jumping to conclusions.

The squad room is buzzing about Dolly Goldberg being found alive. There is a sense of pride that the NYPD had solved another difficult high-profile case, but at the same time, the cops assigned to the GQ case feel deflated. There is a silent consensus that pursuing the love connection has been a waste of time. They have completed phase one of their assignment, all of the preliminary interviews, reports, and background investigations have been completed. Now, many are hoping that they will be assigned to real detective work, like the precinct detectives in the street who are searching for a thief or thieves who broke into GQ's apartment.

Donnellan senses the frustration of his staff, and he feels it himself. He reviews the report from the Tarrant. There are still nine unidentified males whose actions on the video are suspect. The tech unit has extracted still photographs of these individuals from the video. These pictures are being circulated around the city to be viewed by cops, informants and civilians for possible identification. But there are still no positive results.

As soon as Donnellan sits at his desk the phone rings. It's Barry Rosen, who congratulates Donnellan for his help in solving the Goldberg case. He also mentions that he was contacted by the CEO of Tarrant International and he gave his highest recommendation for Donnellan, but as a New Yorker he hoped that Donnellan would stay on the force. Donnellan tells him that police work is in his blood and he's not resigning. Rosen shares his appreciation for the decision and tells Donnellan that politics is in his blood and he also declined an offer from the Tarrant.

When their conversation ends, Donnellan notices that the second line on his phone is still blinking. Its detective David Wang, supervisor of the forensic unit, who tells Donnellan that they have identified the finger-prints of two individuals besides GQ on the telescope: both of whom are in the law enforcement data base. One is Donnellan's and other belongs to an FBI agent named Amanda Blakely. According to her fingerprint sheet she is twenty-eight, five foot eight inches tall, weighs one hundred thirty five pounds, blue eyes, blonde hair and has been in the FBI for three years. Donnellan tells detective Wang to keep this information con-fidential and hand deliver the printout to Chief Dickersen.

When the Chief is told that Donnellan is on the line, she closes the door to her office and picks up the phone. Donnellan explains that she will be receiving a hand delivered envelope from the forensic unit which contains the fingerprints of a young female lifted from GQ's telescope. She is possibly the mystery woman, or maybe not? But there is a twist. The fingerprints belong to a twenty-eight year-old FBI agent named Amanda Blakely. The Chief tries to hide her laugh, but she can't. When she gets her composure she apologizes to Donnellan until she realizes that he is laughing too. Of course, they don't jump to the conclusion that they found the mystery woman, but they also know the FBI and the strict morality clause in their "Code of Conduct."

The Chief tells Donnellan that she is going to handle the initial interview herself and hopefully put Blakely at ease before the FBI makes a federal case out of this. She's going to contact the New York FBI director and make a request to meet with Blakely for a planned conference on women in law enforcement. She will make sure that it is understood that Blakely was highly recommended, and the FBI will have prominent standing at this upcoming conference. As soon as she is contacted by Blakely, she will arrange for an urgent meeting at her office at Police Plaza and hopefully put Blakely's mind at ease and get her help, without any publicity. Otherwise, if the FBI administration got the slightest hint that one of its female agents could be involved in a tryst with a slain actor, it would take months, if ever, to get cooperation.

Donnellan briefly thinks back to a conversation he had with a retired precinct commander who was in charge of the airport when a TWA jet was hijacked at LaGuardia. The commander had three sharpshooters available to take down the hijacker, one from the FBI and the others were from the Port Authority and NYPD. The FBI agent drew the short straw so he would take the first shot if the hijacker slipped-up. The agent took off his coat, took aim and waited until the hijacker tripped on his hostage's foot and she momentarily broke loose from his grip. There was the opening, the agent immediately took two shots and killed the hijacker. The public praised the sharpshooter for rescuing the stewardess, but not J. Edgar Hoover, who reprimanded the agent for being photographed wearing a short-sleeved shirt. Donnellan chuckles as he considers the image of Hoover reading a tabloid headline that one of his agents was doing the horizontal mambo with the playboy of the western world.

The Chief and Donnellan both know about the FBI's distaste for any perception of immorality among their agents. Therefore, the communication with Blakely must be confidential, discreet and thorough; otherwise they could destroy the reputation and career of the agent. As the conversation continues, Donnellan looks on his desk at a newspaper headline: Who is GQ's Mystery Lover? And he thinks to himself, what's next?

The Chief tells Donnellan that, while she is working on interviewing Blakely, he is going to be flying to Los Angeles to quell the media frenzy about a so-called major breakthrough in the GQ case. A reporter on ABC just interviewed a woman who claims that while she was having a relationship with GQ, her former boyfriend threatened her and GQ.

Donnellan calls Mandy in the squad room and relates the details of the woman's claim. Mandy is familiar with the allegation, as she watched the interview on television last night. She tells Donnellan that she has written a summary of the interview, along with a transcript from ABC. He asks her to bring the case file to his office.

She wheels into his office with two copies of the file. They each review the case for a few minutes in silence. The "witness" is one Rhonda Rholla, an aspiring model and actress living with her agent in Hollywood.

"What did you think of her, Mandy?"

"I thought I was watching a movie instead of an interview. Everything about her appeared to be staged. It looked as if she was reading a script for a soap opera. Basically, it looked like she got her fifteen minutes of fame by exploiting the death of GQ. But, I could be wrong."

"I doubt it, Mandy. You're a good judge of people. This whole thing looks phony to me, but I will have to find out for myself."

Detective Dugan waits until Donnellan finishes his meeting with Mandy before he pokes his head into the office.

"Hey Lieutenant," says Dugan smiling. "Pack your bags. You've got a gorgeous broad to interview in LA. I mean drop-dead beautiful. I saw her on ABC. She looked like the winner of a beauty pageant. I got just one question you've got to ask her for me, does her mother fool around? I'm available."

Donnellan tries to smile, but he can't fake it. Dugan senses his frustration and asks him about GQ's wake last night.

"You know, Dugan, we deal with death every day, but it doesn't make it any easier when your best friend or relative dies. This has been my toughest case yet. GQ was a great friend and just an all-around good guy. I just wasn't ready for him to die. His sister is handling things well. But I think everyone loses it when they see the pictures of GQ back when he was Gregory X. Clancy. He's gone for good. What a loss. As you could expect, I was constantly asked about the case. Who do I think the mystery blonde is? Was GQ killed by a jilted lover? I must have been asked those questions a thousand times."

Detective Dugan acknowledges his friend's trouble and nods gracefully, and then walks back to his desk. As Donnellan is completing his review of the case file for Rhonda Rholla and making plans to interview her with detective Harrison, the Chief calls. She had no trouble arranging an early morning meeting with agent Blakely. The Chief asks Donnellan to call her when he lands in L.A. in the morning.

CHAPTER 23

AMANDA BLAKELY ARRIVES AT Police Plaza at seven in the morning to meet with Chief Dickersen. She is wearing a grey blazer, a white blouse and black pants. Her brown hair is cut short and it's obvious to the Chief that her subdued professional attire is an attempt to disguise her stunning beauty. The Chief is not surprised that she's a looker, but her first thought is when did Blakley get her hair colored and cut? The squad room leading to the Chief's office is filled with empty chairs at this time of the morning. The introductions are filled with pleasantries as the Chief invites Blakely to sit in her spacious office while she closes the door.

Dickersen shares with the agent that she has had many difficult challenges rising through the ranks in the so-called "man's" world of law enforcement. Blakeley tells her that she admires her for breaking through the glass ceiling and paving the way for women like her to have opportunities in the FBI. The Chief tells the agent not to kid herself, it's still a man's world in law enforcement and if you make a mistake they'll eat you alive. The two women smile and nod in agreement.

The Chief picks up the envelope on her desk and hands it to Blakely and asks her to open it. The FBI agent looks confused as she takes the fingerprint card from the envelope. "What's this?" she exclaims as she sees her name and fingerprints on the card.

"Look Amanda, I'm going to ask you to trust me. I want to help you, woman to woman. Please just listen to me before you make a decision. There are only three people who know that your fingerprints were lifted from the telescope at GQ's apartment; me, Donnellan and a forensic detective. Now, if this information becomes public, your life will forever be maligned as the mystery woman by tabloid reporters, and forget your FBI career. I can't make this go away, but maybe I can keep you under the radar, but you have to be straight with me and tell me everything about your relationship with GQ." The Chief takes off her jacket. "I'm not going to record this conversation. And I'm not taking any notes . . . just listening."

Tears start rolling down Blakely's cheeks. The Chief passes her a box of tissues. Blakely gathers herself, looks at the Chief and decides to tell her everything. "I met GQ a few months ago at the LA Airport when we both were taking a red eye to the City. The flight was delayed for two hours and I was sitting in the lounge reading *The Cardinal Sins* by Andrew Greeley. GQ sidled next to me and says that's a very interesting book, I read it last week. At first I pretended I didn't know it was him, but when we started to talk I told him that it's nice to meet a world class playboy, but I'm not interested. For some reason, that got his attention. He dropped his guard and started talking with me about his inner feelings. He felt like there was a significant emptiness in his life. At first I thought it was a put-on, but I realized it wasn't as he kept talking. I was surprised and disarmed by his candidness; it completely threw me off. The next thing I know I'm sharing some of my own disappointment about being a woman in a man's world.

"Two hours flew by and then the announcement came to board the plane. GQ arranged for me to be upgraded to first class so that I could sit next to him on the flight. We had a great time and exchanged numbers. After that, we would talk on the phone for hours almost every day; at least a few times each week. It was the strangest thing. Even though we weren't exactly "dating," in the sense of going out and painting the town red, I got to know him better than anyone I've ever known, and felt closer to him than to anyone ever before. We talked about *everything*. At first, he was constantly inviting me to visit him at the Tarrant, but I told him I'm not interested in that sort of thing – you know, a one and done relationship. He understood, and I think he respected it. No one had ever said that to him before. It certainly took things to a different level. He got really serious after that.

"The night before he died, he called me and told me that he can't stop thinking about me and he wants to get off the merry go-round. He's ready to have a real relationship. No more games. I told him that I loved him and would rearrange my schedule and visit him in the morning. I had a mandatory class downtown at noon that I couldn't cancel. The next morning I got to his apartment at about seven. He made a call to his agent and left a message that he won't be available for a week. While he was talking, I went over to the telescope. It was facing downtown, I directed it toward my apartment on 86th Street and I thought to myself: What am I getting myself into? GQ took my hand and without saying a word, we embraced for several minutes. Then we kissed, shared our love for each other and moved to the bedroom. It was all so fast but didn't seem that way. After I showered I realized that I had to get back to my apartment to get ready for my afternoon class, so I quickly dressed, left the Tarrant and took the subway to 86th.

"I rushed to the class at Federal Plaza which didn't end until six. I was trying to decide whether to go home or to GQ's when I heard two coworkers saying that it's a shame what happened to GQ. I asked what happened? When I heard the news I was devastated and had to sit down before I passed out. There was hardly anyone left at the office so I didn't bring too much attention to myself. Anyone watching probably would have thought I was a devoted fan. I finally composed myself and went home. I kept switching from one station to another. All they talked about was the mystery woman, the gorgeous broad; that GQ went out with a bang. I couldn't handle it. I was depressed. I called my office and took a sick day. I decided to keep my relationship to myself. I got my hair colored and cut and then went back to work. I was doing okay . . . until now."

The Chief listened attentively and compassionately to Blakely. The both looked at each other but neither said anything. They were thinking about the situation.

The Chief says, "Before we can come up with a solution, you have to tell me what the condition of GQ was when you left and if you can remember if the door locked when you left the apartment."

Blakely mentions that when she left GQ he was wide awake lying in bed waiting to take a shower. She says, "As I was rushing to leave he told me that he loved me. I said I loved him, too, and rushed out of the apartment. I don't remember if the door completely closed because I saw the elevator was open and ran to get in. There was a man who just exited the elevator and was walking in the opposite direction from me, but I didn't see his face. He wore denim jeans and high top sneakers. Based on the way he walked and dressed, I figure he was in his twenties or thirties but I didn't notice anything unusual about him, not even if he was black or white."

The Chief apologizes for asking a personal question but wants to know if GQ used a condom, because none was found at the apartment. Then Blakely tells her that GQ didn't use protection and that she is not on the pill.

"Whoa, whoa, whoa," says the Chief. "Do you mean it's possible that you're pregnant?" When Blakely starts nodding her head and sobbing, the Chief says, Let's just see what we can do to keep this quiet.

"First off, I'm going to get you assigned to me for the next month. Don't worry I've helped out the FBI so much they should give me a federal pension. Then I'll give you an office down the hall and I want you to review all of the surveillance tapes to see if you can identify the person you saw leaving the elevator and also see if you can spot yourself on the tapes. If and when we capture the perpetrator, we'll find a way to protect your identity. And if reasonable, I will be leaning toward asking the district attorney for a plea bargain to avoid needing witnesses for a trial as long as the perpetrator agrees to a long sentence. When Donnellan calls, I will give him an update, tell him to keep it quiet and see if he has any ideas. Don't worry, you can trust him. We look out for each other."

When they arrive at Los Angeles Airport, Detective Harrison makes a beeline to the car rental agency and gets in line to pick up a car. At the same time, Donnellan finds a private telephone booth and he calls headquarters. Chief Dickersen fills him in on her meeting with the FBI agent. Donnellan scratches his head, wondering, "What's next?" Then he sees Harrison and sprints over to the car.

It's the first time either detective has ever been to California, so Harrison drives cautiously as Donnellan reads the directions and studies a map. The detectives are impressed with the natural beauty and tranquil atmosphere of L.A.'s best Pacific Ocean communities leading up to Malibu. When they arrive at the beachfront villa, the long line of cars parked on both sides of the street is the first clue that this interview will be "Standing Room Only."

"Hey, Lieutenant. GQ's life is not over. Let's make him a star again. Can you imagine the leverage that Rhonda will have after she is interviewed by two New York City Detectives? She will make her love affair with GQ into the most passionate affair since Cleopatra and Julius Caesar."

A camera crew is waiting for the detectives when they pull into the driveway. They are directed to a walkway on the side of the house which leads to a wood framed balcony. This will provide an opportunity for Rhonda to be filmed in a bathing suit with the rolling surf of the ocean in the background. The producer of this "documentary" asks the detectives if they want to have make-up applied before they begin filming.

Donnellan attempts to put an end to the publicity stunt. He tells the camera crew to stop recording. He starts to tell everyone to leave the balcony, when he is confronted by Ron Bell, Rhonda's agent and attorney. They talk privately and agree to set down some ground rules.

Ron Bell invites Donnellan into the kitchen and reminds Donnellan that this is not New York City and his client has no legal obligation to cooperate with the detectives. He tells the Lieutenant that his client is a cooperating witness who has valuable information for the detectives. But, they have to be willing to allow his client to videotape the interview or they can leave.

Donnellan evaluates the offer and senses that the agent is bluffing. He knows that his client has nothing to gain if they leave. They both know that basically this interview is an exercise in futility. However, he also knows that he has traveled over two thousand miles for this interview and he doesn't want to go home empty.

He tells the agent that maybe they can agree to some type of compromise that will satisfy both of their needs. The Lieutenant is well aware that Rhonda and her agent want some type of video evidence that will provide her media exposure. She knows that being interviewed by "real" detectives from New York City about her love life with GQ will unquestionably advance her career

Donnellan tells the talent agent that the NYPD is taking her allegations seriously, but the detectives don't want to reveal the direction of the investigation which could easily be determined by the nature of the questions. Donnellan suggests a three minute film clip of the detectives talking to his client, just introductions and no substance. Then the talent agent will send the film crew home and let the detectives conduct the interview.

The only other option on the table is that the detectives leave and tell their boss that the actress is uncooperative and likely an opportunist pulling a hoax on a homicide investigation. It takes Ron Bell all of thirty seconds before he agrees to Donnellan's proposal.

Rhonda Rholla makes her entrance onto the balcony. The camera crew is capturing her every move. She is a stunning beauty on film, but even better looking in person. The detectives make their entrance. They have a brief introductory interview with Rhonda. Her agent tells the camera crew to "cut."

They stop filming, pack their equipment and leave for the studio. The detectives wait until five minutes have passed before they get down to business.

Detective Harrison does not have a confrontational personality, but he has a way of getting the truth from people. Instead of calling a person a liar and making threats, Harrison's style is to look a person right in the eyes and simply state, "Don't insult my intelligence." Somehow, his body language and sincerity convince most witnesses and defendants to 'give it up.' Harrison is aware that this interview is an insult to his and Donnellan's intelligence, but since there is no sense in making a difficult situation worse, Harrison starts the questioning and lets the actress talk.

Rhonda tells them that she had an intimate relationship with GQ for the last two years. They first met on the set of a made for TV movie about an attorney who falls in love with his client during her divorce. When they met, Rhonda was twenty-three years old and had been living on the West Coast for about a year. She was from Vernon, Connecticut, and was still maintaining a long distance relationship with her high school sweetheart, Brian Rigley.

Her boyfriend, Brian, had proposed to her before she left for California. She didn't accept or reject his proposal, but postponed her decision. Brian was convinced that Rhonda loved only him and eventually would come to her senses and return to Vernon.

After a year in Hollywood, she knew she would never go home again. She wanted to break the news to Brian gently, but he never got the message. When she worked with GQ, she knew for certain it was all over with Brian. Up to that point she had never had an intimate relationship with anyone else but Brian. She said that loving GQ was so natural; it is hard for her to remember who made the first move. Anyway, they began an intermittent love affair that lasted until GQ was killed.

"How and when did you break your relationship with Brian," asks Harrison.

"At first, I stopped calling him or returning his calls. He didn't get it. I had a hard time telling him the truth, because I do love him, but I don't want to marry him."

She looks to the detectives for their approval. They just listen.

"Finally, I decided to give a confidential story to a tabloid that I was having an affair with GQ, she says. I told them that the love scenes in 'Beauty and the Attorney,' were not simulated. Oh, by the way, they weren't . . .So anyway, when the story broke, Brian called and left a message that he's breaking up with me. He was furious and called me all sorts of names. I mean he went ballistic. I never heard him curse like that before. He was scary."

"When did this happen?"

"About eight months ago."

"When you say that Brian went ballistic, did he actually threaten to harm either you or GQ" asks Donnellan.

"Well, I guess he didn't directly threaten me or GQ, but I'm telling you, he was scary crazy."

Harrison looks at Rhonda and reminds her that they will have to get Brian's side of the story, too. He tells her that it is important to remember as clearly as possible because this is a homicide investigation and GQ is dead. This is a serious allegation and the purpose of this interview is to determine if she has any information that could lead them to the murderer of GQ.

"Okay, maybe I overreacted, now that I think of it. I haven't even seen Brian for more than a year and I never remember him hurting anyone. He always treated me like a gentleman would. He wouldn't hurt a fly." Rhonda starts to sob when she realizes the consequence of her publicity stunt.

"Look Rhonda," says Harrison. "We know that you are in a tough business. But we're detectives working on a homicide case. This is not an audition. This is the real deal. Don't insult our intelligence. Did Brian ever threaten you or GQ!"

"No. He would never hurt anyone." She starts crying.

The detectives give her a few minutes to collect herself, and then Donnellan starts asking questions. "Okay Rhonda, let's start looking forward. You see, you've put us and Brian in an awkward position. When you went on TV and started telling anyone who would listen, that you solved GQ's murder, it makes us look bad. Now people want to know who is this person you suspect killed GQ? It doesn't take Sherlock Holmes to figure out that you think it is Brian. So now he is going to be linked to GQ's murder. I think what we have here is a mess. Now, I want you and your agent to do some damage control."

There is silence on the balcony. The only noise is the sound of the waves rushing to the shore. The detectives are not about to make it easy for Rhonda and her agent. They want them to sweat it out for a while before they make a plan. The Lieutenant's beeper starts buzzing. It's Chief Dickersen number. He asks the talent agent if he could use his phone to make a long distance call, he says go right ahead. Harrison stays with the actress and her agent and Donnellan leaves the room to make the call.

CHAPTER 24

DONNELLAN IS KEENLY AWARE that the Chief of Detectives wouldn't contact him unless there was an important development. As soon as the detective enters the talent agent's office he closes the door and calls the Chief.

She tells him that they may have a major break in the GQ case. The Chief had received a call from Jack O'Hea, the Chief of Detectives in the Boston Police Department. He told her that last night the Boston department got an anonymous tip from a "concerned" citizen who said he just kicked the crap out of a drug dealer from New York City who was trying to sell him a Rolex and jewelry stolen from GQ. The dope dealer was apprehended and arrested for possession of stolen property. Boston is keeping the suspect in a holding pen until they hear from New York. The Chief then gives Donnellan the phone number of the supervising detective, Lieutenant Enzo Variello.

Donnellan doesn't trust the security in the talent agent's house. He knows that the possible break in the case must remain confidential until he can interrogate the jailed potential witness and suspect. He tells the Chief he will find a safe phone and call Boston in fifteen minutes and get back to her right away. The actress interview isn't going anywhere. It's an obvious publicity stunt by the actress and her agent to use the media frenzy surrounding GQ's death to further her career. When he reenters the room, he signals to Harrison that it is time to leave. Donnellan walks back to the balcony and doesn't hide his frustration with Rhonda and her agent. "Look, my partner and I just traveled over two thousand miles because you made several false allegations on national television. I am asking both of you not to make a bad situation any worse. As of right now, let's agree to let the New York City Police solve this case." They both agree. The detectives thank the actress and her agent for their cooperation and make a quick exit.

As soon as Harrison exits the driveway, the Lieutenant tells him to head to the airport. As Harrison is driving, Donnellan tells him about the Chief's phone call. Both detectives are anticipating that this could be the break they've been waiting for, but they are both experienced enough to be cautious in their expectations.

As soon as they arrive at LAX, Harrison drops the Lieutenant at the entrance for airport security. Donnellan is met at security by Captain Garcia of the LAX airport police who gives Donnellan access to his office phones. He also makes reservations for the NYPD detectives on the next direct flight to Boston. Donnellan contacts Manhattan South and Dugan answers. He gives him a brief update and Dugan assures him the he will be in Boston in four hours with copies of the surveillance videos and the case files. Donnellan calls the Chief of Detectives with an update.

The detectives are inside the gate waiting to board their flight. The evening news is on the television in the lounge.

'Holy shit!" says Donnellan. "It's Wild Joe Donovan!"

"I thought he was dead," exclaims Harrison.

They ask the bartender to turn up the volume a little so they can hear Donovan. They both listen intently as a panel of experts talk about the changing role of police officers. Basically, most of the experts believe that today's police officer is better educated than in the past. One expert panelist is stating that college education is an important requirement in modern law enforcement and investigators should be more educated since they are always under intense scrutiny by attorneys and the media.

"If I may interrupt," says Wild Joe, "you guys don't know what you're talking about. Dhe cops in dhe old days were every bit as good, if not better dhen dhey are today. The problem is dhat we ain't producing as good of people as we used to. When I was growing up, everyone looked up to dhe cops. We was dhe good guys and people knew it. We didn't need professors to help us because people respected us.

"Look, let me tell ya what happens when people trust dhe police. You don't need a library filled with rules dhat don't help anyone. You just need common sense. I learned dhat my first day in homicide. We get a call about a DOA in the South Bronx. Jim O'Connolly, dhe legendary Homicide Detective, takes me with him on my first case.

"It turns out dhat dhe victim was an Irish woman known in the neighborhood for her temper tantrums. She was built like a middle linebacker and more dhen one neighbor tells us how she would beat her skinny husband like a drum.

"So, on dhis day dhe husband, uh, let's call dhe Irishman Duffy, uh, cause dhat was his name. Well, uh, Duffy comes home after spending eight hours sweeping dhe streets. He no sooner gets in dhe door when his wife starts screaming and shouting. He yells something back to her; she takes offense and trows a frying pan at him. You know, uh, one of dhose cast iron jobs. He picks it up, trows it back at her, and races out the door to the local pub.

"When we enter the bar, everyone immediately knows that we was cops. Jimmy O asks who's Duffy?

"He says, "Oh, for God's sake did she call dhe cops on me?"

"Jimmy O says. "No . . . she's dead." Well, now, Duffy starts crying and sobbing, he can't believe dhat he hurt his wife, he refers to dhe dear woman as a saint. Somehow in this mixed up world dhey were meant for each other.

"We take Duffy downtown. He's sitting in dhe backseat sobbing, no handcuffs, no reading him his Miranda, not necessary. We reach midtown and Jimmy O asks Duffy if he has a dhirst? He says dhat he's a little dry.

"Dhe next thing I know, we are sitting at PJ Clark's drinking beers with our prisoner and some of Jimmy's celebrity friends. After a few drinks, Jimmy says he's in the mood for a pastrami samich. He dhen sends Duffy to the Deli to get sandwiches for everyone at the table.

"It may sound ridiculous to you today, but we was trying to give dhe man a last breath of freedom before he went to dhe big house. He respected us and we respected him."

CHAPTER 25

Lᴉᴇᴜᴛᴇɴᴀɴᴛ Vᴀʀɪᴇʟʟᴏ ɪꜱ ᴡᴀɪᴛɪɴɢ in his office when Donnellan and Harrison arrive at Boston Police headquarters. He invites them into his office and hands each of them a copy of the case file for Jon Cordova, also known as the "Road Runner."

"Let me tell you a little bit about your boy here," says Variello, as he sits on the edge of his desk. "The Road Runner is an over-caffeinated street junkie who bounces up and down the East Coast delivering the product for whoever pays his freight. Last night he delivers some white powder to the syndicate on the North End. Then he rolls up his sleeve and slips a diamond studded Rolex off his arm and whispers it's worth a million bucks, but he'll sell it for five grand. He shows "Smooth Sal" Pignataro, a made-man, the heart with the interlocking GQ engraved on the back of the watch and in a hushed tone says that it belonged to the dead actor from New York. This sets off an alarm since the New England mob boss had already whispered to his associates that the New York "families" are cooperating with the cops to find the killer of the actor.

"So, Smoothie tells his underlings to rough up the Cordova, drop him off on Prince Street, tie him to a streetlight with his jewelry tied around his neck and watch him from a distance until the cops pick him up. Variello gives Donnellan a plastic evidence bag which contains GQ's Rolex, rings and jewelry. Then he hands him the Road Runner's eight page rap sheet filled mostly with drug trafficking and larceny convictions in New York City.

Lieutenant Variello tells Donnellan. "I tried to soften up Cordova to see if I could get a confession and send him on the express train back to New York. I cut him a little slack, before I started playing hardball. He thought that we should roll out the red carpet. I let him dance for a little while before I pulled the carpet from underneath him. I ask him what happened to the actor. He tells me he don't know nothing. I tell him that's not what I hear. He tells me I'm wrong. Then this jailhouse lawyer starts asking me if the Penal Code in Massachusetts is the same as New York. So, I figured I'd put him on ice and let you handle him without any interference from me. I haven't charged him yet. He is being held over there in the quiet room next to my office. I told him I had to handcuff him so he wouldn't play with his Habeas Corpus. Gentlemen, he's all yours."

Lieutenant Variello tells the New York City detectives that the "Road Runner" is complaining that he's hungry. Donnellan asks Variello if he has a take-out menu for a good pizzeria. Variello pulls some papers out of his desk drawer and hands Donnellan a menu from Pino's. He then escorts the detectives to the conference room.

Jon Cordova is seated across from a uniformed Boston Police Officer. He's handcuffed and his hands are resting on the table. Variello directs the police officer to wait in the squad room. Once the New York City detectives are seated opposite the "Road Runner," Variello hands them an envelope containing copies of the Tarrant surveillance tapes. He then returns to his office.

Donnellan studies the menu. He asks Cordova, "Do you want pizza, a calzone or a sub?" The "Road Runner" was expecting the detectives to scream, hit and threaten him, especially since he knew that the dead actor, GQ, was Donnellan's best friend. Caught off balance by the offer, he cautiously orders a large meatball sub. Donnellan chooses the same and Harrison goes for the chicken parm. Donnellan phones in the order.

No other words are spoken. The detectives know Cordova isn't ready to talk yet. The goal is to confuse him, get his mind wandering and trying to figure out what they have up their sleeves. The detectives open their files and silently review the reports that Variello had given them. Occasionally they look up and glance at one another, and then stare intently at the "Road Runner." The detectives want him to feel uncomfortable, to know who the boss is. They want him to realize that whether he cooperates or not, they are walking out of this building as free men and he is not. They don't want him to feel that they need him.

There's a knock on the door. Donnellan steps outside the room and pays the deliveryman. He then returns to his chair and puts the bag of food on the table. A tantalizing aroma fills the room. Donnellan asks Cordova, "Who killed the actor in New York?"

Cordova doesn't respond.

Donnellan says, "Rack your brain and sharpen your memory Cordova, if you know what's good for you. Just don't say a word until you remember who killed the actor."

Cordova curses under his breath.

Donnellan slowly takes two sandwiches out of the bag. They are carefully wrapped in aluminum foil. He leaves Cordova's sub in the bag and simply says, "He who does not talk, does not eat."

Donnellan hands the chicken parm to Harrison. The detective takes a healthy bite of his sandwich and exclaims, "Um um, this chicken parm is packed with flavor!"

Donnellan wolfs down a bite of the meatball sub, shakes his head in delight and smiles at Cordova.

Harrison continues reading the Boston Globe as he eats. Between bites he mentions to Donnellan that the sports writers and fans in Boston are still angry that the baseball players went on strike earlier this year. And with a strike shortened schedule the Red Sox remain stuck in fifth place. They start talking about the old timers like Yogi, Mantle and Mays who played ball for the love of the game. They felt lucky that they got paid to play a kid's game instead of working in a factory or a coal mine.

Suddenly Harrison switches gears and he opens the envelope. He stacks three video tapes on the table and tells Donnellan, "I heard the squad's narrowed down the search for GQ's killer to just eight unidentified individuals on the surveillance tapes. The tech unit has freeze-framed images of each of them. Their pictures will be plastered in every newspaper and television station in the City by tomorrow night." Harrison glares at Cordova and says, "Time is running out to make a deal. Once that ship passes you by and you can't help us anymore, there'll be nothing stopping you from doing a long stretch in Attica as an accessory to a murder."

Donnellan taps his watch and looks at the "Road Runner." It's not rocket science. Cordova knows his back is against the wall. Make a deal with the cops now while he still has a chance. Or, risk doing hard time upstate. Donnellan senses he's ready to talk and he taps his watch again. Cordova nods his head and says:

"All right! All right! I remember. I remember."

"I was staying in New York with a friend of mine. We were crashing in an apartment on the Lower East Side, down around Houston Street. The cat who owned the pad was Jake Moon, we called him "The Merchant." He's a cool dude and always left the door open for stray friends. We were both looking to make a score. We heard that a dealer from uptown was looking to get rid of some Jamaican for two large. We figured we could turn two into ten, but we ain't got two.

"Jake had a girlfriend who works at the Tarrant. She's the only one we know who has that much cash. We take the bus uptown to visit her at work. When we get to the hotel, I stay outside. I don't want to go in because there are a lot of cops in the hotel and I know that there is a warrant out on me.

"Can you help me with that warrant?"

Donnellan and Harrison both nod their heads indicating that they could.

"So, Jake goes into the hotel. I wait about a half hour for him to come across the street. He walks over to me very calm and tells me to just keep walking. I ask him if he saw his girl, he says, "No, but I got some money." We walk to the subway and head uptown to see the dealer, some guy name Henry who was up from Jamaica selling Jamaican.

"Henry wants two grand. "The Merchant" gives him the cash. Then Jake takes out a Rolex, some expensive cuff links and rings. He hands it to Henry. The Jamaican looks at the jewelry. He asks if it's real. Jake says he just rolled a rich dude in the hotel and the jewels are the real deal. The Jamaican hesitates. Jake tells him that the Rolex alone is worth five grand. The Jamaican tells him it's too hot to handle, no deal. We score the pot and go back downtown.

"That night we smoke some of the weed and watch television. "The Merchant" hears the story about the actor getting murdered in the Tarrant. He turns to me and says. "Oh, shit! That's the guy I robbed."

"Jake says he was looking for his girlfriend in the hallway on the 38th floor when he sees a blonde rush out of her apartment right into the elevator. He didn't hear her door slam. He waits until the elevator doors close. Then, he turns around and walks to her apartment. He turns the knob, the door opens. He looks around and he thinks nobody's home. He walks in and sees the money, wallet and jewelry on the dresser. He starts walking toward the loot when a guy walks out of the bathroom. The dude doesn't see him. So, Jake picks up a candlestick off the table. And before the actor knew what happened, Jake clocked him on the back of the head.

"He grabs the loot, sticks the candlestick in his shirt so he doesn't leave any evidence, then he swiftly walks out of the hotel.

"I'm telling you the truth detective. Jake never thought he killed the guy. He was shocked when he found out the guy died. He kept telling me, I swear I didn't hit him that hard."

Lieutenant Donnellan asks the Road Runner, "What happened to the candlestick?"

"Jake still has it in his apartment right on his kitchen table. I told him to get rid of it. You know, it could be used as evidence against him. But for some reason he won't ditch it."

Donnellan takes a video from the envelope, puts it in the VCR and hits the play button. They all watch the video for about five minutes. Then Cordova blurts out. "There he is! That's Jake." Donnellan freezes the picture. "You see the dude walking toward the stairs wearing a white button down shirt, the dungarees and sneakers. The guy in the back, that's Jake."

Donnellan gets the address and phone number for Jake and leaves the room. Harrison asks Lieutenant Variello if they can get the "Road Runner's" statement on video. He calls the tech unit and they make the arrangements.

CHAPTER 26

Sᴇʀɢᴇᴀɴᴛ Hᴇʀʙ Wᴀɢɴᴇʀ ᴀɴsᴡᴇʀs the phone when Donnellan calls Manhattan South. He takes the pertinent information and transfers the call to the Chief of Detectives. Wagner does a criminal background check on Jake Moon. He hits pay dirt. There is a warrant out for Moon for failing to appear at court. This saves time for the police. They have an arrest warrant in hand and that is all they need to apprehend the suspect.

Wagner organizes two teams of detectives from the squad room to assist him on this collar. He doesn't want any mistakes. He calls Chief Dickersen and tells her about the warrant. She directs him to arrest the suspect and keep her informed each step of the way.

The Chief calls the Police Commissioner and Barry Rosen to alert them to a possible break in the GQ case. The public relations team is put on high alert. All they need is Moon.

Wagner drives downtown with three other detectives. They stop in front of Jake Moon's apartment. They walk to the third floor. The apartment door at 3A is partially open. Lead detective Wagner kicks in the door and yells "Freeze! Police!"

There is no movement in the apartment. Sergeant Wagner and the other detectives have their guns drawn. The Sergeant walks into the bedroom and a man pleads with him not to shoot. Wagner asks him for his name. He tells him, Jake Moon. He is arrested and handcuffed. They walk the prisoner into his kitchen.

Wagner sees the candlestick on the kitchen table. He tells Moon to sit down.

The sergeant interrogates the suspect who makes a full confession and admits he hit GQ with the candlestick that is sitting on the kitchen table. Moon repeats that he's sorry, that he never meant to hurt the actor, and that this is all a terrible mistake.

The sergeant directs detective Dugan to call the Chief and Donnellan. Dugan is exhausted from his round trip to Boston, but was energized by the likelihood of a break in the GQ case. He thought this might be his last chance to be part of a major case. He calls the Chief and, then starts to feel a little melancholy. This could be his last case before he is forced into retirement. He gathers himself and makes the long distance call to Boston Police headquarters.

Donnellan answers the phone on the first ring. Dugan tells him that the squad has Moon in custody and that he made a complete confession. Dugan starts to smile to himself as he continues to fill in the details for the Lieutenant. He waits until their conversation is almost over and he takes a short breath. Detective Dugan then gives the commander one last bit of advice as he passes the torch to a new generation of detectives. "Ah, Lieutenant, remember, don't make mysteries!"

CHAPTER 27

THE MAYOR'S OFFICE SCHEDULES a press conference regarding a significant development in the GQ homicide investigation for 11:00 a.m. at Mother Cabrini Hospital. Just before the event begins, the mayor is observed being surrounded by nurses and doctors as they carefully wheel Dolly Goldberg to the makeshift staging area. The Mayor, Police Commissioner, Chief of Detectives, Donnellan, CEO of Tarrant International and many actors, actresses and entertainers are crowded together at the staging area. To the right of the stage, Barry Rosen is whispering to his media sources.

The mayor congratulates the New York City Police Department for going above and beyond the call of duty to capture the perpetrator who assaulted and killed New York City's beloved son, GQ. As soon as the conference ends, Donnellan discreetly slips out a side door and inconspicuously starts walking uptown. As he approaches the Police Academy on Second Avenue, Donnellan feels a spiritual force drawing him toward Epiphany Church. He breaks into a smile as he imagines GQ telling him that, "All surfers know. Don't fight the undertow." So he opens the door, enters the church and lights a candle for GQ. Donnellan is not a religious person, but he appreciates the fellowship, compassion and spirituality of his church community. There are two other parishioners in the church who are silently praying in the back rows. Donnellan walks to the front of the church, sits and reflects upon life with, and now without GQ.

His first thought is of Connor. He thinks with pride that his friend GQ, with all his money had the courage to accept the things he should not change. He did not interfere with the Kelly family. Donnellan thinks to himself that he will keep an eye on Connor from a distance, help him if he can and celebrate his accomplishments privately in accordance with the Kelly code of silence. Donnellan silently laughs as he thinks back to the days when Bernadette left suddenly for Ireland. He remembers GQ putting on a hilarious one-man show at the playground quoting Alfred Lord Tennyson with a mocking British accent: "Tis better to have loved and lost than never to have loved at all." Then he would seamlessly change his character and lean on Donnellan's shoulder and give a sobbing impression of Don Rickles, saying: "I'm so lonely. I need a broad!" He was hysterical. All the guys laughed until tears filled their eyes. GQ fooled everyone, but especially himself.

Donnellan wishes that he could turn back the clock and be a better friend. Then maybe GQ would have confided that he was heartbroken that Bernadette went back to Ireland. But of course Donnellan knows that's a ridiculous notion as they both were just immature teenagers in post-war America. Inexplicably, he gets up, lights another candle and returns to his seat. He's not ready to leave the church yet.

Donnellan's brainwaves crackle with random thoughts of the last few days as he contemplates GQ. He is thankful that Chief Dickersen is his boss. She trusts him, he trusts her. Of course Donnellan would never tell her about his contact with the five families; that would have made her an accessory to an unlawful contact with a criminal enterprise. Undoubtedly she knew he used unorthodox investigative methods throughout this case, especially regarding the help of so called "concerned citizens" in Boston. Donnellan briefly ponders about the reliability of the Road Runner. He is confident the Road Runner will not recant his testimony since his twenty-five thousand dollar reward will be paid in five annual payments. Plus, he said that he voluntarily cooperated with the police in video and signed statements.

Donnellan wonders about Amanda Blakely. He hasn't met her yet, but she has been assigned to Chief Dickersen as the FBI liaison with the NYPD, a prestigious appointment for the FBI. Donnellan thinks back to his last get-together with GQ at the Irish Pavilion. He sensed that GQ wanted to share some exciting news before they rushed out the service exit. Was it about Blakely? Did GQ find what he was looking for? The Chief said Blakely did not jump into bed with GQ, she waited until he was ready to commit to her. When he told Blakely he loved her and was committed to their relationship, she believed him. Donnellan knows that GQ did not lie. That Blakely must be something special. He looks forward to meeting her soon.

Donnellan looks at the stained glass windows surrounding the church and feels the warmth of the sun rays peeking through the glass. He thinks about the support he receives from his wife and family. It's not easy being married to a detective. It takes teamwork and he has the best team. He starts making plans for a nice enjoyable family weekend; maybe a visit to his parents, a football game at West Point, or maybe an early dinner at Sloppy Louie's down near the Fulton Fish Market. Afterwards, they could walk to the World Trade Center and go up to the observation deck. Everyone loves the breathtaking views, especially seeing helicopters flying below. "Whoa," thinks Donnellan as he looks at his watch. "It's time to go back to work."

When he stops for a traffic light on 21st Street, Barry Rosen taps him on the shoulder. They walk together toward Third Avenue and Rosen hails a cab for a ride up to the mayor's residence at Gracie Mansion. As he enters the taxi, Rosen mentions that Mayor Longley is surging in the polls and he's expecting to be reelected in a landslide.

Donnellan half-heartedly congratulates the deputy mayor and just as he's about to close the door, Rosen looks at Donnellan and enthusiastically states that it looks like we will be working together for another four years.

Donnellan thinks to himself, "Fasten your seatbelts boys and girls, this is going to be a bumpy ride."

PART II

WHAT GOES AROUND, COMES AROUND

CHAPTER 28

As DONNELLAN IS WALKING to the Police Academy his mind wanders toward thoughts of Barry Rosen, the invisible hand of city politics. He gives reporters scoops, does favors and makes everyone he meets feel important. Just, don't double-cross him. His memory is long and his vengeance is fierce. Donnellan thinks of one his father's favorite expressions, "Don't mistake a tiger for a pussycat." Rosen is definitely a tiger.

The Police Academy is bustling with activity as Donnellan walks up two flights of stairs and crisscrosses through halls on the way to his office. He's taken by surprise when he enters the squad and the detectives stand, applaud and shout tributes. "Good job! Nice work, Boss! GQ can rest in peace!" Donnellan salutes and graciously thanks his team for their extraordinary effort then he enters his office.

As soon as he sits down, he picks up the phone and calls Chief Dickersen. He was hoping to schedule a meeting and finally meet Amanda Blakely, but that would have to wait at least two weeks since Blakely was visiting her parents in California. The Chief takes the opportunity to thank Donnellan for going above and beyond the call of duty in the hunt for GQ's killer. She also reminds him that his family was tremendously inconvenienced throughout the investigation and maybe he should take some time off to make it up to them. Donnellan thanks the Chief. He says he will consider her suggestion as he picks up the case file on his desk.

The administrative file clerk had clipped a note to the GQ file which was placed at the center of Donnellan's desk. The handwritten note read "Is this file closed, Lieutenant?" All at once the reality that GQ was dead hit him hard. He felt like an energy vampire had sapped his spirit. With more than ten years' experience as a homicide detective, Donnellan naively thought he was immune from the five stages of grief. But, the rules changed when GQ died.

Donnellan skipped over the first stage, denial. He went right to the anger stage as he worked tirelessly for many frenetic weeks in pursuit of his best friend's killer. However, the bereavement process doesn't have an expiration date and subconsciously Donnellan was just starting to grieve the passing of his best friend. Surprisingly, for the first time since he's been "on-the-job," he felt no enthusiasm for the force. He was demoralized and very, very sad.

Out of the blue, Donnellan crossed the threshold to the third stage of grief – Bargaining. On one hand, he was riddled with self-doubt and questioning if could have been a better friend or somehow prevented the death of GQ. He kept trying to challenge his insecurity with thoughts such as, "GQ needs me to be strong." "My family thinks I'm like a rock." "The NYPD counts on me to put a positive face on the department." But his confidence was plummeting. Suddenly, to his squad's surprise, Donnellan took the Chief's advice and decided to take a two-week vacation.

Donnellan is in a daze walking home, but remembers to look skyward and wave to his youngest son before entering the building. Donnellan hits the elevator button for the 7th floor. As he quietly rides up, he imagines GQ whispering in his ear: "You did the best you could! Take care of your family, friends and especially Amanda. You are my watchman!" When the door opens, Patrick runs to his dad and gives him a hug. Donnellan experiences a brief moment of joy for the first time all day. A cheerful Donnellan shares the news about the vacation leave to the delight of his family. This isn't a vacation, but rather a rare opportunity to be a full-time husband and dad for his family.

However, he can't sustain the enjoyment very long and, within a day, he slips into an emotional nosedive. Marian and his children are surprised by his change in behavior. First off, he goes on a media blackout. No television, radio, magazine or other news. He doesn't want to hear, see or read anything about GQ. He is worn-out from the throngs of GQ's real and fictional lovers sensationalizing their passionate affairs to the distracting delight of people all over the world. He just can't take it anymore.

Another change was even more strange. After starting each morning making breakfast for his wife and children, Donnellan would walk his children to school. But instead of taking the shortest and most direct route – which would take him past the Police Academy – he would lead his children through a maze of walkways that snaked through Peter Cooper Village until they exited at 22nd Street so Donnellan didn't have to see his workplace. Once his children entered the school he would continue walking to Third Avenue, make a right turn to 23rd Street and walk to the East River, looping back home. Subconsciously, Donnellan was taking this circuitous route to avoid contact with friends and coworkers.

Marian picked up on his downheartedness in a New York minute, but she didn't know how to approach him. The master of sarcasm was a failure at deception. He was raised to associate heartache as weakness. She had an informal meeting with a social worker friend she worked with at Mount Sinai Hospital who advised her that at this stage of grief it may be it may be best to give Donnellan breathing space to work through his loss. The social worker, in efforts to help ease Marion's concern, cited an ancient proverb –, "When the student is ready, the teacher will appear."

Marian ended her conversation with the social worker on a humorous note when she mentioned how she tried to wake-up Donnellan's cynical Irish wit. Last night she asked Donnellan to come into the living room to watch an aspiring Hollywood starlet on TV. The bleached-blond actress was reporting in vivid detail the tryst she allegedly had with GQ when Marian blurted out, "What a pair of knockers! It's amazing what they can do with a gallon of silicone!" Donnellan faked a laugh and reverted to reading a book in their bedroom.

Most afternoons, while he waited at home for the return of his family, Donnellan was reading books that he had taken from GQ's bookshelves. *The Cardinal Sins, Passages, Crime and Punishment,* and he was even going to attempt to read *Ulysses.* In essence, he was placing himself in a self-imposed quarantine as he sunk deeper into depression. Among his friends he was noticed by his absence. He declined all invitations to come out of his shell, but nothing worked until he accepted an offer he could not refuse. He could never say no to GQ's grandfather, Hughie Clancy.

Mr. Clancy lived on the ground floor of a sparsely furnished two-bedroom apartment on 86th Street in Bay Ridge, Brooklyn. Hughie was the definition of the salt of the earth and was as stubborn as the day is long. Not only did he refuse to accept money from GQ or anyone else; he was genuinely insulted by the insinuation that his home was second-rate. The proud Irish widower was a humble self-educated man revered by his family, neighbors and especially the Irish immigrant community. His lively stories, peppered with wisdom, history and humor were widely sought and generously shared with countless friends.

The door was slightly open when Donnellan arrived at the apartment. Clancy called out in his typical booming voice to invite Donnellan into his home and join him at the kitchen table. After warm greetings and handshakes, Donnellan sat at the table and expressed his condolences to Mr. Clancy. Hughie accepted the expression of sympathy with a somber nod and complimented Donnellan for capturing the murderer. Donnellan just bowed his head in sorrow. The room was silent for a few minutes as the pair quietly reminisced about GQ.

Hughie Clancy knew that Donnellan was dispirited, a feeling that Clancy himself had experienced at a critical point in his life. He hoped that he could enlighten Donnellan to recognize the folly at the root of his unhappiness and regain his self-confidence. Clancy broke the silence.

"John Patrick, as you know I never had any high school or college education, but I know it when a friend is miserable. You can keep on smiling and pretend that you are fine, but it won't fool me. I think that you have been so absorbed in your quest for Gregory's killer that when you reached the end of the hunt, you fell off an emotional cliff. Now that you have time to think, you're second-guessing yourself and wondering how you could have saved Gregory. Am I reading your mail, John Patrick?"

"How did you know that's how I feel? I can't sleep at night without thinking what could I have done? And when people keep congratulating me for capturing the perp, it's like they are sticking a dagger in my back. All I wanted was to be left alone! Now, for the first time in my life, I don't want to go to work. I feel like I'm becoming a hermit. But I don't want to hear any of that psychological bullshit from the human resource counselors trying to help me get in touch with my feelings, so I keep it to myself."

Hughie waits a few seconds and speaks in a very low whisper so only

Donnellan can hear him. "During the War for Irish Independence, I joined the Irish Republican Army and served in the East Mayo Brigade. We didn't have telephones or modern ways to communicate, so we relied on secret messages passed from town to town by bicycle, horseback or passenger train. In 1920, Michael Collins asked for volunteers to come to Dublin to provide protection for Dan Breen and my friend, Sean Treacy. I was just an eighteen-year-old farm boy who had never been to the big city, but I got on the train in Galway to go to Dublin. The British secret police were on the lookout for rebels and they grabbed me before the train left the station. I told them I was going to visit my cousin Nonnie. They called me liar and tried to get me to be an informer. I told them I didn't know anything about the IRA, and that I was just a farm boy. They pulled me off the train, beat me to a pulp and let me walk back to Mayo. Two days later, Sean Treacy was killed in an ambush. I blamed myself. I was a failure, John Patrick. If I had made it to Dublin, Sean would be alive today."

Donnellan sees a tear starting roll from the eye of the old man and says, "Mr. Clancy, you are a hero. Because of you and your friends, Ireland is a free country today. You did the best you could. No one can blame you for Sean Treacy's death."

Hughie Clancy whispers to Donnellan. "No one can blame you for Gregory's death either. So let's just be thankful for the time we had with Gregory."

Donnellan smiles and for the first time in weeks, he feels better. At last, the fifth stage of grief – Acceptance.

Mr. Clancy then reaches behind his chair and puts two small glasses on the table. He asks Donnellan to go into the cabinet by the door and bring over the clear bottle labeled Holy Water. Donnellan thinks to himself that he is about experience some type of age-old Gaelic religious custom. Hughie takes the bottle, and pours a few ounces into each glass. Then he tells Donnellan that he bought this poteen, another name for Irish moonshine, from a farmer in Galway named Walsh. Every time he visits the old sod he smuggles a few bottles of "holy water" to drink on special occasions. With that, they raise their glasses and make a toast to GQ.

CHAPTER 29

O<small>N</small> W<small>EDNESDAY</small> N<small>OVEMBER</small> 4<small>TH</small>, the day after Mayor Longley was reelected; Donnellan leaves his house at the crack of dawn and briskly walks to his office at the Police Academy. He buys a *Daily News* and *New York Post* from his friend Joe at the newspaper stand on 20th Street and First Avenue. Donnellan tucks the papers under his arm and takes the first step to end his media quarantine. He feels rejuvenated and confident as enters the stillness of the early morning detective squad. The midnight shift detectives are huddled at Detective Dugan's desk as he's busy whispering some entertaining stories until he sees Donnellan and he says, "Hi, Boss! Welcome home."

"What are you doing here so early, Dugan?"

"I just updated the GQ case and put the file on your desk boss," replies Dugan with a mischievous smile.

"What do you mean Dugan; I closed that case two weeks ago?"

Donnellan peeks in his office and sees a brown paper bag on the center of his desk. He picks up the bag and pulls out a special GQ Edition of Playboy Magazine with a barely clothed Kenya Holmes on the cover and baring it all in the centerfold. Inside the magazine, there are pictorial spreads of many real and imagined lovers of GQ including Rhonda Rholla and Linda Denniston who is quoted "There may be snow on the roof, but there's heat in the furnace!"

As Donnellan is skimming though the pages, he glances at an amused Dugan who comments that the Denniston broad is well preserved for her age and maybe he would have a shot with her. Donnellan replies that Dugan should wait a few years and see if her eyesight fails, before he makes his move. Donnellan then says that he hasn't been reading the papers or watching television for two weeks. He needed a rest from the GQ sexploitation nonsense. Dugan tells him to hang on to his hat, what started out as a snowball has become an avalanche.

Donnellan opens up the *Daily News* and there are six stories about GQ's love life. The media and public are still captivated by GQ's mystery lover, the beautiful blonde who raced from the Tarrant on that fateful morning. Who is she? Where is she? Why is she hiding? Playboy is offering her a quarter million to pose topless for the magazine and penthouse is offering a million dollars for a full spread. *The Daily News* and *New York Post* are offering readers a reward for anyone who calls their tip line and correctly identifies the mystery woman.

Donnellan thinks to himself that Amanda probably went home to California for a few weeks hoping that the public would forget all about GQ and their curiosity about the mystery woman would just fade away like old soldiers. No such luck for Amanda. The public's spellbound fascination about every aspect of GQ's love life is still soaring, especially the quest to find his last lover.

He throws the newspapers into the trash, stares at a stack of messages and calls Chief Dickersen. She welcomes him back to work. He thanks her for suggesting he take some time off and mentions that he had self-sequestered himself, like a juror, for the last two weeks. She tells him that the fun and games reach new heights every day and if you can't laugh, then you cry. They schedule an early afternoon meeting for Donnellan to finally meet Agent Blakely.

Chief Dickersen is an extraordinary supervisor and manager. Her leadership approach is to give directives that are clear, fair and easy-to-understand. She was a true change agent for the NYPD, particularly for the detectives assigned to her department at headquarters. First off, she knew from the first day that she entered the police academy that some cops resented her for being a woman, some because she was black, some because she was college-educated and others, well they just don't like themselves or anyone else.

As she moved up the ranks of the department, the Chief was mentored by a cadre of astute friends in Harlem, but she was well aware that there were opportunists examining her every move, hoping to capitalize on any misstep. The day she was promoted to Chief of Detectives she had a meeting with all of the detectives and staff who worked at the police headquarters. She started by thanking the team for their dedication to the citizens of New York City and their service to the department. She then stipulated that, forthwith , certain rules and procedures will be enforced for all personnel in the detective bureau. Simply put, no sexism, racism, alcohol consumption, cursing, yelling, or insults will be tolerated in the workplace. She made it clear that any violation of these rules will result in disciplinary action. There was no mixed message in her statement.

After he hung up with the Chief, Donnellan turned to the thick stack of messages on his desk and started returning calls. His next call was to Barry Rosen. Donnellan congratulated the deputy mayor on the landslide reelection of Mayor Longley. Donnellan was expecting the deputy's mood to be elevated after such a triumphant victory, but he sensed a slight angst in Rosen's voice. It took almost ten minutes before the deputy mayor told Donnellan that a source at the *Daily News* suspects that a rogue reporter at the *News* is moonlighting as a stringer for the tabloid, *Sunsational Inquirer*.

The reporter, Bernard Toomey, is from Bay Ridge and he slipped into GQ's wake pretending to be a supportive neighbor. Somehow he got an inkling that GQ had an illegitimate son and he has been snooping around Stuy Town looking for clues. He is making his bones at the *Sunsational* writing totally fabricated titillating revelations about GQ's sexual exploits.

Rosen tells Donnellan to stay cool, he has a plan. He will arrange to have the editor invite Toomey to the *Daily News* headquarters tomorrow afternoon to discuss a new assignment for the reporter. Once Toomey is settled in a conference room, there will be a knock on the door and Rosen and Donnellan will take a seat at the table and the editor will leave.

Donnellan thinks that back in the old days before the widespread acceptance of tell-all journalism, no reporter in his right mind would even think of publishing outright lies about the sex life of a public figure, especially when the police were involved. He thinks back to JFK, whose extramarital transgressions were kept out of the public eye for decades after he was assassinated. He remembers when one of the old-time cops assigned to the presidential detail told him about a visit that JFK had to the City, where the secret service agents were in a panic when the president ditched them. The cops located him at the Waldorf Astoria.

Donnellan ponders a few different approaches he might take with Toomey. He immediately rules out any kind of physical intimidation, but it's too soon for him make a plan. He will wait until he meets the reporter to assess the situation. Yet, Toomey's reporting definitely is an issue he must address before it gets out-of-hand.

He looks at his watch and realizes it's not even nine o'clock. Then he picks up the phone to return Brady Finnegan's call. He suspects that one of Finnegan's associates is calling in a *marker*. Donnellan thinks, well that didn't take long. It takes five rings before Finnegan answers the phone. They agree to meet on Friday morning at seven. Nothing, more is said.

The phone rings, Donnellan picks it up and is greeted by Captain Rivera. They exchange a few courtesies, then Rivera tells him that the One-Six is swarming with private investigators and reporters trying to locate GQ's mystery woman. There's money on the street for the Tarrant's surveillance tapes or any information about the blonde. He's even noticed some of the cops snooping around trying to get some of the reward money. Donnellan thanks him for the heads-up and hopes that maybe someday the media will let his friend GQ rest in peace.

He decides to return one more phone call before he gets on with reviewing the active cases and meeting with his squad. He calls Father Francis Principe, a Catholic Police Chaplain, who taught GQ and Donnellan when they were high school students. The priest answers on the second ring and they agree to meet for an early lunch in Little Italy.

Father Principe and Donnellan reminisce about GQ and his zest for life as they indulge in a sumptuous meal at Angelo's Restaurant on Mulberry Street. The priest laughed when he told Donnellan that the last time he saw him, GQ was trying to get him to give up his celibate life and go on a date with a divorced talent agent. Then Father Principe asked Donnellan how he's handling the loss of his best friend. Donnellan said it was tough times for a while, but now he is doing fine. The priest tells him to call anytime if he ever needs to talk. Then he takes out his official police chaplain card, writes down his beeper and home phone number, and gives it to Donnellan.

As they exit the restaurant and go their separate ways, Donnellan thinks back to his electrifying high school years when he and GQ were coached by Father Principe. But that was then, and this is now. So Donnellan picks up the pace and walks briskly to Police Headquarters to meet the Chief and FBI Agent Blakely.

CHAPTER 30

THE CHIEF OF DETECTIVES Office is bustling with activity when Donnellan arrives for his meeting with Dickersen. He arrives early so he can express his gratitude to the detectives, administrators, tech units, and secretaries who are the backbone of the department. The Chief gives him time to work the crowd before she waves for him to come into her office. She closes the door and tells her secretary to hold all calls. She conveys her condolences again for the murder of GQ and asks Donnellan if he's ready to get back to work.

He thanks the Chief for her consideration, and tells her, "Yes I'm back." She listens, evaluates his demeanor and concludes that he's ready to go. She tells him that the mayor is very appreciative that the police department, particularly to you and me, handled the two most high-profile cases this year with such competency and effectiveness.

"Barry Rosen asked me if I would like a promotion to Deputy Commissioner which would open up my job for you. I told him thank you but I want to stay as Chief of Detectives and I recommended you for the Deputy's job if you want it, John."

"Thanks Chief, but I don't want to make a move, so can we just keep it the way it is for now?"

She was not surprised by Donnellan's decision and told him that he can stay at Manhattan South as long as she is the chief. Then she changed the subject to Amanda Blakely.

"When I first found out about Blakely and GQ, I didn't know what to think. My main goal was to solve the GQ homicide and maybe we would need her as a witness. But from the first moment we met, I knew that she was an exceptional woman, FBI agent and, most importantly, a first-class human being. At first I had her reviewing the surveillance tapes, as a sort of exercise before I figured out what to do next. But she took the assignment seriously and made quite an impression.

"She made a chronological time-stamped chart identifying all known individuals in each tape, along with a concise summary. This was particularly helpful to convince Jake Moon to take a plea deal. As a result of her remarkable ability and work ethic, I contacted the New York FBI Director and had her assigned as my personal liaison with the FBI. As you know, the FBI calls on us all the time to assist them with their task forces, search warrants and fugitive investigations. We now have Blakely coordinating the labyrinth of law enforcement investigations throughout the city. Her office is three doors down, let's go meet her."

Amanda Blakely has a spacious office by New York City standards. Her desk is relatively sparse and uncluttered, with a memo pad in the center and a conference telephone with three lines to the left. Behind her chair is a blackboard easel with the heading "Westies," and a flow chart populated with circles and arrows. Blakely is absorbed in a file when the Chief knocks on her door. She invites Donnellan and the Chief to sit and puts the file in her cabinet drawer. Donnellan smiles and introduces himself.

He is surprised by her professional appearance and deportment. Somehow he had visualized the "the mystery woman" as someone like Rhonda Rholla with a college degree. But Amanda was not a flighty actress chasing glitter and stardom, rather she was blazing a trail for equality in a "man's world." He also wondered what happened to the "gorgeous blonde broad," since the FBI agent had short brown hair and was wearing a grey business suit with a white open-collared shirt.

Chief Dickersen stays in the office just long enough to make the introductions, but wants to give the agent and Donnellan some time together to talk about GQ. So she leaves the office and closes the door. Amanda expresses her condolences to Donnellan for the death of his best friend. He thanks her and conveys his sympathies to her for the loss of GQ. He notices a tear running down the side of her cheek and gives her time to collect herself.

Amanda tells him that GQ shared many stories of his lifelong friendship with Donnellan and she feels like she's known him for a long time. Donnellan tells Amanda that the Chief had told him about Amanda's relationship with GQ and how they met at the airport and would talk almost every day until GQ died. Donnellan confides that the day before his death, GQ was exceptionally spirited and wanted to tell him about some type of life changing leap in his life. Donnellan sensed that GQ was finally at peace with himself. But when the crowd at the Irish Pavilion started rushing toward GQ, they had to make a quick exit.

Agent Blakely was assessing whether she could trust Donnellan. The Chief told her she could trust him, but she wanted to judge for herself before she would tell him about her total relationship with GQ. After forty-five minutes of conversation, Amanda had no doubt that she could confide in Donnellan. She took a deep breath and said. "I took three weeks' vacation to visit my family in California and decide whether I would come back to New York. It wasn't because of my job or fear of being discovered as the mystery woman, though that would add insult to injury. It was because, when I missed my period for the second time, I knew I was pregnant and GQ was the father."

Donnellan was momentarily stunned by Blakely's revelation and was barely able to keep from saying, "Holy shit!" Instead he whispered "Congratulations! Amanda is there anything I can do for you?"

The FBI agent replied, "Thank you, Lieutenant. But I think I have everything under control for now. My plan is to move back to California in January and live with my parents and raise my babies as a full time mom."

"Babies!" exclaims Donnellan.

"You heard that right Lieutenant, I am having twins. I will submit my letter of resignation to the FBI in the middle of December and ask for a leave of absence so I can keep my health insurance. Hopefully, they will approve my request."

"You should ask the Chief for some help with that, she has clout!" says Donnellan.

"I already did," says Blakely. "The Chief was the first person I spoke with after I missed my second period. Somehow, I knew I could trust her and I was right. Although she is a devout Christian, she does not judge people. Her first question to me, woman to woman, was if I going to keep the baby. I told her absolutely and she was delighted about my decision. We talked about my options, including staying in the FBI and living as a single parent in New York. She told me that she could help me find child care services and would make certain that the bosses stay out of my way.

"I thanked her for her support, but I have a loyal and supportive family in California and that is where I want to raise my children. The Chief then offered to be my intermediary with my request for a leave of absence. She said; "Less words: More power!" Then, she drafted a letter for me to review. In essence, the letter simply thanks the FBI for the opportunity to provide service to the citizens of the United States, followed by a straightforward request for a one-year leave of absence to address a personal family crisis.

"The Chief gave me advice on handling the birth certificates for my twins. We decided that for the father's name I would put down G. Xavier Clancy and hope that no snooping reporter ever figures who the father was. So for the next six weeks I'm an FBI agent working for the Chief of Detectives."

"I can see why GQ fell in love with you Amanda, you are a special lady," says Donnellan. "Just remember, no matter where or when, you can count on me."

The phone rings, Blakely answers with one hand, signals with the other that Donnellan can call her, and he quietly leaves her office and closes the door. Chief Dickersen's secretary tells Donnellan that the Chief is in a meeting upstairs with the Commissioner and probably won't be back until tomorrow. He thanks her for the update, looks at his watch and decides it's time to go home.

CHAPTER 31

THURSDAY MORNING AND DONNELLAN is in his office before seven. He believes that he must work countless hours on the job supervising the active investigations, in order to justify the extra time he spends filling in the remaining pieces of the GQ jigsaw puzzle. Fortunately, he has the support of his team of seasoned detectives who operate at the highest professional level. Donnellan spends almost five hours in the morning with case meetings, file reviews and phone calls to the medical examiner before he stops to think about his upcoming meeting.

He looks at his watch and hurriedly leaves his office for his appointment with Barry Rosen at the *News* Building on 42nd Street. Most tourists visit this landmark skyscraper because it was used as the model for the *Daily Planet* in the first two Superman movies with Christopher Reeve. As he enters the *News* building he hears a parent telling his embarrassed teenage son: "Look! Up in the sky! It's a bird! It's a plane! It's Superman!"

Barry Rosen is waiting in the lobby and mingling by the elevator with two beat reporters. He sees Donnellan and gives him a hand signal to wait one minute in the lobby. He understands that Donnellan does not want to socialize with reporters as they are instinctively curious. When the reporters get on the elevator and the door closes, Rosen hit the button, waits for an empty elevator and signals Donnellan to get in the car with him. He hits the twelfth floor button and they talk briefly until the door opens.

Kieran McNamara is waiting in his office for their arrival. He invites them into his office and closes the door. He expresses his condolences to Donnellan for the loss of his best friend and hopes that the *News* was respectful about GQ's death. Nothing is said about the search for the mystery woman. That is unspoken because in the cutthroat business of selling newspapers, the *News* can't afford to ignore the public's voracious appetite about anything sexually related to GQ, or else their circulation, advertising and profit margin would sink. Donnellan understands this dilemma, but is also irritated at the current state of sensational journalism.

McNamara is well aware of the purpose of the secret meeting that Rosen wants with Toomey. The editor will cooperate with any request from the deputy mayor, who is one of the paper's best sources. All three men understand that they have a codependent relationship, but they also have professional ethics, a moral compass and compassion. They spend about half an hour sharing good-humored stories and experiences while they wait patiently for the arrival of Toomey. The phone rings, the editor answers, gets up and leaves for a meeting in the conference room.

Bernard Toomey is excited and nervous as he sits across from his boss. He hopes that he is going to be commended for his three part series on the life of Robert Moses and maybe get a promotion, but he is also uneasy about his tabloid moonlighting. Kieran McNamara congratulates Toomey on his recent columns and tells him that he has potential as a reporter. Then he starts talking about the significance of values in journalism and the importance of trust and reputation.

Toomey is starting to worry about where this conversation is going. Then there is a knock on the door and Rosen and Donnellan sit down across from Toomey. McNamara then leaves the room. Toomey is dumbfounded and horrified.

Rosen speaks first and asks Toomey, "Do you know who I am?"

Toomey nods.

Rosen then takes the latest issue of the *Sunsational Inquirer* out of his briefcase and opens it up to the explosive headline. "Did the teenage GQ father a child?"

Rosen stands, yelling and cursing at Toomey, telling him he will never work in this town. He starts to lunge at Toomey and Donnellan holds him down and escorts him to the door. He then sits across from Toomey for a one-on-one conversation.

The reporter is petrified and wonders what will happen next. Donnellan speaks in a low voice and reassures Toomey that he can make things better for him. Donnellan says, "I know your Uncle Jack, he's a sergeant in the One-O-Eight in Queens, but I want to keep him out of this mess. Let's work together, alright?"

Toomey nods emphatically yes and Donnellan reaches across the table and they shake hands. Donnellan states, "First off, let's not bullshit each other. You were at GQ's wake in Brooklyn, supposedly as a sympathetic neighbor supporting the family. You knew it was a private service not open to reporters, but you couldn't help yourself could you?"

"I'm sorry, Lieutenant but I did go there to pay my respects and I waited to see you in person because I've seen you on TV and read about you in the papers. But when I heard GQ's sister's keening outburst, I was bowled over and chills ran up my spine. I didn't know what happened. So I stayed longer and followed some of the Stuy Town crew to the Irish Haven. Then I put the pieces together that maybe the Kelly kid was really GQ's son. I'm sorry, Sir. I shouldn't have done it, but please help me?"

"Okay Bernard, I will help you. But first off, stop thinking that the Kelly kid is GQ's son. He has two parents that raised him from birth and you will never be able to prove that they are not his biological parents. But let me tell you about Connor Kelly. He is very private teenager who wants to be a doctor. I spoke with him two days ago and he told me that he plans to go to Regis High School, and then wants to join the ROTC at Boston College and finally finish his education at Georgetown Medical School. He wants to be a military surgeon, like Hawkeye Pierce, Alan Alda's character in MASH. So, let's not rain on his parade."

"What should I do, Lieutenant?"

Donnellan asks Toomey to help him think of a way out of this quagmire. The cat is out of the bag as a result of Toomey's breathless headlines about GQ's illegitimate son, so that has to be addressed first. "Well," says Donnellan, "the only thing I can think of is misdirection. Let's go with the out-of-wedlock child, but let's put him on the west coast living in an upscale orphanage near Hollywood, if such a thing exists. Make up a story, create a fictional teenage lover. Use your imagination. The *Sunsational* is all bullshit anyway, so just add some more crap to the pile. Once you get the story published, quit that rag and get on with your life. Then, I can help you make amends with Rosen and McNamara, if you still want to be a journalist." Donnellan then tells Toomey to just stay cool, and he is going to talk with Rosen and McNamara to smooth things over.

The deputy mayor and editor are conversing when Donnellan enters the room. He tells them that Toomey is scared, remorseful and cooperative. Plus, his Uncle Jack, a sergeant in the PD, is a Bay Ridge boy and friend of Hughie Clancy, so we can be assured of his cooperation. Donnellan asks McNamara to keep Toomey in the fold, but keep a close eye on him. He then tells them about his plan for Toomey to keep moonlighting for the *Sunsational* but redirect the out-of-wedlock story to an orphanage in California.

Rosen likes the plan and says he will work with Toomey on a truly scandalous and erotic story that is fitting for a tabloid that has published stories such as "Arkansas Woman Is Abducted by UFO and Gives Birth to an Alien!" After the laughter subsides, Donnellan says it's time to smoke the peace pipe with Toomey.

Toomey is nervously waiting when they reenter the conference room. McNamara takes the lead and tells him that he is glad that Toomey has straightened out the misunderstanding with the Lieutenant. Then he tells him that he will have a rare opportunity to work on his article with the deputy mayor.

Just as the meeting is ending, Donnellan takes out his business card, writes down his beeper and a private phone number, and hands the card to Toomey. He asks Toomey if he has a private home phone line. Toomey tells him that he doesn't and that he still lives with his parents, but he has a beeper. Donnellan then tells him that if he gets a beeper call with the numbers 171717 that's a signal for Toomey to call him. But then again, if he has an urgent need to reach Donnellan don't hesitate to call. Rosen and Donnellan then shake hands with the editor and reporter and head back to their respective offices.

The squad is fairly quiet at 6:00 p.m., when Donnellan checks in at Manhattan South before heading home. He reviews the detective roster and notices that next week Detective Rosa Hernandez is being transferred from the Major Crimes Unit to Manhattan South Homicide. He appreciates that Chief Dickersen expedited his request to add Hernandez to his squad. He calls Sergeant Kevin Driscoll and gives him a quick update. The desk sergeant at the 16th Precinct tells Donnellan that Sergeant Driscoll is in the house and he transfers the call to the plainclothes unit.

The sergeant picks up the phone on the second ring and states, flatly: "Driscoll."

"Hi, Kevin. It's Donnellan. I just thought I'd let you know that I followed up on your request to transfer detective Hernandez to my squad. She starts next Monday."

"Just don't tell her I had anything to do with this, Lieutenant."

"Don't worry, Driscoll. You didn't have anything to do with it. We needed a Spanish speaking detective with her skills and she was by far the best out there. But your support didn't hurt."

"Thanks, Donnellan. Rosa is an exceptional detective and an even a better person. My divorce was so bitter I promised myself I would never get married again, but yesterday I visited *Teddy the Jeweler* on Canal Street and bought an engagement ring. If Rosa accepts my proposal this weekend, I want you at my wedding."

Donnellan momentarily remembers when Driscoll was lying unconscious at Saint Vincent's Hospital and Rosa held his hand and stayed by his side. He tells Driscoll, "Excellent, but don't pop the champagne until she says, Yes."

"No champagne for us Lieutenant," says Driscoll. "We don't drink alcohol."

"I'm glad to hear that, Kevin. Because I've always said that guns and alcohol don't mix." Donnellan ends the call by offering his optimistic congratulations. After he hangs up the phone, he picks up the detailed chart on his desk and does one more review of his active case summaries.

But before he leaves, he decides to follow up with Amanda Blakely. She answers on the first ring and mentions that she was hoping to get a tour of Stuy Town before she leaves for California. He invites her for dinner at his house on Saturday at six so she can meet his wife and family. She is pleasantly surprised by the offer, and accepts the invitation.

CHAPTER 32

THE ALARM WAKES UP Donnellan at 5:30 a.m. He shifts into high gear for his early morning meeting with Brady Finnegan. As he walks toward the East River to get his car, which is parked on a pier at 23rd Street, Donnellan starts to wonder what's in store for him. His experience when *markers* are called in by the five families is that it usually involves asking an assistant district attorney to consider a plea bargain for a reduced sentence for one of their associates as a reward for their cooperation.

He starts his car, drives over to the garden hose at the corner of the lot, gets out, rinses off the bird droppings, then drives to the Wholesale Tire and Repair Company. He tells the mechanic he wants a grease and oil, and to also check his tires. He walks into Finnegan's office and closes the door. They exchange the usual pleasantries, but this is not a social call. Finnegan asks the lieutenant what he knows about the hit man, Cornelius "Cruel" O'Toole.

Donnellan is curious about the question because it's common knowledge that O'Toole is a vicious murderer and is number three on the FBI's Most Wanted List. Finnegan then tells him that O'Toole started out as an enforcer for the *Westies*, the last remnant of the Irish gangs in Hell's Kitchen, and then started contracting his brutal services for hire, including torturing and killing clients that were protected by the crime families throughout the Northeast region.

"What do they want me to do about O'Toole?" says Donnellan.

"The families are getting impatient waiting for the FBI and other police departments. They want you to capture or kill O'Toole," whispers Finnegan.

"Okay, let me think about it," replies Donnellan. "I can't make any promises. If the bureau hasn't caught him yet, I don't know what I can do. But I'll give it a shot."

There's a knock at the door and a mechanic tells Donnellan that his car is ready. Finnegan stands, shakes Donnellan's hand, offers his condolences for the death of GQ and says sorry for your troubles. Donnellan thinks to himself, "Not as sorry as I am." He drives back to the pier on 23rd Street, parks and starts walking toward the Police Academy. As he walks, he thinks back to the flow chart headline at Blakely's office; *Westies*.

With no O'Toole homicides in his jurisdiction, he's going to have to be careful about getting involved in the investigation, but the FBI Task force does give him an opening. Plus, he remembers that Dugan did some work on that case about a year ago, so he decides to talk to Dugan first.

As usual when he enters the squad room, Brendon Dugan is sitting at his desk reading the *News* and making comments under his breath. Donnellan waves his hand and Dugan takes a chair in his office. He tells Dugan that Amanda Blakely is now coordinating the FBI's O'Toole Task Force and he would like to help her out. Dugan is puzzled, but he keeps to his philosophy, don't make mysteries.

Dugan says, "O'Toole's old man was on the job in the early sixties. A good cop, never in trouble. He spent most of his time in the traffic division, mostly at the Lincoln Tunnel. One cold winter morning he got hit by a truck skidding on the ice. The poor guy died two weeks later, leaving a widow with four young kids including the outlaw. The widow, she survives on a small pension and by working as a cleaning woman. Her two daughters and one son do the right thing and work hard for a better life. But, Cornelius, he was trouble from the beginning, a juvenile delinquent at 14, 15 and 16. He always got a light sentence by claiming he was depressed because of his father's accidental death, and his Pop being a dead cop, he always got sympathy.

"The older he got, the eviler he got. He is more than a hitman; he's a sick bastard who tortures his victims. You know, like in that Clint Eastwood movie, *The Good, The Bad and The Ugly*, O'Toole is the ugly. He also gets his jollies agitating the cops. He's been known to approach cops on the beat or in parked radio cars and flash his father's badge, claim to be on the job, then call the FBI and laugh about his antics.

"He's a tricky hump who knows how to disguise his appearance and sinister personality. About six months ago, the state police thought they had him boxed in near the Delaware River, but they lost him when he vanished into thin air on the Pennsylvania border.

"It turned out he knew some back roads in that area because he worked for a few summers at some whitewater rafting companies when he was a teenager. He was also arrested twice in New York and once in Pennsylvania for assault and battery."

Donnellan sizes up Dugan's rundown and asks him to find out if there have been any new developments in the task force.

CHAPTER 33

Marian Donnellan is surprised, but not shocked that her husband invited a law enforcement colleague for dinner on a Saturday night. Yet, she is somewhat puzzled that the guest is a female FBI agent. Marian is not suspicious that her husband is keeping a lover on the side, she trusts him completely, but still it is odd. As she searches up and down the aisles at Gristedes, she decides that she will follow her mother's advice and have no expectations and just enjoy the moment. So, since she will be serving dinner for her children and her guest she decides on the comfort food choice of a garden salad, chicken parmesan, penne pasta and frozen peas.

As she walks down 20th Street pulling her shopping cart full of groceries, she's still mystified about this female agent who was some sort of "friend" of GQ's. Then she wonders, what kind of "friend?" Strange isn't it? Then she thinks, Donnellan knows the truth about her but he's playing dumb and he won't even give her a hint. Marian smiles and thinks to herself that in four hours the Amanda Blakely magical mystery tour is coming to Stuy Town.

The house is unusually quiet as Marian unpacks the groceries and makes preparations for dinner. Her sons, Patrick and Sean are playing roller hockey at Epiphany School and Norah is playing basketball against her downtown rival at the Immaculate Conception parish on 14th Street. Donnellan is an assistant coach for Norah's team and he tries his best to be supportive to all the players and keep his comical witticisms to himself.

The basketball game is a nail biter, tied right up to the final seconds when Norah is fouled going toward the basket. Norah goes to the foul line with two chances to win the game. The coach calls a time out which gives Donnellan a chance to whisper words of encouragement to his daughter. Norah goes to the line, the referee hands her the ball. She bounces it three times, looks straight ahead, shoots the ball at the basket, where it hits the backboard and falls right into the hoop. Her Epiphany teammates, coaches and fans erupt in cheers.

After the game, Donnellan and his daughter walk to Epiphany to meet her brothers and go home together. Patrick and Sean keep their roller skates on and roll down the sidewalk swinging their hockey sticks back and forth. It's almost five o'clock when they get home, which doesn't give them much time to get ready to meet their dinner guest.

Amanda leaves her apartment, stops at the local bakery, buys a chocolate cake, some cookies, and takes a quick cab ride to 20th Street. She thinks back to her last night with GQ. He wanted to take her to Stuy Town and show her where he roamed as a kid and introduce her to his favorite people, Marian and John Donnellan. He wanted her to experience their family, their love for each other and their children. He wanted Amanda to share that type of life with him. He wanted more than a fling, he wanted a partner and a family. He told her how much he loved her, then he was killed.

It was a bold move for Amanda to accept an invitation to Donnellan's house, but she wanted to experience the GQ childhood, before she left for California to start a new life and raise her children. She was ready to leave New York and was not sure if she would ever come back to the city. She even doubts that she can even stay here six more weeks. Every day is harder and harder; she just wants to go home to her parents, brother Jack, and sisters Ava and Margot.

The cab stops, she pays the fare, enters the building, gets on the elevator, goes to Donnellan's apartment, takes a deep breath and rings the doorbell. Marian doesn't bother looking in the peephole. She knows her guest has arrived. They exchange warm greetings as Amanda hands Marian two dessert boxes. John is right behind his wife and he welcomes the FBI agent to his house and formally introduces his wife and children. Norah is particularly excited to meet a female FBI agent and starts asking rapid fire questions about firearms training and what different cities she's worked in, until her mother tells her to give Amanda a little time to unwind.

Marian is somewhat apologetic as she suggests that maybe they should get ready for dinner right away since she has three hungry children waiting to eat. Amanda understands completely as she's from a big family. Once everyone is seated at the table, they bless themselves and say their grace before meals in unison. Then they start talking and eating. Amanda is asking and answering questions between bites, and also taking mental notes on parenting as she interacts with the Donnellan family. She especially enjoys talking with Marian about her experiences growing up in Stuy Town and her friendship with GQ. When the meal is over, Donnellan senses that the two women would appreciate some alone time, so, he excuses himself to go tell a story to the kids before he lets them watch TV in their room.

Donnellan is a hilarious storyteller and a master of Irish, British, Jewish, and Italian dialects. The women can hear the continuous laughter coming from the back bedroom as Donnellan makes up one outrageous tale after another. Amanda offers to help clean up, but instead Marian pours two glasses of wine and suggests they move into the living room and talk. Amanda declines the wine and asks for a glass of orange juice. Marian is slightly perplexed and thinks maybe there's an FBI rule about drinking alcohol when you're on call.

There was an immediate friendship between the women. Within an hour they felt like they knew each other for years. At one point, Marian again asked Amanda how she met GQ and how well did she know him. Amanda kept her true relationship a secret as she talked about her frequent conversations with GQ, but Marian noticed tears welling in the corner of her eyes. She instinctively knew there was more to the story. Then Marian started getting teary. Without warning, Amanda cried out "I miss him so much."

Marian whispered to Amanda, "What's wrong dear, you can trust me. I love GQ, too."

Amanda sobs that she's the mystery woman. She tells Marian that GQ was ready to settle down with her and wanted to have a family like the Donnellans. She says that GQ was going to introduce her to them when he made his return to Stuy Town. Marian hugs Amanda and says she is sorry. Then Amanda tells her that she is pregnant with GQ's babies. Marian thinks to herself, "Oh, my God!" Then she whispers that Amanda should let Donnellan know her situation.

Amanda tells her that the only people who know her situation are Donnellan and Chief Dickersen. At first Marian is let down that her husband kept this secret, but on second thought she respects his integrity. When Donnellan enters the living room it is obvious that Amanda has a new friend which pleases him. He doesn't like keeping secrets like this from his wife. At nine o'clock Amanda is ready to go home. Donnellan insists on going with her until she gets into a cab.

As they walk toward First Avenue, Donnellan is unexpectedly approached by Joan Kelly who is walking home with her son Connor. Donnellan stops and introduces them to the FBI Agent. Joan asks Donnellan if he could talk with her privately for just a minute. Amanda signals to Donnellan to go talk with Kelly as she understands that some people are afraid to call the police, but will report crimes to friends they trust in law enforcement.

Donnellan moves twenty feet inside the traffic circle and Joan confides that they had a meeting yesterday with GQ's attorney, Steve Cohen, and he has set up a trust for Connor with more than a million dollars. Joan says that she was assured by Cohen that the trust is safeguarded and tamper-proofed, but she is still frightened that Connor's secret will be exposed soon, especially with that snooping reporter from the *Sunsational* asking all sorts of questions in Stuy Town about GQ's illegitimate son.

Donnellan says, "Keep the faith, Joan. Everything will be fine. I had a meeting with the snooping reporter and he won't be creeping around Stuy Town or writing about Connor. Let's just say he had a religious experience and now he's on our side. As far as Steve Cohen, he's my good friend, like a brother. His word is his bond. You can trust him and never hesitate to call him if you have any concerns, he will never let you down."

Tears start rolling from Joan's eyes. She gives Donnellan a hug and says, "Thank you, John from the bottom of my heart. Now I can sleep at night."

While Donnellan is talking with Joan, Amanda strikes up a conversation with Connor to distract him from whatever it is that his mother needs to confide in Donnellan. She asks him how he's doing in school. He says that he is a good student and wants to be a doctor. "Wow," says Amanda "is there any special reason that you want to be a doctor, Connor?"

"Well," says Connor, "my mother's youngest brother Raymond was severely wounded in Viet Nam and he's still a patient at the VA Hospital on 23rd Street. She visits my uncle at least once a week and sometimes I go with her. She told me that Uncle Raymond was a brilliant student who wanted to be a writer like Ernest Hemingway. My mother told my uncle when he graduated from Brooklyn College, to go to officer training school and get a commission as a lieutenant in the Army, but he wanted to be on the frontline, like Hemmingway did when he enlisted as an ambulance driver in Italy in World War I. My uncle never wrote his story because, while he was on patrol in Viet Nam, he stepped on a land mine and lost his right leg. Even worse, he became totally delusional. He hears imaginary voices and he's paranoid. But for some reason, when he sees my mother and me, he relaxes and seems happy. I told my mother that someday I will be a doctor and try to help Uncle Raymond get better. So that's my goal."

After hearing Connor's story, Amanda is a little choked-up, but she keeps it to herself. She takes a business card from her purse and she writes down two phone numbers on the back, the first is hers and the second is her father's best friend, Captain Edmund Heenan, M.D. When Donnellan and Mrs. Kelly come back, Amanda mentions her appreciation of Connor's goal and hands Joan her FBI business card, telling her that she will be talking to Captain Heenan about Connor's interest in military medicine and, if he would like, she could arrange for him to have a conversation with the doctor. Joan expresses her gratitude, then takes the card and hands it Connor. He studies both sides of the FBI Agent's business card, thanks Amanda and he promises that he will be calling her soon. Connor puts the card in his pocket and he and his mother continue their walk home.

As Amanda and Donnellan resume walking, she tells Donnellan that she hopes she wasn't out-of-line giving Joan Kelly her home phone number. Donnellan assures her that as a parent of a young teenager, Joan appreciates positive role models for her son to help keep him on the straight and narrow and away from drugs and dropouts. She tells Donnellan she didn't know what came over her because she rarely ever gives anyone her home number, and never to a stranger. Amanda mentions that maybe it is just her intuition, but for some reason she felt that she could help Connor reach his dreams. Donnellan nods in agreement.

When they reach First Avenue, Amanda hails a cab and heads home. Donnellan has a mischievous feeling when she leaves that he is in the presence of GQ. He laughs out loud as he thinks about Sigmund Freud's assessment of the Irish. "That it is one race of people for whom psychanalysis is of no use whatsoever."

CHAPTER 34

Monday morning Donnellan walks briskly to the academy. He is aware that a drowning victim was discovered in the Hudson River just off South Street Seaport. He throws some quarters in the bowl at the newsstand and picks up a few newspapers. His thoughts are about the dead man. He wonders if the floater took his own life and jumped from one of the bridges, or accidentally fell in the river or was intentionally murdered. Whatever the circumstance, the body is at the morgue and the autopsy will determine the cause of death.

The night shift detectives have been canvassing the area, and talking to potential witnesses at the seaport. Donnellan suspects there haven't been any promising leads or he would have been contacted at home. The squad room is quiet when he arrives at his desk. He puts down the papers and sees a headline "Two Weddings and a Funeral at South Street" with pictures of brides on either side of a bouquet of flowers floating in the Hudson River. Donnellan shakes his head and throws the papers in the trash.

The phone rings and Doc Weinstein tells him that the floater was strangled before he was tossed in the river. He says the victim had no identification, was Asian, most likely of Chinese descent, in his early twenties, five foot seven, one hundred and forty five pounds, muscular with short cropped black hair, and goes on to give other descriptive characteristics similar to thousands of young men in Chinatown.

Donnellan understands that the residents of Chinatown have their own culture and don't trust the City to solve their problems. They have their own way of keeping their neighborhood safe and only contact the police if a crime is committed by an outsider. Otherwise many of the residents pretend they don't understand English and will not cooperate with the police. So Donnellan makes a call to his friend Georgy Ling, a businessman with a direct line to the Godfather of Chinatown. Ling tells him that he knows who the floater was, why he was strangled and who did it. He also says that the Godfather of Chinatown has already solved the crime. Georgy Ling then agrees to a meet Donnellan for lunch at the Ye Olde Chop House, downtown next to Trinity Church.

Donnellan calls the deputy mayor, and then calls Bernard Toomey's beeper, leaving the number: 171717. Toomey calls at once on the private line. Donnellan tells him that he has a scoop and to meet him at the corner of Broadway and Thames Street at noon. He tells Toomey to wear a jacket and tie because the restaurant they are going to has a dress code. He also tells him, "No games. No tape recorders. Don't even bring a pad or pen."

Toomey is waiting when Donnellan arrives. They exchange polite greetings then head downstairs from the sidewalk into the restaurant, below the Trinity Building. The Chop House is the oldest restaurant in the City, established 1800. The three martini lunch is alive and well there. They are promptly seated at a table for three. Donnellan orders three diet cokes. Ling appears out of nowhere and sits between them. Donnellan introduces him simply as his friend.

Donnellan tells Toomey, "The dead man that was pulled from the Hudson River was murdered. But the perpetrator will never be prosecuted because of the Chinatown culture of secrecy. Nevertheless, the victim had a name and his story should be told. So my friend is going tell you about him and you can decide if you agree with me."

Georgy sips his soda, then says. "It took Tommy Hon almost a year to get from Hong Kong to Chinatown. He was an indentured servant who started his journey on a freighter from China to South Africa, then on to Europe. He could have stopped in either of those locations to work in a kitchen and pay off his debt, but he wanted to be an American. So his ship left Europe and he and ten other laborers were picked up by a small boat off the coast of New Jersey and transported to lower Manhattan. He worked seven days a week and in his spare time he learned English. He also dated a Chinese American woman and was hoping to marry her, start a family and own his own restaurant. He even picked a location for his restaurant on the corner of New Utrecht Avenue and 44th Street in Borough Park.

"Two days ago, Tommy was gambling at an after-hours poker game sponsored by the Godfather. Tommy hit the jackpot and he was on his way to becoming a business owner. But one of the losing players waited in the street for him. He strangled Tommy, stole his money, and threw him in the river. The Godfather, he believes in an eye for an eye, and he doesn't want gamblers who play by his rules to be 'iced.' So you can expect another floater to come ashore in the next day or two on the beach at Coney Island."

Ling finishes whispering his story and swiftly leaves the table and walks out the front door. Toomey is dumbfounded and speechless. Donnellan tells him to research the story, write a draft article and show it to McNamara. He tells Toomey that the deputy mayor already knows this story and the *Daily News* editor had been briefed. Then Donnellan asks him for an update on the GQ misdirection story.

Toomey says. "When I wrote the first article saying that GQ sired an illegitimate son, a dozen women from coast to coast claimed that GQ fathered their child. One aspiring adult movie actress even sent her erotic photo portfolio for me use in a follow-up story. So, I spoke to Mr. Rosen and our plan is to use some of the risqué pictures for next month's cover and my article will stress her California lifestyle and her alleged tryst with GQ. After that, the next month I will feature more sensational pictures of the starlet, but will refute her assertion and write that there is no evidence to support her claim that GQ fathered her twelve-year-old son.

"I sent the erotic pictures and my draft articles to the deputy mayor and he likes my writing skills. I told him after I'm done with this scheme, I'm quitting the *Sunsational* for good. Mr. Rosen told me that after I quit the tabloid he would have a job for me in the mayor's media relations department."

Though he tries not to be, Donnellan is entertained by the creativity of Rosen and Toomey and thinks to himself, "What a pair!" Donnellan smiles, buys Toomey lunch then leaves to visit Amanda Blakely at Police Headquarters.

CHAPTER 35

Police headquarters is pulsating with exhaustive activity as the department is trying to put a lid on the crime wave that has been plaguing the city for the last few years. Donnellan rushes right up to the Chief of Detectives' office for quick unannounced meeting with Chief Dickersen and Agent Blakely. When he reaches the Chief's office, her secretary tells him that the Chief is at City Hall for a press conference with the mayor. Donnellan continues walking and is invited into Amanda Blakely's office. The flow chart with the "Westies" heading is still behind her desk. Before he sits down, he takes a closer look at the chart and follows the arrows and circles that end with O'Toole.

Amanda is curious about Donnellan's interest in connecting the "Westies" to the *Cruel* O'Toole task force. Then he tells her that the oldest detective in his squad, Brendon Dugan, spent some time on the task force because he was a friend of O'Toole's father. And so, before he is forced to retire, Donnellan would like to help Dugan have one more chance to arrest O'Toole. Then, Donnellan asks the ultimate question, "How can I help?"

The FBI Agent goes to the cabinet and takes out a file, reviews it and says: "The Task Force is supervised by Mike Scuderi from New York City Headquarters. We have been working with all of the Northeast state and local police departments to capture the fugitive. It appears that O'Toole only travels by car, motorcycle or off-road vehicle based on the geographic locations of his crimes and sightings.

He's a merciless sociopath who has tortured his victims with guns, knives, chainsaws and, even, his bare hands. The Rhode Island police almost had him last month, but he escaped by jumping in the river at night and swimming two miles downstream, stealing a boat, then carjacking a car.

"After he escaped, he called the FBI Hotline, identified himself and laughed about killing two people in Providence. Let me show you the chart I made plotting the dates of the known sightings of O'Toole. I think I have identified a behavior pattern. The most common location for O'Toole sightings is along the Delaware River from New York, Pennsylvania and New Jersey."

Donnellan then mentions that O'Toole worked for a whitewater rafting company in that area as a teenager, which Blakely knew from her review of the file. Blakely then said that confidential sources have informed the task force that O'Toole has associations with two biker gangs in upstate New York and Pennsylvania who are protecting him. Blakely hands Donnellan the file which he reviews. He tells Blakely that he agrees that O'Toole is probably hiding somewhere upstate near the Delaware River.

Donnellan then tells her that he and Dugan are planning to take a trip upstate tomorrow to poke around in the Delaware River region upstate. She says that she will contact the task force and the state police on both sides of the river to let them know he'll be in the area. Before Donnellan leaves, he compliments her on her first-rate investigative methods. He also mentions that she has two new friends for life, him and Marian.

Even though it was his day off, Dugan is sitting at his desk reading the *News* when Donnellan enters the squad room. He continues to wonder about what will happen to Dugan when he is forced into retirement. Donnellan has investigated too many suicides by distraught cops and he takes Dugan's situation seriously. He thinks, "I'll have to ask the chief if there's any way we can keep Dugan in the department."

When Dugan sees Donnellan he says: "Hey, Boss! What do ya hear? What do ya say?"

"I hear the Poconos are beautiful this time of year" says Donnellan. "I thought you and me could go on a field trip upstate tomorrow to see if there have been any O'Toole sightings. We can do lunch at The Toast and Grill, a biker joint near the Delaware River. The locals describe it as the best 'bucket of blood' in town."

"I can't wait," says Dugan. "Should I bring a camera and take pictures?"

Dugan picks Donnellan up at Stuy Town at nine o'clock. They drive two hours north of the City, take Route 84 west, and then head north when they reach Route 97. They climb the winding road that hugs the edge of a mountain and provides a terrifying, panoramic view of the Delaware River below. They stop at the Hawk's Nest scenic overlook and wait for FBI agents Scuderi and Blakely. Donnellan walks to the edge of the wall and glances down at the powerful flow of the Delaware River. He stares at the whitewater splashing furiously against the rocks and boulders. There are still a few rafts at some vacant campsites, but there are no people to be found anywhere near the river.

An unmarked car pulls up next to them and Scuderi rolls down his window. He tells Dugan and Donnellan that the FBI and state police are on high alert. Then he hands Donnellan two devices, a transmitter so the FBI can monitor their visit to the Toast and Grill, and a recorder so they can record it. Donnellan takes the transmitter and hands the recorder back to the agents. He tells them that he won't record the visit because they may get tapped down by the bikers. The only things that they are carrying are their guns which they have tucked into their pants near their belt buckle. They will leave the transmitter in the car under the dashboard and a shotgun in the trunk.

CHAPTER 36

DONNELLAN ARRIVES AT THE Toast and Grill at eleven forty-five and parks next to a Ford pickup truck with an empty gun rack attached to the cab. There are four other cars and five motorcycles parked in the lot. As they enter the honky-tonk, they are both wearing over-sized hooded sweatshirts. Dugan's is a brown and tan camouflage with ARMY embroidered on the front. Donnellan's is gray with NYU stitched in the front. When they enter the local hangout they are greeted by the bartender, a fiftyish heavy set woman named Vicky with two gold caps on her front teeth. She asks them if they are lost. They tell her that they were just stopping for lunch.

Vicky tells them to sit anywhere they want and she will take their order. Dugan says let me get a beer first, then sits at the bar while Donnellan grabs a local paper and finds a table with a view of the parking lot and front door. As Dugan is looking at the beers on tap, Vicky asks if they are cops. Dugan was expecting this question and tells her that his nephew is a life insurance salesman.

He says, "Don't ask my nephew any questions otherwise he will spend an hour telling you about life insurance. I retired from the NYPD ten years ago and bought a little cabin up in Sullivan County near my sister's family. Guess who wants to sell them insurance?" They both glare at Donnellan who is quietly reading the paper. They continue their conversation and Vicky tells him that she has lived in the area all her life, has three sons and points to a long-haired biker playing pool and says that's my oldest son Kurt. Dugan says that he's a big boy and Vicky tells him that her son is a lumberjack and truck driver, when he works.

Then Dugan tells her, "You know I used to work with a cop who died in a truck accident a long time ago. He had a son who worked up here as a teenager and disappeared into the wind. It's too bad he never came back, some of us cops set up a fund to help him."

Vicky pours Dugan a beer and says, "You know my son told me about one of the bikers he rides with, Steel Neel, who told him that his old man was a cop who was killed in a truck accident. He was in here last night and was as drunk as a skunk. He'll probably be in soon for a little bit of the hair of the dog that bit him."

"Really," says Dugan as they hear the rumbling roar of several motorcycles pulling into the parking lot. Donnellan is looking intently out the window at six bikers walking into the hangout. The first one in the door is huge, at least three-hundred and fifty pounds. The guys at the pool table call him "Zeus." The next three bikers scope out the place, glare at Dugan at the bar with Vicky and signal all clear. Then Steel Neel enters, sees Dugan, then Donnellan and he starts running out the door. Donnellan jumps from his seat and runs to the door, Zeus tries to block him. Donnellan takes out his gun, sticks it in the big man's belly and tells him, "Move or I'll cut you a new asshole." Zeus moves fast and the two cops run to their car and transmit to the FBI agents that O'Toole is racing north on Route 97 riding a motorcycle.

The agents notify the state police then head north in pursuit. Sirens start blaring on both sides of the river. O'Toole starts to cross the Delaware at the historic one lane Roebling Bridge, but he stops suddenly when he sees the Pennsylvania Troopers coming towards him. He changes direction and starts recklessly driving south on 97, but the New York Troopers have him cornered from the north and south. He jumps off his motorcycle and starts running down to the river. Dugan slams on the brakes and Donnellan leaps from the car before it comes to a full stop, hitting the ground in a flat-out sprint.

O'Toole stops, turns around, starts laughing and takes two wild shots at Donnellan. Then he races toward the river bank, grabs a raft and starts paddling down the river. Donnellan tucks his gun back in his belt and keeps running, grabs a raft and starts paddling after O'Toole. But Donnellan is not an experienced rafter and quickly gets caught in the rapids and stranded awkwardly on a boulder. O'Toole stops his raft on the river bank, laughs like a maniac and fires two more shots at Donnellan. The bullets ricochet off the rocks and put a hole in the rubber raft leaving Donnellan defenselessly clinging to the boulder.

O'Toole screams to Donnellan that he's going to give him the "coup de grâce" and put him out of his misery. Cruel O'Toole stands, takes careful aim and is about to shoot when his raft is jolted by a whitewater rapid. O'Toole falls overboard with his foot tangled in the webbing of the raft. He starts floating rapidly down the river bobbing up and down behind his raft, hitting rock after rock until finally he submerges underwater and out of sight as his raft continues down-stream toward Route 84.

The New York State troopers pull O'Toole's drowned body from the river at the same time Amanda is carefully walking from rock to rock until she is close enough to toss Donnellan a rescue line. Once he has a good grip on the line, the Pennsylvania State Troopers and FBI agent Scuderi pull him to safety. Other than a few superficial bruises, Donnellan is in one piece, but totally exhausted and freezing cold. The troopers hand him some dry clothes and Amanda hands him a blanket.

Donnellan looks across the river and notices a cluster of police cars, recues ambulances, fire trucks, reporters and camera crews. He gets in the car with Dugan. The FBI agents pull up next to him and Scuderi tells him that O'Toole drowned in the river and now there's a media frenzy about *Cruel* O'Toole's last stand.

Donnellan nods his head and tells Dugan it's time to go. Dugan has a mischievous grin on his face as he drives south on the Pennsylvania side of the Delaware River toward New Jersey. "Okay," says Donnellan, "Go ahead and say what's on your mind."

"Well," says Dugan, "I was just thinking how strange life can be. This morning I thought we'd be sending O'Toole up the river." Donnellan shakes his head and smiles at Dugan, then puts his head back and sleeps until he's dropped off on 20th Street.

Marian and her children are excited when Donnellan enters the apartment. Norah is the first one to tell him that he was on all of the television stations. They showed him climbing out of the river with the help of state troopers and FBI agents.

Sean says, "Daddy you killed Cruel O'Toole, you're famous."

Donnellan tries to calm down his children and tells them that he gets no joy out of people dying, even villains like O'Toole.

The television is still on and they hear the reporters talking about the O'Toole capture. The family watches the news together. Donnellan sees himself straining to get out of the river holding on to a rope that is being pulled by firefighters, troopers and agents. Then he notices that the film crew is also focused on the female FBI agent standing on the rocks, the only woman involved in the rescue. Donnellan thinks to himself that the last thing Amanda wants is publicity.

The phone rings and Donnellan picks it up. It's his brother Craig offering his congratulations. He tells him that he's glad he was wearing the NYU sweatshirt he gave him. Then he says that he picked up an early edition of the News and Donnellan's rescue is on the cover. Craig mentions in jest that the FBI agent who rescued him is a "looker."

When Donnellan tells his wife about his brother's call, Marian calls Amanda. She picks up the phone on the first ring and is relieved to hear from Marian. She mentions that she's feeling emotionally exhausted, but physically fine. Then she tells Marian that she can't do this anymore and she's resigning from the FBI tomorrow. Donnellan gets on the phone and reassures her that he's okay and he convinces her to talk with the Chief before she submits her resignation. They agree to meet in the morning at seven o'clock. Donnellan then calls the Chief and she tells Donnellan to meet her at six.

CHAPTER 37

THE CHIEF OF DETECTIVES had been at her office for more than an hour when Donnellan arrives at six. She congratulates him on capturing O'Toole. He nods and tells her that the credit should go to Blakely and Dugan. Then he asks her if she can find a way to keep Dugan in the department after he is forced to retire. She says that she already solved that problem and will hire him as her personal consultant. Donnellan thanks her.

The Chief tells Donnellan that she had a long conversation with Amanda last night and they have a plan. First, and foremost, she is leaving for California on December 15th and she won't be coming back to the City for a long time. Her main goal is the health of her babies. But she does need to keep her health insurance for at least a year if not more, so we have to tread carefully with the FBI. It turns out they are going to offer her a promotion and make her the face for the FBI to help them recruit talented women for the bureau.

The media office of the FBI wanted to use pictures of her when she graduated from Quantico in their recruitment brochures. Donnellan looks at the photos of Amanda when she had long blonde hair and he briefly imagines the mind-boggling effect for the mass media if they ever discovered that GQ's mystery woman was the beautiful FBI agent who rescued him. Donnellan thinks back to one his father's favorite expressions. "Truth is stranger than fiction."

Amanda enters the Chief's office at seven and gives big hugs to the

Chief and Donnellan. The Chief tells Amanda that she has been in touch with the deputy director of the FBI and that the Bureau greatly appreciates her many contributions to the O'Toole Task Force. He understands that the events leading to the capture and death of O'Toole may have influenced her decision to reconsider a career as an FBI agent. In light of these circumstances, the FBI agrees to grant Blakely's request for a two-year leave of absence effective January 1, 1982 through December 31st, 1984. Furthermore, The FBI will not use any photos or images of agent Blakely in any media guides, brochures or other correspondence. The Chief then hands Amanda a draft letter for her review and approval. Amanda reads and signs the letter.

A tear starts rolling down her cheeks and she thanks the Chief for all of her wisdom, help and most importantly her friendship. Amanda then gets up from her chair to leave, hugs the Chief and promises her that they are friends for life. The Chief tells Amanda to hold off on the goodbyes for now, because she still has six more weeks of work at police headquarters. The Chief has already designed a plan to keep Amanda off the frontline but still tap into her financial crime investigative expertise. She assigns Amanda to work with her on writing an easy-to-use handbook to help police supervisors coordinate complex investigations. That way, Amanda can experience a few uneventful and peaceful weeks in the city, before she starts a new life with her children in California.

PART III

THE LAST CALL

CHAPTER 38

Mike Scuderi, the supervising FBI agent in charge of the New York City Region, receives an urgent call for help at 3:00 a.m. from the Deputy Director in charge of the FBI's White Collar Crime Unit, Anna Rivera-Kenny. He quickly gets dressed and meets her at the FBI Office at Federal Plaza in downtown Manhattan.

She explains, "The white collar crime unit was actively investigating a multi-million, possibly billion dollar, insider trading and tax evasion fraud with the help of a cooperating informant. The investigation is in the very early stages and the confidential informant, an executive at the SEC, agreed to wear a wire for all of his contacts with the international crime network. On two occasions, a driver from the crime network drove him to Atlantic City for payoffs in the form of gambling chips. On both occasions he was wired and followed by a surveillance team consisting of four agents in two cars. The trips were routine, documented and unremarkable.

"Yesterday, the informant received an unusual message from the crime network that he was going to be picked up downtown for a payout in Atlantic City. We wired him up and added an additional team for the surveillance. But we lost him when they changed the route and went north instead of south to Atlantic City. The driver took the informant to some biker bar on the New York side of the Delaware River where the informant was drugged and tossed into the river to drown. This situation is even worse than it looks Mike.

At this point we don't know anything about the international crime network. Who are they? How much money did they steal? Who killed our informant? We need your help."

Mike Scuderi says, "Why didn't you give me a heads up that you had an undercover operation going on through my region? I know exactly where that biker bar is. With one call, I could have helped you find the informant before they killed him."

"It was top secret on a strict need-to-know basis," she replies. Then they listen to the tape of the informant's wire from beginning to end. Scuderi tells the Deputy Director that they should bring Agent Amanda Blakely in on this case because she is familiar with the detectives mentioned on the tape and she is the FBI's liaison with the NYPD. Rivera-Kenny reluctantly agrees to bring her in on the case.

At five o'clock, Mike Scuderi and Anna Rivera-Kenny bring Amanda Blakely up to speed on the investigation and they listen to the recording together. Scuderi and Blakely recommend that the FBI should reach out to the NYPD for help on the homicide investigation, especially since two detectives, Donnellan and Dugan, are mentioned on the tape.

The Deputy Director says, "How do we know if we can trust the Chief of Detectives to keep this undercover operation top secret? Remember, "Loose lips sink ships" and there are already too many people in the loop."

Amanda Blakely has heard enough and since she knows she's quitting in a few weeks, she feels free to express her opinion without fear.

"Would you stop with this need-to-know bullshit, please?" she says. "Don't you have any respect for Scuderi or me? Do you think we would suggest that you bring in the Chief of Detectives if we had any doubt that we could trust her? You had an informant who trusted you with his life; and he's dead. You don't know who killed him or who stole millions from the government. You better start learning how to trust the right people if you want to solve this horrific case. The NYPD has the best homicide detectives in the world, and we need them. Time is wasting and killers are on the loose. I suggest that we meet with the Chief, Donnellan and Dugan ASAP if we ever want to solve this gruesome murder."

"All right, all right," says Rivera-Kenny. "But do we really need to bring in the old guy. How's he going to help?"

Scuderi then reminds the Deputy Director that Dugan is mentioned on the tape and we should let the Chief of Detectives decide who attends the meeting. Reluctantly, the Deputy Director agrees that the Chief of Detectives will supervise the homicide investigation.

CHAPTER 39

DONNELLAN SIPS HIS FIRST mug of black coffee as he watches Channel 7's Eyewitness News. Three reported homicides overnight, two in Brooklyn and the other in Staten Island. He leisurely walks into the kitchen thinking maybe it will be a calm day in Manhattan. All of a sudden he hears the buzzing sound of his beeper mixed in with the murmur of the television reporters. He walks to the table, picks up the beeper and sees the familiar number of the Chief of Detectives.

At six-thirty in the morning Donnellan knows this is not a social call. He quickly gets dressed and leaves his Stuyvesant Town apartment. He walks briskly four blocks to his office at the Police Academy. Brendon Dugan, who is now just four months away from mandatory retirement, is reading the *Daily News* when Donnellan enters the squad room. "Hey Boss, looks like some kind of government banker drowned in the Delaware River right near where *Cruel O'Toole* almost gave you the coup de grâce."

Donnellan grabs the paper and zooms in on the report. "The body of Austin R. Northgate, the Deputy Director of the Securities and Exchange Commission, was discovered floating in the Delaware River near the New York/Pennsylvania border by a kayaker yesterday evening. The deceased was dressed in his usual business attire and his wallet and jewelry were on his person. The New York and Pennsylvania State police, as well as the FBI, are actively investigating the cause of death but there is no sign of foul play and the police have not ruled out suicide."

Donnellan has a pensive and quizzical look on his face as he hands the paper back to Dugan and enters his office. He turns the page of his calendar to November 17th, 1981. He sits in his chair, grabs the phone and calls the Chief of Detectives. Emma Dickersen answers on the first ring. He starts to ask about the beep, but she cuts him off in mid-sentence.

"Mike Scuderi, Amanda Blakely and a supervisor from DC have requested an urgent meeting at Police Plaza this morning to talk with me, you and Dugan. It has something to do with the Fed who drowned in the Delaware River. They don't think it was an accident or suicide and they need our help. Can you wake up Dugan and get downtown a.s.a.p.?"

"Dugan's already here, Chief. We'll be at headquarters in twenty minutes."

Donnellan sticks his notepad in the inside pocket of his blazer and heads over to Dugan's desk and says, "Scuderi scheduled an emergency meeting with the Chief and some bigwig from DC. It has something to do with the Fed who drowned upstate. They want to meet with both of us."

Dugan is surprised, puzzled and rejuvenated. He dreads the thought of retirement and being sent out to pasture to die in leisurely surroundings like an old horse from the mounted division. He was expecting that with just four months left in his police career he would be relegated to the role of squad gopher since he wouldn't be around to close any new cases. He thinks about putting his papers in every day to avoid the humiliation of being patronized by his colleagues, but he doesn't know how to leave the job he loves. Now for some unknown reason, he's back in the saddle again. Dugan takes the keys for the squad car off the hook and he and Donnellan rush off to headquarters.

The ride down to Police Plaza is fairly quiet for the detectives as each one is trying to figure out why the FBI wants to meet them about a drowning on the Pennsylvania border. They are both thinking back to the day that Donnellan was almost killed on the Delaware River by the *Westie* hitman, Cruel O'Toole. But O'Toole is dead and that case is closed, so why are we meeting with the FBI? Dugan parks the car at headquarters and they both hurry toward the main entrance. There's very little activity at Police Plaza at seven-thirty in the morning. The detectives are not distracted by greetings from friends in the department. They quickly enter the Chief's office and the three of them go to the conference room to meet with the FBI Agents.

CHAPTER 40

THE FBI AGENTS HAD a private meeting with Chief Dickersen when they arrived at Police Plaza. Mike Scuderi handled the introductions. "Lieutenant Donnellan, Detective Dugan, I would like you to meet the Deputy Director in charge of the FBI's White Collar Crime Unit, Anna Rivera-Kenny."

The detectives shake hands with the agents, take the notepads out of their jackets and sit at the table. Across from them the FBI agents have their notebooks, charts, and a recording machine. Scuderi explains to his associate that it is standard for detectives in the City to only carry a small notepad that fits in their pocket so they always have their hands free in case they need to reach for their gun. He further explains that with the gang wars and drug-infused crime continuing to wreak unprecedented violence in every borough, New York City is on pace to reach two thousand homicides in just this year alone. Chief Dickersen acknowledges the brutality of the crime wave and emphasizes that it is a nationwide problem not limited to New York. Then she asks the agents to explain the purpose of the meeting.

Before Agent Rivera-Kenny has a chance to speak, Mike Scuderi gives the detectives a brief biographical of the Deputy Director. She graduated from NYU Law School at the top of her class and was immediately hired by the US Attorney's Office. She worked for five years in the Justice Department's Organized Crime Task Force and was a lead prosecutor on the ABSCAM corruption investigation.

Rivera-Kenny politely interrupts her colleague because she doesn't want him to appear to one-up the detectives.

She breaks in politely, "I appreciate my colleague's introduction, but I'm here because I need your help. Are you familiar with the inner workings of the stock market and banking industry? Insider trading, tax evasion, shell companies, international organized crime networks and the privacy rules of Swiss bank accounts?"

The Chief nods. She is very familiar with these issues as she works closely with the New York State Attorney General's Financial Crimes Unit. Donnellan and Dugan shake their heads no.

Rivera-Kenny continues. "Although it sounds like you would need an army of accountants and lawyers to investigate these types of crimes, what you really need are cutting-edge detectives. That's why we're here. Let me explain.

"An international association of thieves has been stealing hundreds of millions of dollars from the United States government and corporations for several years and we didn't even know it was happening. That is until Austin R. Northgate, the Deputy Director of the Securities and Exchange Commission, got scared and told his attorney that he was being paid big bucks to give confidential information to an international network of European investment bankers and their organized crime syndicate.

"Northgate had a big mouth and used to have a few drinks in Washington before he came back to the City. One night he was overheard bragging to a friend that he could make a lot of money in stock the market because he had inside information on whether corporate mergers would be approved or rejected and either way he could make a fortune. It wasn't long before he had a new friend who promised total secrecy, who would set up two anonymous offshore accounts, one for each of them to profit from his privileged information. It started small as usual, but when word spread in the underworld that they had a golden goose in the SEC, the fraud skyrocketed. By the time Northgate realized what happened, he was in deep with no good way out.

"The mobsters shared the treasure and even gave Northgate cover to spend his newfound wealth. Did you notice when you read about his drowning that he had won the largest jackpot ever in Atlantic City? That was a setup. After that, he would take occasional trips to the casinos after a profitable tip and even though he didn't bet, he always cashed in thousands of chips.

"But when Northgate heard whispers that an attorney from the SEC Enforcement Division named Jason Friedman Breen started an insider corruption investigation, he lawyered up at lightning speed and came to the FBI begging for a deal. We got him wired up and followed him back and forth to Atlantic City after he tipped off his conspirators. It ran like clockwork. But last Friday his underground network unexpectedly directed him to go to Atlantic City for a meeting. We put three cars on surveillance, but lost him at the Pennsylvania border."

Anna stops to catch her breath and Dugan asks her and Scuderi how could they lose an undercover informant going from Manhattan to Atlantic City in upstate New York? She hits the play button on the tape machine.

"Hey, Louie. Why are we taking the Thruway to get to Atlantic City?"

"It'll just be a quick stop. I have to pick up another passenger at a town near the Delaware River."

"You're kidding me! I used to live near the Delaware River until my father lost his job back in the sixties. We had to move to the City and live with my grandparents until he got a job with the Post Office."

Scuderi stops the tape and explains that there were three cars in the surveillance team. The lead car was ahead of the confidential witness taking the standard itinerary of the previous trips: across the George Washington Bridge and then south on the Jersey Turnpike. The other two cars took turns following behind the target at a close range of fifty to one hundred yards. But when the target turned north on the Palisades Parkway the lead car was out of range for the surveillance. The two tailing cars kept their positions until the target made a sudden exit off Route 84 just before Pennsylvania.

Now there was only one car following and soon they lose sight of the target. It was night time and the winding mountain roads were poorly lit. They could still hear the conversations because the transmitter had a 10 mile radius on a clear night.

The Deputy Director continues, "To make matters worse, there was a motorcycle accident on Route 97 near the Hawk's Nest overlook and a mob of bikers were blocking the road in both directions as they surrounded the victim. So, our team was stuck in gridlock. We couldn't identify ourselves and clear out the bikers at that point because we didn't know if the confidential informant was in danger. So we crisscrossed a few back country roads until we got to the Toast and Grill. The parking lot was almost empty and there was no sign of Louie's car. At that point we put an all-points bulletin out on the car. The message was clear, stop the car, the New York plates are stolen, the driver and passengers should be considered armed and dangerous, if and when driver and passengers are apprehended, contact the FBI immediately.

CHAPTER 41

T<small>HE</small> FBI A<small>GENTS ARE</small> uneasy acknowledging that their surveillance teams lost their confidential informant, even though it was not due to a blunder or incompetence. Chief Dickersen assures them that surveillance teams did everything possible to protect their informant but undercover work is always risky. Donnellan and Dugan nod in agreement. Scuderi mentions that he didn't know about the surveillance because headquarters kept a tight lid on this case. Then he hits the play button.

"Here we are," says the driver.

"Holy shit," says Northgate. "Louie, I haven't been in this bar since I was a kid. We used to call this dive the "Last Call" because they stayed open late and never proofed teenagers."

Northgate and the driver are heard entering the Toast and Grill. There are low murmuring conversations mixed with the loud laughing of several men. The barmaid points out an empty table in a quiet corner of the restaurant. Northgate and the driver he calls Louie are heard sitting at a table.

The driver speaks: "The families had to save you from a contract put out by the Ukrainian."

"What! " says Northgate. "Who's the Ukrainian and why is he after me?"

"The Ukrainian is the boss of the Eastern European crime network and he's made a lot of money from your tips for the last five years. He also has a mole who works in the SEC who watches your every move. So, he was surprised when he didn't get any insider notice about government approval for the biggest merger of the year, between an American mining company and a Japanese mining company.

"The Ukrainian figures that you double crossed him and made a side deal for yourself instead of sharing the wealth. So out of courtesy he contacts the families and tells the bosses that he's going to put you to sleep. But to the families you are the golden goose, so we want to protect you."

Northgate is stunned and replies, "I didn't double cross any-body. The SEC kept me out of the negotiations this time because it was a secret deal between the Vice-President and the Japanese Prime Minister. I didn't find out about the merger till I read it in the paper."

"Look, we handled it for you, you are safe. But listen, the Ukrainian is from the old school and he still thinks you're a rat. The best thing you can do is write him a letter and tell him it was a misunderstand-ing. Here take my pen and this notepad and write this down. I don't even know the Ukrainian's name so just write.

"I am sorry that I let you down. I hope you understand. Now sign your name and give me the pen and paper."

The Deputy Director hits the stop button and, looking directly at Chief Dickersen, says, "All the agents on my team, including me, told the US Attorney assigned to this investigation that we wanted to let Northgate tip off the syndicate about the merger or else we could sabotage the investigation and even worse put our informant in grave danger. But, Eric Hunter is a political animal who was afraid of being labeled an incompetent amateur if he knowingly allowed a criminal enterprise to steal millions from the government. So, he went to the Director and we were overruled.

"We tried to prepare Northgate for the possibility that his change of behavior could raise suspicions. We rehearsed several different answers he could give if he was confronted about the merger, but we still felt he was in jeopardy. That's why we added another car to the surveillance team."

The Deputy Director then hits the play button. The murmur of various conversations and loud laughing continues to be heard until a door opens and there's a moment of complete silence, followed by a rowdy chuckling voice saying to the biker gang customers, "Hey, Zeus! I haven't seen you move so fast since Donnellan threatened to cut you a new asshole."

Zeus, the three-hundred and fifty pound giant who is known for lifting his Harley Davidson over his head is heard replying, "If I ever get ahold of Donnellan, I am going to put his feet in one hand and his head in the other and play him like an accordion."

A female voice is heard saying, "You can have Donnellan, but leave the old detective alone, he's all mine."

Mike Scuderi fast forwards through a few minutes of inaudible laughter and talking then goes back to play.

"Hey, Spider. This is Austin, the guy I told you about. He's going down to Atlantic City to try his luck at the poker tables."

The Spider responds, "Hey, Louie, can I hitch a ride? I have a delivery to make in AC."

"Yeah, you can come along, but you have to sit up front with me."

The Spider then says he will get a round of drinks before they leave, but first he walks over to a group of bikers who gather around him and block him from the view of Northgate. Then, as the Spider walks toward the bar, all of the bikers leave. As the roaring sound of motorcycles fills the air, the Spider gets a beer for Northgate and a club soda for Louie and himself. There's a chilling silence on the tape until they hear the sound of clinking glasses and Northgate is heard saying, "This is my last toast at the Last Call."

Donnellan can't help but think to himself, "Truer words were never spoken."

CHAPTER 42

The Spider, Louie and Northgate are heard walking to the car. Northgate is heard complaining that he feels weak and needs help getting into the backseat. Louie is heard telling him to relax and he can sleep on the trip to Atlantic City. There's an eerie hush as the recording moves forward. No conversation. Just breathing sounds. Suddenly the car stops. The two front doors open, then a back door. The next sound is Northgate's body being dragged out of the car and the struggle to prop him up on a ledge at the Roebling Bridge. The last sound is a body splashing into the water.

The conference room is silent as all of the investigators digest what they just heard. Chief Dickersen breaks the ice. "First of all," she says. "We will do anything we can to help you solve this case. Whoever's responsible for the death of Northgate and stealing millions from the government must be caught and prosecuted. I don't quite know how you expect us to help, but keep in mind that we live in "Fear City." My budget is always under the microscope, so I have to carefully assess my commitment to reassign elite detectives to help the FBI when we are in the worst crime wave in New York City history."

The Deputy Director responds, "I understand your constraints, Chief, but I think I can solve this problem. The FBI has approved reimbursing the NYPD dollar for dollar for all of the man-hour costs you incur during this investigation. In addition, we will give the NYPD ten percent of any money recovered, which we expect will be in the millions of dollars."

"That helps," the Chief says, "but how do you think we can assist you?"

"Let me explain," answers the deputy director. "We have a full blown mystery on our hands. We were very early in our investigation when Northgate died. We know his associates were stealing millions with his inside tips, but we don't know who they are or where the money went. Plus, we don't know anything about Louie or the Spider. The license plates on the Lincoln Continental were stolen and we don't have any idea where the hitmen went after they drowned the confidential informant. So, our approach is for the FBI under the supervision of Agent Blakely, to work with the SEC and follow the money. At the same time, we envision that the NYPD would the hit the street, identify and apprehend the hitmen, and climb the ladder toward the kingpins. Basically, we want to squeeze the network from top to bottom."

Donnellan quips, "Like an accordion!"

Dugan is the only one who laughs.

Chief Dickersen decides it's time to take a quick fifteen minute break. She directs her detectives to her office and closes the door. First, she wants Donnellan and Dugan to know she would understand if they decline to get involved in this case. For Dugan, he might want to retire peacefully into his job as a consultant. For Donnellan, he may not want to socialize with Zeus and his biker friends. Both detectives assure the Chief that they are totally onboard. The three detectives come up with a quick-thinking plan and reenter the conference room.

"Time is not on our side," says the Chief. "So, we must move without delay. Donnellan and Dugan are well-known homicide detectives to the customers at the Toast and Grill. When they enter the hangout, the bikers will be on defense and think that they are going to be arrested. Donnellan will put them at ease and say he needs their help solving a suicide by drowning of a New York City resident with a huge life insurance policy. Donnellan will round up the bikers and move them to the tables at the far corner of the restaurant. He will distract them with a group interview, giving them all a chance to get their jollies lying to the famous detective. Donnellan will pass around a picture of Northgate as he talks.

"Dugan on the other hand, will be uninterested in the whole group session and wander over to talk with the bartender. He'll make some small talk and whisper to her that all the bikers are liars and Donnellan is wasting his time. He'll tell her that the town is swarming with cops and if these guys keep lying to Donnellan they're looking at state prison time, but she can help keep them out of jail. It's a long shot, but maybe she'll cough up some useful information. If not, Plan B is to arrest every biker who frequents the Toast and Grill for interfering with a police investigation and see if anyone will cooperate to avoid prison."

"Lieutenant Donnellan," cautions the deputy director. "Aren't you concerned about meeting with those bikers by yourself, especially since you've been threatened?"

"Not really Anna. I've been around bikers before and I know how they roll. As far as Zeus goes, he'll either be my new best friend or I *will* cut him a new asshole."

Chief Dickersen interrupts Donnellan and gets back on track. The Chief makes it clear that the plan is filled with holes, but they are running out of options. She further states that as soon as Dugan and Donnellan enter the Toast and Grill there will be visible NYPD and New York State Police presence around the perimeter of the restaurant in case of a brawl. After the Chief finishes outlining the line of attack, Donnellan looks at his watch. It's almost ten-thirty. He starts to get a little anxiety, as he has a lot to do and little time to do it. His first stop will be a brief visit to Austin Northgate's wife, Emily, to offer his condolences and, if she's receptive, he will talk with her about her deceased husband.

Donnellan then interrupts the multiple cross conversations by blurting out. "Could we wrap this up quickly, I have an early dinner date with Zeus."

The Chief and the Deputy Director agree that Amanda Blakely should be the point person to coordinate this task force as liaison between the NYPD and FBI. The Chief then releases Donnellan and Dugan from the meeting. They go directly to the Upper West Side to visit Emily Northgate.

The homicide detectives know well that each individual experiences the death of a close relative in his or her own unique way, especially when the cause of death is homicide or suicide. Emily Northgate answers the doorbell and invites the detectives into her apartment as her youngest daughter clings to her dress. The detectives express their condolences for her loss.

"I think I know why you're here, detectives," whispers Northgate, so her two older children could not hear the conversation. "But I already told the FBI and State Police that I never knew anything about my husband's insider trading or even that he was cooperating with the FBI. This has all been such a shock to me and now people are thinking he took his own life because he was ashamed to tell me and his family the truth." She starts to cry, but gains her composure.

Donnellan speaks to her in a low voice. "Mrs. Northgate, we don't believe your husband took his own life. He made a huge mistake, but he voluntarily confessed to the FBI and agreed to cooperate in their investigation of a sophisticated criminal network. But before I share my reason that I suspect your husband was murdered, I have to ask if you can keep this a secret for a day or two?" She nods her head in agreement. "Okay," says Donnellan. "Either today or tomorrow you are going receive an envelope in the mail with no return address that will be postmarked from some town upstate. Inside will be a hand-written letter from your husband apologizing for his mistakes. It will look like a suicide note, but we have reason to believe that your husband was forced to write this letter by the two people who killed him."

"Oh, my God!" cries Mrs. Northgate. "I can't believe this is happening."

"I'm sorry to share this information, but I don't want you to be the last person to know the truth. We are on the trail of your husband's killers and we want them to believe that we are treating your husband's death as a suicide, so they may let their guard down and make a mistake. Can you stay strong for a few more days? I assure you that the FBI, State Police and the NYPD are working together to apprehend the evil people who drowned your husband."

She whispers, "Get them. Get them. Get them."

Donnellan then asks her, if possible, when the suspicious envelope arrives in the mail, don't open it. He writes down a phone number and asks her to call Manhattan South Homicide as soon as she gets the envelope. A detective will then pick up the envelope and take it to the forensic unit to dust the envelope and letter for fingerprints. Mrs. Northgate says that the mail is usually delivered to her apartment building at one o'clock in the afternoon and she will be on the ground floor waiting for the mail carrier. The detectives offer their sympathies again and then head back to the Police Academy.

CHAPTER 43

Dugan and Donnellan make a very quick visit to Manhattan South Homicide to see if there are any updates to the plan. All systems are Go. They grab a quick sandwich, gas up the car and start driving to the rest area on Route 84 in Port Jervis, NY.

While he's driving north on the Thruway, Dugan says, "This is my last hurrah, Boss. I appreciate what you and the Chief have done with giving me a rope to stretch my time on the job. But I can't do it. It's time for me to cut the cord and start a new life. I have to do it sometime and this is it. I don't have a plan. I never had a plan. I just did what I had to do and made a good life. When I came on the job I had no plan except to work hard and do the right thing. When I retire I'll figure out how to enjoy my life. But just do me one favor. No party. I would just like to go quietly into the night and stay in touch with a few close friends like you, Harrison and the Chief."

"I understand, no party," replies Donnellan. "Let's not get sentimental, Dugan, but I'm glad that we're getting one more chance to rock the boat." Dugan laughs and says, "Just don't push me overboard."

The rest area at Port Jervis is jam packed with law enforcement vehicles. Dugan parks next to Chief Dickersen. She tells them that a few undercovers have made passes by the Toast and Grill and the bikers have filled the parking lot. Donnellan gives the Chief the thumbs up and Dugan starts driving toward the restaurant. Neither detective has any sense of anxiety; basically they feel like it's a walk in the park. Dugan parks the squad car between two Harleys. Donnellan opens the door, enters the joint and yells, "Police!" Everyone is quiet and stares at Donnellan.

Zeus is the first one to speak and he is angry. "Hey, Donnellan. You've got a lot of balls. The last time you were here you stuck your gun in my gut and told me you were gonna cut me a new asshole!"

Donnellan responds in a loud angry voice. 'Did I pull the trigger, Zeus? Did I stare down the barrel your maniac friend Cruel O'Toole's gun? Did he try to kill me? Did I come back here and arrest you and every member of your gang for conspiring to kill a police office? No!

"So let's start over. I'm here because a government banker from the City drowned in the Delaware yesterday and his old lady is getting a big insurance payout. I want to know whether he took his own life or was murdered. I heard he might have come here for a drink before he died so let's all sit down and talk."

Donnellan directs the bikers to connect a few tables length wise so they can all sit down at one long table with Donnellan at the head. After everyone is seated Donnellan says, "Hey, Dugan. You go stand over by the bar and watch my back."

Donnellan then starts going around the table asking each person to identify themselves. He's not taking notes and doesn't care if they give real, false or nicknames. He just keeps the conversation going.

Dugan drifts over to the bar and greets the bartender. "Hey, sweetheart. Are you still single?"

She smiles and nods. She asks "How bout you honey?"

Dugan snickers and says, "No rings ever on my fingers. I guess I married the job and had no time for a personal life. Now I'm being forced to put in my papers and I'll have to start over. It's time sweetheart, things are changing too fast for me. I'm from the old school. You know. No games. Just straight up with people.

"Look at Donnellan sitting there with all those bikers. He knows they're going to lie about that banker being in this joint before he drowned. You know lying to a cop is a crime? We know he was here with the Spider and what's the name of the other guy?"

"You mean the Shamrock?"

"Yeah, yeah that guy. He's a bad man."

"He's more than bad, Dugan. He's evil. He's a hitman for hire."

"No shit. I've been around a long time and I don't remember him coming into the city."

"Hey, honey" says Dugan. "What's your name again? I can't forget your pretty face, but I'm bad with names."

"It's Vicky."

"Hey, Vicky. How about getting me a beer and one for yourself."

She pours two beers and they give a toast to Dugan's retirement. He takes two gulps from his beer and then asks Vicky "How'd the Spider get the bikers to block the road."

She whispers, "The Spider pulled out a roll of fifties and got the bikers' attention in a hurry. Somebody had given him a boatload of money. He even gave me a fifty."

"Do you still have it?"

Vicky opened up the cash register and lifted the tray and says, "Yup, it still there."

Dugan scans the bar and sees a small Styrofoam cup and asks her to stick that fifty in the cup and slip it to him. He takes out his wallet and grabs four twenties and slides it to her. He tells her to keep the change for her tip. Then he asks her if she would like to meet him in the City for lunch someday. She says she would like that. He gives her his home and work number.

Donnellan sounds like he's getting ready to wrap up his group therapy session with the bikers. So, Dugan takes the opportunity to ask a few quick questions.

"Hey, Vicky. Why would the Shamrock need the Spider to take down a patsy like the banker?"

Vicky whispers, "The Spider is some kind of scientist that can put people to sleep and make it look like an accident. The Shamrock is a straight hitman who will kill you with a pistol, bury you in concrete and make sure the body and weapon disappears without a trace."

"So, it looks like the Spider was Plan A and the Shamrock was Plan B. Either way," says Dugan, "the Fed was going to the big bank in the sky."

Dugan sticks the Styrofoam cup in the inside pocket of his jacket and walks over to the table and says, "Let's wrap up this bullshit session Boss. The troopers and TPF are getting hungry."

All the bikers perk up and stare at Donnellan. They knew that the state troopers were tough cops who held a grudge. It was also well-known in the outlaw world that the cops in the NYPD's tactical patrol force (TPF) were young, at least six feet tall, and trained to hit hard.

Dugan continues, "What do you think, we came up here without backup? Donnellan is just warming you up for the troopers. We're in their territory and they don't want anyone thinking that they're not good enough to handle this investigation. I'm warning you! Don't lie to them. They already know the Fed was here with the Shamrock and the Spider before they drowned the Fed. They also know that you bikers staged a phony accident to block the road to help them. Just remember, if you go up the river for a stretch, the Shamrock and Spider will be laughing behind your back."

Donnellan stands up. He has everyone's full attention. "Look," he says and opens his jacket. "I have no recorder. I took no notes or names. I just came here to talk with you. The bosses asked me to wear a transmitter so they could storm this joint if there was any trouble. I told them I wouldn't. They asked how we'd know if there's a brawl? I told them to listen for the gun shots."

There is mild laughter in the room.

"Look, don't lie to these guys. Maybe we can consider the road blockade a misunderstanding if we get your help. I don't like to say this when I'm out of my jurisdiction, but a resident of my territory was drowned in this river, so if you have information you can call me direct. Just call the city police and ask to be connected to Manhattan South Homicide. If I'm not in I'll get back to you."

Dugan tells everyone to stay put and he and Donnellan walk out the door.

The Toast and Grill is surrounded by the New York State Police. Captain Arthur Treaney, the supervising officer of the state troopers, is stationed at the NYPD Mobile Command Center with Chief Dickersen, the Captain of the TPF, and FBI Agent Mike Scuderi. Donnellan gives a concise briefing of the first stage of the operation. Dugan and Donnellan initial and date the Styrofoam cup and Scuderi places it in an FBI evidence envelope. The FBI agent then initials and dates the envelope and hands it to a waiting agent who transports it to Washington for a priority forensic examination.

The Chief thanks the Captain and his unit for their support and releases the tactical patrol force to return to the City. Captain Treaney is further debriefed by the Chief, Donnellan and Dugan. They come to a consensus on the next stage of the operation: Treaney and his troopers will attempt to identify and interview everyone at the restaurant, including the bartender Vicky. Unless there's an outstanding warrant for any of the bikers, they will not make any arrests pending the outcome of the ongoing investigation. Before the Captain leaves the command center, he assures the Chief that he will have a full report of all interviews within twenty-four hours and he will have a trooper deliver it to her at headquarters. The Chief thanks him and his staff for their dedication and support. The NYPD detectives then return to the city.

As Donnellan is driving back to the city, he observes that Dugan is surprisingly quiet. It's like he's preoccupied, but in a pleasant way. He waits until they reach the Tappan Zee Bridge then says, "Hey, Dugan. You were amazing today. I don't know what kind of magic you have with the ladies, but somehow you charmed the bartender to give up the Shamrock and the Spider. How do these gangsters come up with these names anyway? And what's with the Shamrock? Is the hitman trying to give the Irish a bad name. Why couldn't he be like the Spider and take a nickname like the wolf or the bear or the ground hog or any other indistinguishable name? Let's hope he has a long time to repent for disgracing our ancestors."

Donnellan expected Dugan to go into a hilarious tirade on the Shamrock, but instead he was very defensive and said, "The bartender, her name is Vicky. She's good people. I didn't bamboozle her. She knew what she was doing. One of her sons is a biker who rides with those guys. She knew that if everyone stayed silent, the only people going to prison for the murder of the Fed were the bikers. That's why I opened my big mouth so those macho jerks you were talking to get a wake-up call and wouldn't lie to protect the Shamrock and Spider."

"Whoa," thought Donnellan "There's more to this story, but I'm not going to stir the pot." He changed the subject and they talked about the Giants and Jets until he dropped Dugan at his apartment building on 96th and Lexington.

Dugan appeared awkwardly content as he exited the car. He went right to the Deli and ordered roast beef on a roll and two Schaefer beers to wash it down. His one-bedroom apartment looked almost the same as it did forty years ago. The couch, the leather chair, the pictures on the walls, even the lamps were the same. The only thing that was up-to-date was the color television in his living room. As soon as he changed into his pajamas, Dugan sat in his chair, turned on the television, popped open a beer and started eating his sandwich. He laughed out loud as he watched his favorite cop show, *Barney Miller*. He stayed up to watch the *Tonight Show*, but fell asleep in his chair before he set his alarm clock. A rare slip-up for the old detective.

CHAPTER 44

THE SHAMROCK AND THE Spider changed the license plates on the Lincoln right after they dropped Northgate into the river. They put on a set of Maryland plates registered to a phantom corporation and they weaved their way south on the Pennsylvania side of the river. They kept quiet until they reached Route 84. It was well-known that the Shamrock's real name wasn't Louie, it was Payton Patrick O'Leary. But on the other hand, the Spider's identity was a mystery.

As they cruised along the interstate highway, the Spider wondered aloud. "How'd you get the stiff to write the letter?'

The Shamrock starts to laugh. "I told him the Ukrainian put a contract on his head and I was here to protect him."

"He believed that line of bullshit! I thought this guy was supposed to be smart."

"He probably watched too many James Bond movies and thought SPECTRE was after him," laughs the Shamrock. "If he only knew it was a couple of gangsters from Philly and Jersey."

"Be careful though," says the Spider. "Your fingerprints are on the envelope and letter."

"I got an alibi to cover that, if I get caught. I'll say the banker asked me to drive him upstate. I got a receipt from the George Washington Bridge to prove it. He wants to stop at a bar for a drink in his old neighborhood. I go into the joint with him. He has a beer, writes a letter, puts it in an envelope and then gives it to me to hold. While we're in the restaurant some guy hears we're going to Atlantic City and he pays me a hundred dollars – cash – to tag along. When we leave the joint the Fed tells me he wants to spend some time alone, so I stop the car near the bridge and he gets out. He asks me to go mail the letter he gave me, and says that he's changed his mind about going to the casinos. I tell him I'll drive him home, but he says he has a friend picking him up at the bridge in a little while. So, I mailed the letter and drove some guy whose nickname was some kind of insect like a fly or mosquito or something to AC and went home."

The Spider has a quiet a laugh hearing the alibi and says, "You are kidding me right? Who could believe that story?"

The Shamrock responds, "No one has to believe the story, it just has to put a reasonable doubt in the mind of one juror that the Fed killed himself. Besides, I'll never talk to the cops without my lawyer present. Plus, I doubt the cops will ever figure out that we drowned the Fed."

They park next to the only car in the parking lot when they arrive at the Port Jervis Post Office. The Shamrock takes the letter and deposits it into the post box, then he turns and asks the Spider, "What's your name and where are you from?"

The Spider doesn't answer and quickly gets into his getaway car and waves goodbye. The Shamrock is fuming that he was disrespected and drives like a madman to Philadelphia.

The Spider doesn't like being a passenger, so after they burst out the post office lot he tells his driver, Mike Hansen, to get off the highway before they hit the Thruway so they can change sides. The Spider gets behind the wheel and his partner lights up a joint. They pass it back and forth as they drive slowly north on the Thruway. It's definitely strong stuff and the Spider starts to weave toward the white lines as he drives slower and more erratic.

"Oh shit," he says when he sees the flashing red lights of a state trooper pulling him over.

He sobers up right away and tells Hanson to open his window and toss the beeper and the bag of chemicals. He keeps driving slowly on the shoulder of the road trying to get as much distance as possible. The trooper pulls up next to him and the Spider stops the car.

The state cop stays in his car and speaks into his microphone commanding the driver and passenger to get out of the car and put their hands up. He waits and watches them until two backup troopers arrive. The two suspects are then patted down, handcuffed and transported to the local jail to be booked for grand theft auto, possession of a controlled substance, reckless driving, driving while impaired and resisting arrest.

CHAPTER 45

DONNELLAN ARRIVES AT THE squad room at seven o'clock the morning after visiting the Toast and Grill. He checks his messages and reviews updates on the Northgate investigation. The mysterious letter arrived on schedule for Emily Northgate yesterday and it was couriered to the FBI for priority forensic investigation. The case is breaking fast, but it still needs many finishing pieces. Donnellan looks out his door at the squad room and he sees that Dugan is still not in yet. But he can't wait any longer and calls the Chief. She answers on the second ring and she tells Donnellan that she wants him and Dugan to attend at a meeting with the FBI at her office at nine.

The phone rings at seven-thirty and wakes Dugan out of a deep sleep. He is lying in his reclining chair and the television is still on.

He answers his home phone the same as at work, with a half-bark. "Dugan."

He's stunned when he hears a female voice respond.

"I hope I didn't call too early, Dugan, but I was wondering if you were serious about a date in the City. I have the weekend off, so I'm available."

Dugan is caught off guard, but does not want to let his chance for an actual date pass him by. He thinks quickly, "Hey, Vicky! This is great. How bout you spend the whole weekend in the city, doll. I'll put you up at the Tarrant. I know people there and I'll get you a room with great views of the city. Let's start with lunch on Saturday, sweetheart. Don't worry. No funny stuff. You get your own room. I stay in my apartment. We'll just have a good time. Deal?"

Vicky says deal and gives Dugan her phone number. He tells her he can't talk now because he has to get to work. As soon as he hangs up, the phone rings again. It's Donnellan. He tells Dugan to get to the Chief's office by nine for a meeting with the FBI.

Dugan is the last person to arrive at the conference room and he sits next to Donnellan. There's one additional person from yesterday's meeting at the table, Jason F. Breen from the SEC. The Chief opens the meeting by saying there have been several major breakthroughs in the investigation.

"We now know that Austin Northgate was murdered by two mob connected hitmen, the Shamrock and an individual known only as the Spider. We have obtained a fifty dollar bill from a witness that may have the Spider's fingerprints. Although getting a good print off a bill is difficult for a forensic lab because so many hands may have touched the bill, the FBI has leading-edge technology, so we have a better than even chance of getting a print. The state police have interviewed many witnesses who corroborate the presence of the Shamrock and Spider with Northgate on the night of the drowning and the state police investigation is ongoing."

Deputy Director Anna Rivera-Kenny speaks for the agents, "For the last 24 hours, agent Blakely, SEC Enforcement agent Breen and I have been plotting the transaction patterns of Northgate's offshore account, held under a pseudonym. Basically, he and the criminal network he conspired with had readily available investment tools to exploit his confidential information. As long as they had the inside track they made millions whether a merger was approved or rejected. Our review of Northgate's illegal offshore accounts reflects a pattern of high-speed investments that were held for the briefest period possible.

"As for Northgate's link to an international criminal syndicate, we looked for multinational investors with similar trading patterns to his and found none. Instead, we discovered multiple duplicate transactions that were domestically initiated from a Philadelphia brokerage firm, which then transferred the profits to a bank in Bermuda, which wired the profits to a privately owned bank in the Cayman Islands.

"By chance, the Cayman Island bank was already cooperating with the Justice Department on a money laundering investigation regarding a South American drug cartel. We contacted the US Attorney directing that investigation and all of the illegal accounts we identified have been frozen and civil proceedings have been initiated to seize all of the ill-gotten money which will be in the hundreds of millions. We do not anticipate that anyone will come forward to challenge the forfeiture of the ill-gotten money as they would immediately be charged with racketeering under the RICO statute. "

The Chief says, "Well done," to the FBI and SEC agents. "But we're not at the finish line yet. We still have two murderers on the run."

There's a knock on the door and the Chief's assistant peeks in and says there's and urgent call for agent Scuderi. He excuses himself and says that he told the forensic team to call him if there are any breaks in the case.

While they are waiting for Scuderi to return to the conference room, the Deputy Director compliments Dugan and says, "Detective Dugan, when I first heard the Chief outline the strategy for breaking this case I must admit I thought there's no way this can work. Quite frankly, I thought she was kidding. But now I'm a believer."

Donnellan is thinking to himself, "Stop now. Don't go there." But she continues.

"You must be the most charming detective ever to get the bartender to spill the goods on the Shamrock and Spider and then get her fifty dollar bill."

Donnellan thinks to himself, "Uh Oh" He looks at Dugan's face getting redder and decides to lighten up the meeting before Dugan spoils the party.

"Anna," he says, "Dugan is like Sherlock Holmes without the pipe. He's a regular hound of the Baskervilles. Actually, all kidding aside, when we devised our initial plan, the Chief and I knew there was only one detective who could make our plan work and that was Dugan. Not because he's a sweet talker, quite the opposite. He respects people, gains their trust and they tell the truth."

Scuderi returns just in the nick of time. He says, "Payton Patrick O'Leary, also known as the Shamrock was, arrested by the FBI in an early morning raid at his home in Philadelphia. And his fingerprints were identified on the envelope and letter sent to Mrs. Northgate.

"But we may have trouble finding the Spider because a confidential informant in Philadelphia said that last night the Shamrock put a fifty-thousand dollar contract out on the Spider's head. So he may be dead and buried already."

Chief Dickersen says that last night the state got a few leads on the Spider. A few of the bikers thought the Spider was some type of mad scientist who might be from Canada. But we don't have any positive identity yet.

Dugan can no longer bottle-up his frustrations and blurts out, "I'm so sick and tired that every time one of these street hoods has the slightest bit of talent, all of a sudden they are glorified as some type of genius. The Spider poisoned a patsy. What do we think, he invented poison? Socrates poisoned himself two-thousand years ago. Let's stop idolizing these hoodlums with names like the Spider, the Serpent and the Grisly. Call them what they are – back-stabbing murderers."

Suddenly, there's a knock at the door. The Chief's assistant says there's an urgent call for agent Scuderi. He asks if he can take the call in the conference room. She says, "Yes."

CHAPTER 46

THE FBI AGENT PRESSES the speaker button on the phone in the center of the table and says, "Scuderi." The caller identifies himself as Jack Starno, the FBI agent in command of the forensic unit.

Starno then reports, "We lifted a clean fingerprint off the fifty dollar bill. It belongs to a convicted criminal from New York State who is currently on parole for manufacturing controlled substances, possession and sale of such. The convicted felon, Walter L. Taylor, also known as the Chemist, has a last known address in Saranac, NY, near the Canadian border. Taylor was arrested last night by New York State troopers for various offenses and is currently being held in a jail in Kingston, NY. Taylor's full rap sheet was faxed to you five minutes ago."

Scuderi thanks the agent and hangs up the phone. The Chief immediately ends the meeting and states: "I have to contact Captain Treaney, fill him in on the latest developments and ask if he would let Donnellan get the first crack at the Spider. Meanwhile, the FBI agents can continue to build a case against the Shamrock and pursue the financial crimes investigation. Let's all meet here tomorrow at nine for an update."

The Chief then asks Dugan to get the car and get himself ready for another road trip. She asks Donnellan to come with her to her office where she will call Captain Treaney.

Once Donnellan closes the door, the Chief says, "What's with

Dugan? I thought he was going to explode at the meeting. I was waiting for him to start analyzing the meaning of life according to Aristotle after he ended his outburst talking about Socrates. Do you think he's okay for a trip to Kingston?"

"I think he's just a little tired, Chief. He'll be fine by the time we get to Kingston."

"He's not tired Donnellan. He's in love with the barmaid! I can see it written all over his face. His nerves are on edge because he wonders if he's too old for her or if she's just playing him."

"I think you're right, Chief. I'll try to calm him down on the trip."

The Chief then calls Captain Treaney and puts him on speaker phone. She congratulates the state troopers for helping to break this case and then she tells him that the Spider is in custody in Kingston. Treaney agrees to meet Donnellan at the jail in Kingston. Also, he will have the Spider transferred into an isolated jail cell to make certain that he's in the dark about the bounty on his head and to protect him from harm. Donnellan then races down to meet Dugan.

They speed all the way up the Thruway with the red lights flashing on the squad car. Captain Treaney and two state troopers stand up and greet the detectives when they reach the jail. The state troopers are neatly dressed in their uniforms and move with military precision. Donnellan wears his classic blue blazer, grey pants, white shirt, and tie. Dugan . . . well, Dugan is Dugan. He's wearing his favorite twenty-five year old brown checkered jacket with patches on the elbows, black pants, brown shoes and a wide tie that was popular in the fifties. Despite his appearance, the troopers are impressed with how Dugan broke this case and refer to him as a legend.

The Captain and Donnellan go into a private office to discuss the interrogation of Taylor. They agree that the troopers should enter first and take the cuffs off the suspect. Once the Captain is seated across from the suspect, the troopers will leave and Donnellan will enter the interrogation room and close the door.

Captain Treaney sits upright staring at the suspect as Donnellan enters the room. The Spider whispers to himself, "Oh shit."

Donnellan loosens his tie and puts a toothpick in the side of his mouth. He reviews a report and says "You're a dead man walking, Taylor."

"How so," says the Spider.

"The Shamrock put fifty grand on your head last night and, if you made it to Albany you'd be swimming with the Fed in the big river in the sky."

The Spider responds, "What are you talking about? What Shamrock? I don't know no Shamrock and I never poisoned anyone."

The Captain keeps staring at the suspect as Donnellan says, "Funny you should mention that, about the poisoning, because no one said anything about you poisoning anyone. That's quite a slip. Guilty conscience? Anyway, let's cut the crap. The Fed you drowned was wearing a wire and we've got you on tape getting him a beer, dragging him out of the car and pushing him off the bridge. We're the only ones who can save your life because the contract from the Shamrock will follow you to prison, so you'll have to watch your back every minute of every day. Fifty grand is a lot of money, especially in the big house."

"Okay, okay, I'll cooperate, but I tell you, I didn't poison the Fed, I dropped a few Quaaludes into his beer. What are you going to do for me? Cut me loose? Reduce my sentence? What's in it for me?"

Captain Treaney speaks up, "Taylor, you're from Saranac right?"

Taylor nods.

"Do you know anyone who works in Dannemora?"

Taylor says his uncle, three cousins, many neighbors and friends work there. The remote maximum security prison is the biggest employer in the region, close to the Canadian border.

"Well if you convince me that you're not going to hand us a load of bullshit, I may be able let you do time in Dannemora, where you may have some people watching your back. Otherwise, we ship you to Attica or Sing Sing and you're on your own."

Donnellan hits the play button and they listen to the tape from beginning to end. The Captain takes out a pad and starts writing while Donnellan asks Taylor a few more questions. When Captain Treaney is finished writing, he hands Taylor a written statement to sign. The statement starts with "I, Walter L. Taylor, also knowns as the Chemist and the Spider, voluntarily provide this statement. No threats or promises have been made to me."

The statement is a concise summary of his involvement in the murder of Austin Northgate, ending with his signature declaring that the statement is true. The Captain and Donnellan sign as witnesses. Taylor is then moved to a protective custody section of the jail. And Donnellan and Dugan head back to the City.

CHAPTER 47

Donnellan drives the squad car back to the city and fills in Dugan on the Spider's interrogation and statement. Dugan is amazed and says, "That's the first time I ever heard a defendant copping a plea to go to 'Little Siberia'. That's the coldest maximum security prison in New York. No one has ever, or will ever, escape from Dannemora. It's a frozen fortress in the middle of nowhere."

The detectives agree that with the Northgate tape, the Spider's statement, witness interviews and the fingerprint evidence, the homicide investigation is basically wrapped-up. They presume that both suspects will try to plea bargain rather than go to trial and risk getting the maximum sentence. Certainly, both murderers will be imprisoned for many decades. Dugan is visibly relieved that the Spider cooperated because he didn't want Vicky to be a key witness if either suspect went to trial. So, now he has one less thing to worry about this weekend.

Dugan stays quiet for another twenty minutes before he murmurs, "Do you think I'm too old to change my ways? You know what they say; you can't teach an old dog new tricks."

"You're not too old to fall in love or have a relationship, if that's what you mean. Look Dugan, this case is pretty much signed, sealed and delivered, so if you want to call Vicky, just call her."

"She called me this morning," replies Dugan.

"No shit," smirks Donnellan. "That explains your attitude this morning. I thought you were going off the deep end."

"She's coming down for the weekend, Boss. Oh, can you do me a solid and see if you can get her a great room with a view at the Tarrant, I don't care what it costs."

"Sure, Dugan. Consider it done."

"I'm really nervous about this," Dugan says as he takes a deep breath. "This will be my first date in more than thirty years. It's giving me the jitters."

"Dugan, have some fun for a change, enjoy being in new love. This weekend you'll spend time window shopping and seeing the sights, like Rockefeller Center, the Empire State Building and Saint Patrick's Cathedral. You'll feel like a teenager again. Me on the other hand, I've turned the clock in the other direction and will spend my weekend like a senior citizen in old love. For example, after church on Sunday with the family, if Marian asked me to go shopping on Fifth Avenue, I'd say, "No thanks, honey. Why don't you ask your sister, Clare? The Giants are playing the Cowboys this afternoon."

Dugan finally breaks down and laughs.

"Just take it slow, Dugan, and have a good time. Life is too short," declares Donnellan. "Last month I buried my best friend and I will never get used to life without GQ. It's sad to say that he would have traded all of his legendary romances, if he could have shared more time with his true love."

"Was that the mystery woman Donnellan?"

"That's right Dugan; the mystery woman, GQ's last lover was his true love."

"Hold on Donnellan. So, you know who she is and you didn't tell me?"

"I promised her I would protect her identity. The only ones who know about her are me, the Chief and my wife. When we found her fingerprints on the telescope in GQ's apartment I was on my way to California, so the Chief interviewed her one on one, woman to woman. The mystery woman told the Chief everything and pleaded with her to keep it a secret, because the publicity would have wrecked her and her children's lives."

"I get it, the mystery woman has kids," says Dugan. "What? Was she married and doing GQ on the side?"

"Not married, no kids yet, but two on the way."

"So what's the big deal, GQ's girlfriend is pregnant. That's no big scandal today," says Dugan.

Donnellan's feeling a little uneasy talking about GQ's mystery woman and tries to change the subject. "Let's talk about you Dugan. You're alive and kicking. You put more than forty years in on the job. You earned a chance to enjoy your retirement years. Don't be a hermit. Go out and enjoy yourself."

"Nice try, Donnellan. Do you think I'm going to let you off that easy? You trusted me with your life at that biker bar. You can trust that I will keep the identity of GQ's lover a secret. I don't know her, I'll never meet her and I'll never talk to her. So don't make a mystery, just give it up. If you don't, I'll have to go down to Evidence, get those prints, and figure it out myself. I'm a pretty good detective you know."

"You might be a good detective Dugan, but you will never find those prints. They have dematerialized. Gone in the ether." Dugan stares at Donnellan, his mix of frustration and admiration clearly evident. Donnellan relishes the moment.

"All right, all right," he says. "But let's get back to the case for a minute. What'd you think of the FBI agents on this case?"

"Scuderi's good people, he's been around the block a few times. The Deputy Director's way above my pay grade and the pretty brunette with short hair is a mover and shaker. Basically, they're solid and so is the guy from the SEC." He looks at Donnellan and wonders out loud, "What are you smiling about?"

"Dugan, before September 10th, Amanda Blakely, the pretty brunette, was a beautiful blonde with long flowing hair. She was GQ's dream girl and all he wanted was to spend the rest of his life with her, and only her. She's leaving in a few weeks for California to live with her parents and give birth to her twins. Then she wants to anonymously start a new chapter in her life. Now you know why I kept it a secret."

Dugan is speechless for a few minutes, and then whispers as if in a trance, "I'll take this secret to my grave, Donnellan. I'll take this secret to my grave."

"Just don't overreact when you see Amanda tomorrow morning. But considering your outburst today, nothing you do or say at the meeting will surprise anyone."

CHAPTER 48

THE MEETING AT POLICE Plaza is mildly celebratory as all investigators are amazed that they solved in two long days what seemed like an impossible task. There was only one addition to yesterday's meeting; Captain Arthur Treaney was invited to attend by Chief Dickersen.

The FBI Deputy Director Anna River-Kenny summed up the case as follows:

"Just a few short days ago I asked the FBI and NYPD to do the unimaginable. To solve a major financial crime and homicide, without knowing how the financial crimes were committed or the identity of the murderers. The probability of solving any of these crimes was slim at best, but all of you working tirelessly achieved the gold medal in law enforcement. Today as we speak, the Shamrock is in federal custody with no bail, the Spider has cooperated and is in state custody and hundreds of millions of stolen dollars are being returned to the citizens of the United States."

The Deputy Director then reads a congratulatory letter from the Director of the FBI addressed to all those around the table and the meeting ends on a high note.

Dugan and Donnellan slip out of headquarters and head up to the Westside to pay their respects to Emily Northgate. She invites them into her living room and they all sit down.

Donnellan speaks for the detectives. "Mrs. Northgate, we are truly sorry to have to visit you for the second time to offer our condolences on the tragic death of your husband. But we thought it was important to give you the most accurate information straight from us. First off, we are confident that your husband didn't take his own life. Rather, he was poisoned by two mob-connected hitmen and thrown in the river to drown. The two murderers who are responsible for his death have been arrested and will probably spend the rest of their lives in prison. Your husband was cooperating with the FBI and he helped the government seize hundreds of millions of stolen dollars and break up a crime syndicate. We know that there is nothing we can do or say to make the pain of this loss any easier." Dugan and Donnellan then stand and Mrs. Northgate thanks the detectives for sharing the results of the investigation in person.

Before heading back to Police Plaza, Donnellan drops Dugan off at his apartment so he can get a haircut and buy some new clothes for his date with Vicky. Donnellan then turns the car onto the FDR Drive and coasts downtown at high speed with the windows down and the sunlight reflecting off the East River to his left. He drives past the sentries at One Police Plaza, with a nod and a wave, and parks right in front. He moves with purpose on his way to the Chief's office to review the Shamrock and Spider case file with her. Amanda knocks and enters the office. She tells them that she's leaving tomorrow to spend Thanksgiving with her family in California. Donnellan offers to drive her to the airport and she accepts the invitation.

On Saturday morning, Marian and Donnellan pick up Amanda and take her to JFK Airport. They wait with her at the gate until her plane is ready to board. Just before she gets on the plane, Marian asks her, "Have you thought about names for your twins, Amanda?"

Amanda smiles and says, "I'm naming my son Gregory and my daughter Quinn. So I'll always have GQ in my life."

As they wave goodbye, Donnellan takes hold of his wife's hand and says, "How would you like to go window shopping on Fifth Avenue after church tomorrow?" Marian hesitates at first and then replies, "Sure, honey. That would be great. But aren't the Giants playing the Cowboys?"

Donnellan says, "Who cares."

Old Love is New Love

EPILOGUE

Thanksgiving
November 26, 1981

THANKSGIVING WAS USUALLY AN enjoyable day for Donnellan, but not this year. He woke up early and kept reminding himself to be thankful for the many blessings in his life and make the most of the chance to celebrate the holiday with family and friends. But he couldn't shake the thought that this was his first Thanksgiving without GQ. He tried to conceal his grief, but, by ten o'clock, it was apparent to his wife that Donnellan wasn't Donnellan. She hoped that he would snap out of his sadness in time to enjoy Thanksgiving, but she understood that he was still grieving the loss of his best friend. When Donnellan asked if he had time to make a quick trip to Brooklyn to visit Mr. Clancy, she encouraged him to hurry up and go. She thought, if anyone can raise his spirits it's Hughie Clancy.

The first stop Donnellan made in Brooklyn was to buy some crumb buns and jelly donuts for Mr. Clancy at his favorite bakery near Our Lady of Perpetual Help Basilica. From there it was a quick ride to 86th Street. Donnellan knocked on the door and Hughie shouted out, "Come in. The door is open."

Donnellan entered the apartment, placed the bakery box on the table and greeted the old Irishman with a warm handshake and said, "I hope you don't mind my unannounced visit Mr. Clancy, but I've been thinking of GQ all morning and I just felt that I needed to see how you are doing."

"John Patrick, you're always welcome in my house, no need for an invitation. Please sit down and, by the way, Happy Thanksgiving. I'm doing as well, or better, than any man approaching his ninetieth year. I'm glad you stopped by, I might need to ask you a big favor."

"Anything for you, Mr. Clancy."

Hughie then takes out two small glasses from the shelf behind his chair and points to the cabinet with the bottles labeled Holy Water. Donnellan knows the drill and hands a bottle to Mr. Clancy, who pours some poteen in each glass and says, "Before we have a toast to Gregory let's talk about you. It's a tough Thanksgiving for both of us, John Patrick, without Gregory. But let me tell you how I've learned to cope with sorrow throughout my life. I think about the tides in the ocean. When the tide is high, it's like exhilarating joy. When the tide is low, it's like sorrow and sadness. But just like the tides in the ocean our feelings change throughout the day, every day. This morning you woke up with the blues. Accept that it is understandable to feel sad that your best friend just died, but don't let that low tide linger too long, especially when you have so much to be thankful for.

"Now let's raise a glass and pray that Gregory is resting comfortably with God in heaven."

Donnellan has a smile on his face for the first time today as he clinks his glass and toasts GQ. He fakes a cough as he swallows the poteen, which burns his throat like a raging fire. He manages to whisper in a raspy voice. "You mentioned you might need a big favor. How can I help Mr. Clancy?"

"Does your cousin Sean Timothy still fly for Aer Lingus?"

Donnellan nods.

"Well, I don't know if you noticed but I have only one bottle of poteen left in my cabinet and I'm no longer healthy enough to travel back home. So, I was wondering if Sean could pick up a few jars for me?"

Donnellan considers his options and assures Hughie Clancy that Sean will help him, but he asks, "How is Sean going to find the farmer who makes the home brew?"

"Ask Sean to go to the police station in Galway and ask for my nephew, Captain Bryan Belton. Tell him Uncle Hughie needs some medicine, he'll know what I want. You know John Patrick this poteen is like mother's milk for my arthritis."

Donnellan thinks to himself, "Mother's milk. That poteen could take the barnacles off a battleship." Instead, he politely tells Hughie to consider it done. As he gets up to leave, Donnellan says, "There's one more thing I think you should know, Mr. Clancy. You know all that media coverage about GQ's love life that made him look like a lightweight goofball. It's all bullshit. GQ did have many romantic lovers, that much is true. But in the end he was searching for a meaningful relationship and he finally found his true love, and was committed to her, and only her. She's truly a special lady, Mr. Clancy. She's hiding in public view because she fears that if her identity is revealed, it will ruin her life and GQ's twins who she hopes to give birth to this spring."

"Holy shit, Donnellan. Now I've heard everything. Will I ever get to meet this fine young lass," asks Mr. Clancy, completely amazed

"Sorry I can't make any promises, because I'm sworn to secrecy. But I assure you that I will watch over her children like they were my own."

Hughie understands Donnellan's dilemma, thanks him for sharing his secret and keeps thinking about GQ's mysterious love. Donnellan drives back to Stuyvesant Town with a grin from ear to ear.

As soon as he opens the door to his apartment the phone rings. Marian answers on the first ring and tells Donnellan, "It's Dugan." Donnellan goes into his bedroom, closes the door and picks up the phone.

"Hey Boss. Just thought I'd give you a quick hello to see how you are doing."

"Where have you been, Dugan? I haven't seen or heard from you since Friday?"

"Well let's see, I met Vicky at the Tarrant on Saturday. Oh, by the way, great room with a view of the park and it was "on the arm." You know – free. So, we go to Sardis's for lunch. She really digs all the celebrity pictures and the tourists gawking at us like we was some kind of celebrities ourselves. You shoulda seen Vicky, she was all decked out and beautiful. So, then we do the midtown highlights, Saint Pat's, 30 Rock, you know the drill. So, for dinner I take her to Windows on the World and we have a table by a window. What a view. So she says, "Dugan." I like that she calls me Dugan; that's all anyone has called me for forty years. She says, "Dugan I'm like you. I don't play games. That bed at the Tarrant is big enough for both of us, so don't stop at your apartment when we leave. You won't need your pajamas and I brought an extra toothbrush." So, I spent the week upstate with Vicky and I'm in love for the first time in my life.

"Long story short, for now I'm living in an apartment above the Toast and Grill and having the time of my life. But really, the reason I called was I was thinking about GQ and I wanted to see how you're doing."

"Well, Dugan, I'm doing fine, but not as good as you. Keep the party going and I'll see you on Monday."

Donnellan walks into the kitchen and tells Marian about Dugan's love life. She simply says, "Now I've heard everything."

Suddenly his beeper buzzes and Donnellan sees it's the Chief's number. He goes back to the bedroom and calls Emma Dickersen who tells him, "I just got back from the Macy's Thanksgiving Day Parade. It was actually a lot of fun and there were no police-related incidents. I sat with the Mayor, Lefty and the Commissioner. But the reason I contacted you was to see how you are doing today."

"Thanks, Chief. I had a hard time this morning, but I'm feeling great now. How about you? What are your plans for the rest of the day?"

"Well, at four o'clock I volunteer to serve turkey dinners at my church. Then at six, I'm going to a sunset service – I don't know why they call it that when sunset is at 4:30 – and by ten I'll be totally exhausted and sound asleep."

Donnellan thanks her again for the call and returns to the kitchen to help Marian prepare their family's dinner.

At the same time, on the west coast it's still morning and Amanda is just finishing having breakfast with her parents. They are very supportive, yet extremely puzzled by the mysterious death of the unnamed father of her soon to be born children. Amanda sympathizes with their curiosity and tearfully comes clean, telling them everything.

"Wow" is all her father can say as her mother removes the latest People Magazine from the table, the one with the headline "Who was GQ's Mystery Lover?"

Amanda breaks the silence with a laugh and tells her Mom, "Don't worry, I've seen all the headlines. Now you know that the mystery woman is moving back home to be with her Momma and Poppa."

The Blakely's promise Amanda that they will do everything possible to protect her and their soon to be grandchildren.

Sunday, November 29, 1981

Donnellan is waiting for Amanda when she arrives at noon at JFK Airport. They walk to the parking garage and put her luggage in the car. As Donnellan drives out of the airport, he tells Amanda that he would like to make one stop in Brooklyn for a quick visit with GQ's grandfather. Amanda is hesitant at first, but she is excited to meet Hughie Clancy because she knew how much GQ loved and revered his grandfather.

Donnellan knocks on the door and Hughie replies in his usual manner, "Come in. The door is open."

Donnellan walks in first, followed by Amanda. Hughie knows right away who she is. She says. "It's a pleasure to meet you, Mr. Clancy. GQ told me many times how much he learned from you and how he loved and admired you."

"Please call me grandpa, just like Gregory did. You are such a beautiful and magnificent woman, no wonder Gregory fell in love with you at first sight. I only wish my dear wife could be here to share this moment."

Hughie grabs his cane and asks Donnellan to help him stand up. Hughie then walks over to his statue of the Blessed Mother and takes the rosary beads from the statue, places them around Amanda's neck and says, "When my wife Oona left Ireland as a stowaway child on a cargo ship, the only thing her Momma and Poppa had to give her was these rosary beads. Once she arrived in America, she never went anywhere without them. She truly believed that these beads gave her special protection throughout her life's journey. Please keep this special gift in memory of my Gregory who brought nothing but love and laughter into my life from his first breath till his last."

Tears rolled from Amada's eyes as she thanked Mr. Clancy for his glorious gift and promised to keep it as a family heirloom. Amanda gave Hughie a big hug before leaving and promised to call and write him often.

Donnellan drops Amanda off at her apartment, drives downtown, parks his car and starts walking home. He stops for a red light on 23rd Street and he hears a teenager breathlessly calling, "Hi, Mr. Donnellan!" He turns to see Connor Kelly running to catch up to him.

"Hi, Connor. Slow down and catch your breath. It's good to see you."

"I was just visiting my Uncle Raymond at the VA Hospital and I saw you waiting for a green light."

"Is there something you wanted to ask me?" says Donnellan.

"Well, I was just wondering what ever happened to GQ's mystery woman. Did you ever find her?"

"Connor, the GQ investigation is closed and the man who killed him pled guilty and will be in prison for a long time. I'm surprised that you're still following the case."

"Everyone at school is talking about GQ. He was famous, but he started out just like us. You know, from Stuy Town, went to Epiphany, no silver spoon and no favors. So, around here he's a legend. Plus, it's still all over the news every day. My friends and I have a little game when we walk down the street. If one of us sees a sees a pretty woman we say; I found her. Then the rest of us will say something like, not his type, too short, too tall, too old, married with children, sometimes the contest goes on for days.

"I know it's a game, but I really feel like I have something in common with GQ and I have my own theory about finding the mystery woman. Most of my friends pick tall blondes with hair down to their shoulders, but I think GQ's girlfriend must be really smart since everyone is looking for her and she still hasn't been caught. So she probably dyed her hair brown or black and cut it short to avoid detection. I also take our game a more seriously than those guys, because I wouldn't be surprised if she actually showed up here on 20th Street just to see where GQ lived as a teenager."

Donnellan clears his throat to hide his laugh as he thinks to himself, "Holy shit! This kid has some serious voltage." Connor notices a mischievous smile on Donnellan's face and he thinks maybe he's going to give me a clue. For the briefest moment, Donnellan considers asking Connor to share more of his thoughts about the mystery woman, but quickly comes to his senses and says simply,

"It's not a mystery, Connor; it's a secret."

ACKNOWLEDGEMENTS

FIRST, AND FOREMOST, I would like to thank Jonathan Donnellan for sharing his wisdom, guidance and enthusiasm in every phase of the publication of *Damage Control*. Jonathan is the son of my father's best friend in the NYPD (Lieutenant John Donnellan) and my mother's best friend, Jean Donnellan. As I got closer to finishing the early drafts of this book, I called Jonathan to ask if it would be acceptable to name the main character after his deceased father, John Donnellan. Jonathan answered with a heartfelt yes! I then asked with humility if he would read my draft manuscript and give me his professional feedback.

Jonathan, a lawyer and law professor, gave me two choices with regard to his commentaries. As a lifelong friend he would only give me his most positive viewpoints so as not to damage our friendship. Or, he would give his candid opinion with no holds barred like he does for his law students and fellow attorneys. I chose the latter, and I am grateful. The DNA of his truly exceptional insight is integrated throughout *Damage Control*. Of course it helps that Jonathan was raised by the real John Donnellan whose fingerprints are throughout the book. I have a debt of gratitude to Jonathan's sister who encouraged me to finish my book every time I saw her. Thank you, Amanda.

I also wish to thank all of the investigators, detectives, attorneys, auditors and coworkers I had the privilege of working with at the New York State Attorney General's Office. A special thank you to retired senior investigator, Thomas McBride, and three former FBI Special Agents: my former Chief Investigator, the late Warren J. Donovan; my supervisor for twenty years, Anthony J. Scuderi; and my mentor and friend, the late Bernard T. Fusco.

I especially want to recognize my good friend and partner Frank Keenan who retired from the NYPD as a Detective Sergeant in the Manhattan South Homicide Bureau. Frank had a remarkable career in law enforcement and shared many stories with brilliant insight and humor. I seriously told him many times that he should write a book, but unfortunately he died soon after his retirement in 1992. It was a few months after Frank's death that I woke up in the middle of the night, and for the first time in my life, I thought about writing a book and sowed the seeds for *Damage Control*.

I am grateful for the opportunity to have worked as a Clinical Associate Professor under the leadership of Frances L. Brisbane, Ph.D., a former Dean of the School of Social Welfare and current Vice-President for Health Sciences Workforce Diversity at Stony Brook University. I am also thankful for the opportunity to work with many talented colleagues at Stony Brook University, especially Marvin L. Colson, Johnny Colon and Mamie Gladden.

Thank you to my cultured friend and avid reader, Nancy Johnson, who judiciously reviewed my draft manuscripts and provided her editing and astute suggestions. Thank you also to her husband, Andy Johnson, for his patience and support.

A special thank you to my son-in-law Jason Friedman who provided me with support, insight and his sharp-edged writing skills. Jason is a brilliant attorney, but an even better father and husband.

Thank you to my cousin, Mary Arre, who was the first person to see the early draft of "Damage Control," twenty-five years ago when she transcribed my handwritten pages into typed text. Mary has graciously shared her expertise right through to the final update of this book.

Most of all, thank you to my mother, Elizabeth Ann "Betty Meade" Cassidy who listened attentively as I read her every draft of every chapter of "Damage Control." Her encouraging response was always the same. "I want to hear more!"

SPECIAL TRIBUTE
HUGH "JOE" CASSIDY (1925-2011)

I OWE A SPECIAL DEBT of gratitude to my father, Hugh "Joe" Cassidy who spent many months working and sharing his expertise with me on every phase of this book until his death in 2011. He began his 30-year career with the New York City Police Department when he returned to Brooklyn after participating in five shore invasions with the Marines and Army as a Coast Guard "frogman" in the Philippine Islands during World War II. He rose through the ranks of the NYPD: Patrolman, Sergeant, Lieutenant, Detective Squad Commander (ten years), Captain, Precinct Commander and retiring as a Deputy Inspector. He was truly an amazing person, and an even better parent. I am blessed. All of the police procedures and many of the characters in Damage Control have origins in stories whispered in his ears, which he then whispered in mine. If he were here today he certainly would insist that I mention his two namesakes.

Hugh Brendon Cassidy (1903-1982)

Joe Cassidy's father was his best friend, role model and my grand-father, Hugh Brendon Cassidy. He was the devoted husband of Winnifred Cregg Cassidy and father of six sons (all United States military veterans) and two daughters. Hugh Brendon Cassidy was a soldier in the Irish Republican Army, East Mayo Brigade, (1916-1923), IRA Record No. MD/321883, and a proud immigrant to the United States who worked for 45 years in the New York City subway system. Hugh Brendon never said goodbye to family and friends, instead he smiled and said like a true subway motorman, "see you on the eastbound!"

Hugh J.B. Cassidy III (1948-1986)

Joe Cassidy's oldest son and my brother, Hugh J.B. Cassidy III, received many scholastic honors at Epiphany School, Cardinal Hayes High School and at Stony Brook University where he was a founder of the Riding Club. When the door opened for Hugh to enter the equestrian world at Stony Brook University, he pursued his passion with boundless energy and became a nationally respected horse-man, judge, show manager, trainer and owner of Long Island's his-toric equestrian parkland, Old Field Farm. Thirty years after Hugh's death, I found and published his handwritten manuscript in which he shares his expertise as a horseman and advocates for the compas-sionate treatment of horses. All proceeds for Hugh's book, "Thoughts on Horsemanship" are donated to Old Field Farm Ltd., a charitable foundation that serves as a cultural and educational platform for horse sports-past, present and future.

ABOUT THE AUTHOR

Thomas M. Cassidy is a former senior investigator who spent 20 years battling crime for the New State Attorney General. Other experiences include appointments as a Clinical Associate Professor at the School of Social Welfare at Stony Brook University, as a Research Fellow for the American Institute for Economic Research and an appointment as a Senior Fellow at the Institute for SocioEconomic Studies.

Tom, a member of Mystery Writers of America, is the author of: "Elder Care/What to Look For/What to Look Out For!" (New Horizon Press), "How To Choose Retirement Housing," an Economic Education Bulletin published by the American Institute for Economic Research, and co-editor along with Dr. Lynn M. Tepper, an Associate Clinical Professor at Columbia University, of a college textbook, "Multidisciplinary Perspectives on Aging" (Springer Publishing Company).

Articles by Thomas M. Cassidy have appeared in many newspapers across the United States, including *The Washington Post, The New York Times, Daily News, Investor's Business Daily, Buffalo News, Star-Ledger, Gannett Suburban Newspapers,* and *Personal Financial Planning.* Tom has appeared on NBC (TODAY), CBS, CNN, PBS, FOX, and many other television and radio programs across the country.

COMING SOON!
GRAVE DANGER

FBI SPECIAL AGENT AMANDA Blakey delays her return to California. And, Detective Brendon Dugan postpones his retirement when he goes undercover to prosecute the operator of an illegal nursing home who's been fleecing, abusing and even killing elderly victims for years.

While the detectives from Manhattan South Homicide are building a solid case against the evil elder abuser, the tables are turned on Lieutenant John Patrick Donnellan and the hunter becomes the hunted. I hope you enjoy a few pages from an early chapter of the soon to be released sequel to *Damage Control.*

GRAVE DANGER

On Tuesday, December 1, 1981, FBI Special Agent Amanda Blakely is reviewing her notes at Police Headquarters when the Chief of Detectives, Emma Dickersen, enters the conference room with a senior investigator from the New York State Attorney General's Medicaid Fraud Control Unit. Rory Keegan, RN, is not your typical nurse or investigator. His nickname, "Chainsaw," might be your first clue. He received his nursing education as part of a program to train cops for a second career if they decide to retire after 20 years. Keegan, a former sergeant in the motorcycle squad, is a straight talker who doesn't mince his words. He speaks as soon as everyone is seated,

"Yesterday when I got the call from the Chief, I went right to Bellevue to review the patient chart for Margaret Moore with the director of nursing in the emergency room." He pauses, and offers his condolences to Amanda Blakely, then continues. "The records reflect that Moore was comatose and barely breathing when she was transferred to the hospital emergency room by ambulance from a residence on 8th Street. She was described by her next of kin, Ellen Mills, as an elderly relative in the end stage of cancer. Her weight was listed at seventy-seven pounds. There was no indication of physical abuse. Moore died twenty hours after arriving at the hospital.

"Ellen Mills notified the hospital that Moore had prepaid for her casket and burial plot, so her remains were sent to a funeral home in Queens. She was buried in Calvary Cemetery two weeks ago. There was no autopsy due to her age and diagnosis. I contacted the medical examiner and he assured me that he will conduct a priority autopsy on Moore after we have her casket disinterred from the cemetery.

"Next I contacted Hector Ruiz, a Medicare investigator who provided me with a printout of Moore's medical billing history. Her primary physician was identified as Dr. Tomaso Romano. I interview Dr. Romano at his office on Christopher Street and we reviewed Moore's medical history. Romano said that Margaret Moore had a difficult life because her mother died at her birth and her father blamed Margaret for her mother's death. She spiraled into a deep depression due to her torturous childhood and after a failed suicide attempt at age fifteen she was transferred to a state psychiatric hospital where she resided until her eighteenth birthday. She tried to become a nun, but was rejected for mental health reasons. Then she went to work at the New York City library where she worked for more than fifty years.

"Dr. Romano advised that Moore was his patient for more than thirty years and she had no history of cancer. He described Moore as an extremely devout Catholic who attended church every day. She did not smoke or abuse alcohol. She was slightly overweight and had Type 2 Diabetes which was being managed successfully with diet and medications even though Dr. Romano and Moore shared a passion for the desserts at the Ferrara Bakery.

"Dr. Romano stated that he had not seen Moore in four months and she was scheduled to see him in late January. He never heard of Ellen Mills and was not aware that Moore was under her care. At this point, I showed the doctor the picture of Moore from Bellevue. He gasped and had to sit down. All he could say was, oh my God! What have they done to her?" Keegan pauses to review his notes and passes around copies of Moore's patient charts.

The Chief asks Amanda Blakely what she learned from her uncle.

"According to my Uncle Robert, his cousin Margaret worked for more than fifty years at the New York City Public Library in midtown Manhattan. She was not a hoarder, but was close to being one. She scrimped and saved as much as possible and had a nest egg of more than $100,000, plus a pension and Social Security. In August she slipped in the shower and fractured her hip and she refused to have surgery. She felt it would not help her as she has been disabled most of her life. But now her handicap was much worse and she could no longer live independently. She needed help with bathing, toileting and dressing. The hospital gave her a list of three nursing homes, but she was outraged when she found out it would cost her $3,500 a month. Then someone told her about a nurse who would take care of her for $1,000 a month. So she called Ellen Mills and moved in with her.

"Uncle Robert flew to the City and stayed at his cousin's apartment on 12th Street while she was in the hospital. He said the nursing home had a bed and furniture for Margaret, so he cleaned out her apartment and donated most of her furniture and household items to the Saint Vincent DePaul Society. He went with his cousin when she was admitted to the nursing home and brought her clothes, personal items and financial records. He said that Ellen Mills appeared polite and compassionate at all times. She said she has been a nurse for twenty years and she was very upset that so many elderly people never received the compassionate care that they needed and deserved. Finally she had enough and decided that she would take things into her own hands and start caring for patients in her own residence to give older people the kindhearted care they ought to have in their later years.

"Uncle Robert described the residence as a huge ground floor apartment with at least four bedrooms and two bathrooms. He thought it might have been a doctor's office before she took over the residence. Mills said that she only has beds for three patients at a time. He described Margaret's room as fairly large by City standards. It was furnished with a hospital bed, recliner and a wheelchair. The only other person that Uncle Robert saw was a powerfully built young man named Ronald, whom Mills referred to as her son. He was also told that two residents, an elderly man and woman were sleeping and the doors to their rooms were closed.

"There were a few strange things that Uncle Robert noticed. The windows in the apartment were covered by dark curtains so no one could see in or out. Another surprise was that there were several expensive antique clocks and lamps in the living room. Uncle Robert, being a collector himself, was going inquire about a few of her antiques but he was running late and needed to catch a plane and go home.

"He did say Mills told him that the best thing he could do was to leave Margaret alone for a few months so she could get acclimated to her new surroundings without interference from friends and family. Then she said that she would contact him when the time was right for him to call or visit. My uncle said he basically forgot about her until Thanksgiving when the family got together and wondered how Cousin Margaret was doing."

The Chief asks Keegan if he ever heard of anything like this before. Keegan replies, "Unfortunately, underground caregiving is on the rise because people are living longer and Medicare only pays for short term rehabilitation nursing home care. So, if you need custodial nursing home care, it can cost you four grand a month. It's a tough situation because people don't want to spend all of their life's savings on the one place they never want to go to. Last week I had lunch with a nursing home administrator and even he told me that his mother said to him and I quote, "If you ever stick me in your nursing home, I'll kick your ass from here to Canarsie!"

"Basically, the middle class people with savings or a house are caught in a vicious Catch-22. They have to give away their money or pay for care until they are destitute enough to qualify for Medicaid, the government program for the poor. So people hire unlicensed caregivers off-the-books to stretch their money. But, I've never heard of anything this vile. Oh yeah, I checked with the health department and Mills isn't an RN or even a high school graduate! She worked as psych aide at Creedmoor for ten years and was fired for stealing from her patients."

The Chief asks Keegan what he thinks would be the best way to get the evidence to put this psychopath behind bars for many years. "Ideally," says Keegan. "It would be to conduct a sting operation and have a cop pose as a patient, get wired up and go the inside this hell hole."

Keegan is interrupted when Dugan knocks and enters the room.

He quickly assess that everyone is staring at him, the oldest detective in the department. Dugan is puzzled and says;

"What, what, what's going on?" No one answers, and you could cut the silence with a knife. Dugan continues, "I get it Donnellan, you're planning my retirement party. I told you Donnellan, I don't want a party, just let me go out quietly."

Donnellan senses that Dugan is stressed about the prospects of his imminent retirement and other life changing events. Plus he knows Dugan's philosophy, don't make mysteries. So, he speaks up.

"Hey, Dugan, we're not planning your party. We've got a huge problem. A homicidal matron on 8th Street has been fleecing and killing elderly victims' right under our noses. We're trying to figure out the best way to send her to the big house for a long, long time. It turns out that one of Amanda's relatives may have been her latest victim. So just sit down and help us figure this out."

Dugan scans the room as he sits and says, "Hey Keegan, what are you doing here? I thought you retired three years ago."

"I got my twenty in and now I'm an investigator for the Attorney General's Office. I'll be straight with you Dugan, the reason we were staring at you is that you're the best shot we have of sending that wicked witch up the river. If we can get a cop to go undercover and get inside her torture chamber we can shut her down forever. Amanda's already volunteered to pose as the daughter. Would you be willing to go undercover as an Alzheimer's patient?"

"Holy shit! This is unbelievable! Let me think about it for a few minutes. Hey Keegan, can't you find another cop to do it. You've got a lot of old timers at the AG's office," says a distressed Dugan.

"We do have some old warhorses who could do it Dugan," states Keegan. "But, that will take me time because first I have to find out who is available and who would volunteer. Seeing as the Chief wants to shut this operator down tomorrow, it's either you or we drop the undercover operation and arrest her on the evidence we already have."

Amanda has two pictures in her hand as she speaks to Dugan. "Normally I would keep quiet, because this is a police matter not an FBI investigation. But, I'm convinced that Ellen Mills murdered my uncle's cousin in the most painful way. Look at this picture of Margaret from a year ago." Dugan sees an overweight healthy woman smiling as she sits at a family Thanksgiving dinner.

"Now look at her when she was admitted to Bellevue last month." Dugan sees a comatose skeletal woman with almost no flesh on her body.

"All Right! All Right! I'll do it. Just tell me what I have to do."